MW01136257

AUNT BESSIE'S HOLIDAY

AN ISLE OF MAN COZY MYSTERY

DIANA XARISSA

❋ Created with Vellum

For Kevin, for everything he does for us.

AUTHOR'S NOTE

It's hard for me to believe it, but this is the eighth book in the Isle of Man Cozy Mystery series. As ever, it can be read on its own, but I do think the series is best read in order (alphabetically by the last word of the title).

The first thing to note about this book is that I've used the word holiday in the British rather than the American sense. (In US terms, this book is about Aunt Bessie's Vacation.)

Otherwise, if you've read the other books in the series, you'll know all about Bessie's origins (in my romance *Island Inheritance)* and that I use British spellings and phrases, except where Americanisms sneak in, as I'm living in the US now and tend to talk and think in American English on a daily basis. I hope I've managed to find the right balance between the different English languages so that the book is enjoyable on both sides of the Atlantic, as well as in Canada, Australia, New Zealand and anywhere else anyone chooses to read it.

This is a work of fiction and all of the characters are fictional creations. Any resemblance they may have to any real persons, living or dead, is entirely coincidental.

The story is primarily set in a fictional holiday park in the Lake District in England. When we lived on the island we frequently visited holiday parks, and the one in this story is a mix of several different parks with many fictional elements added. (If you want more information about holiday parks in general, please see the notes at the end of the book. As far as I know, there really isn't anything quite like them in the US.) Torver Castle is also entirely fictional.

Those of you who have read my romances will have already heard the story of the ghost in Castle Rushen who can help women identify their true love. That story is fictional. To the best of my knowledge, Charlotte de la Tremouille does not haunt the castle.

As ever, I love hearing from readers. My contact details are at the end of the book.

CHAPTER 1

"I didn't even remember entering the contest," Doona told Bessie. "So winning was a huge surprise."

"I don't think I know anyone who's ever won anything like this," Bessie replied. "A week's holiday is a wonderful prize."

The friends were sitting in the kitchen of Bessie's small cottage, enjoying tea and biscuits. Doona had rung less than an hour ago to tell Bessie that she had exciting news. At Bessie's invitation, she'd driven over to the cottage immediately.

"I know. Now I'm ever so glad I didn't take any holiday time in the summer," Doona said. "I can take a week off now and no one can complain."

"I'm sure John wouldn't complain."

"He might not, but Anna surely would," Doona retorted, frowning.

Bessie nodded, remembering what Doona had told her about the policewoman who had recently joined the staff at the small Laxey branch of the Isle of Man Constabulary. Anna Lambert had been hired from across to assist with the day-to-day operations of the small station. Apparently, this was to allow John Rockwell, who was in charge of policing for Laxey and Lonan, to spend more time in the field and on investigative work. From what Doona had said, Anna's arrival wasn't going as smoothly as everyone had hoped.

"So, which week are you going on your wonderful surprise holiday?" Bessie asked, hoping to distract Doona from complaining about her new boss and ruining her excitement over her unexpected good fortune.

"I'm supposed to travel on the 18th," Doona replied.

"Well, it all sounds wonderful," Bessie said. "I've never been to a holiday park like that, but the brochure looks tempting." She picked the glossy pamphlet up from the table where Doona had left it and flipped through it for a second time. "There's certainly a lot to do."

"Yeah, most of it for families and small children," Doona said with a sigh. "I wasn't sure I wanted to go at all, but on page six there's a list of activities for adults."

Bessie turned to the correct page and read aloud from the brochure. "Here we are, 'Coming to Lakeview Holiday Park without children? Try your hand at pottery, watercolour painting, or pencil sketching. Our heated, indoor water complex is open all day with special evening hours where selected pools are for adults only. We have aerobics and yoga classes, crazy golf, woodland walks and tours of nearby Torver Castle, one of the most haunted castles in the whole of the British Isles, also available for our adult guests.'"

"And there are a bunch of restaurants," Doona added. "Look on page eight."

Bessie turned the page. "Chinese, Italian, French and American," she read down the list. "With an Indian takeaway, pizza delivery and a grocery shop on-site, you certainly won't starve."

Doona laughed. "I'm sure I'll come back at least ten pounds heavier," she remarked. "I'm ignoring the exercise classes. But did you see the French-style patisserie?"

Bessie looked at the photograph of éclairs and profiteroles piled on top of one another and dripping with chocolate sauce. "Maybe fifteen pounds," she murmured as her mouth watered.

"And it's all included in my prize," Doona added. "Anything and everything that I want to do and all the food. It's the greatest prize ever. It's almost too good to be true."

"It all sounds wonderful," Bessie said with genuine enthusiasm. "And I think you could really do with a break as well. I'll miss you, but I'm sure you'll have a lovely time."

Doona nodded. "But I was thinking," she said to Bessie. "Maybe you'd like to come along?"

Bessie sat back in her chair, feeling surprised. "But this is your special holiday," she said after a moment.

"And it will be much more fun with a friend along," Doona replied.

The pair were unlikely friends. Doona, with her highlighted brown hair and bright green eyes, courtesy of coloured-contact lenses, was twice divorced and in her forties. She worked at the front desk of the Laxey Constabulary. After having grown up in the south of the island, she'd only moved to Laxey two years earlier when she'd been in the middle of a very difficult divorce. At the time she'd hoped the change of scenery and the new job would help her get over her broken heart.

Bessie was probably twice her age. She'd lived in Laxey, in her small cottage right on the beach, for all of her adult life after a childhood spent in America. Over the years, Bessie had come to love her short grey hair, which matched her eyes. While Doona was comfortably plump, Bessie had always been slender and that hadn't changed with age. Bessie had never married and never held down a paying job. She kept busy acting as an honourary aunt to just about every child in Laxey and doing research at the Manx Museum into the history of the island she called home and loved immensely.

They'd met in a Manx language class just days after Doona had moved into her new home in the village. Their friendship was forged over shared struggles with the difficult Celtic language. Bessie provided Doona with the support she needed as she worked her way through the breakup of her marriage. Now the pair spent as much time together as their busy schedules allowed, with Doona being the one offering support to Bessie as the older woman found herself caught up in multiple murder investigations recently.

"As I said, everything is paid for," Doona reminded her. "I'm allowed to bring up to three guests. Our accommodation is in one of their lakeside cabins and we'll have two bedrooms and two bathrooms, so we won't have to share. I thought you might like a chance to get away for a week and just relax. Of course, you can also do as many of the activities as you like."

Bessie flipped through the brochure again, looking at all the glossy photos of families appearing to be having a wonderful time. She was very tempted.

"You can try rock climbing and inline skating if you want," Doona teased. "Or you can tour that haunted castle and try some pencil sketching. We can do things together or just meet up for the occasional meal and do our own thing, whichever you prefer."

"It's your holiday," Bessie argued. "You should do what you want to do."

"I intend to," Doona replied. "I'll make my list of activities and then you can decide which ones you'd like to do as well, if any. I don't plan to try rock climbing, but if you decide to try it, I want to be there to watch."

Bessie laughed. "I think watercolours and sketching are a bit more my sort of thing," she told her friend. "And I wouldn't mind touring a haunted castle, either."

"So you'll come?" Doona asked.

"If you're sure you want me to," Bessie replied.

"Hurrah!" Doona shouted. She gave Bessie a hug. "I didn't want to say this before, but I really, really don't want to go on my own," she confided to her friend. "I'm sure the whole place will be filled with happy families. I'm afraid I'd be quite lonely."

Bessie smiled and patted Doona's hand. "If you'd told me that in the beginning, I wouldn't have hesitated for an instant. I'm sure we'll have a good time."

"We are definitely going to have a good time," Doona said emphatically.

The days seemed to fly past, at least for Bessie, and she soon found herself packing and getting ready for her week away. The night before their early morning departure, John Rockwell insisted on throwing them a small going-away party. Bessie suggested they have the party at her cottage, as that was an easy place for everyone to gather.

"Bessie, are you all packed and ready to go?" he asked when he arrived a short time before the party was due to start. Bessie hugged the tall, dark-haired man, feeling relieved to see that he'd regained at least some of the weight he'd lost recently. His stunning green eyes were bright and his smile seemed genuine.

"I think so," Bessie told him. "At least as much as I can be. Some things will have to be added in the morning, of course."

"I'm glad you're going with Doona," he said in a confiding tone. "I think she'd get rather bored on her own."

Bessie shrugged. "I never get bored on my own," she said firmly. "But I've had a great many years to get used to being alone."

John nodded. "It does take some getting used to," he said ruefully.

"How are you coping?" Bessie asked, feeling as if she'd said the wrong thing. John and his wife, Sue, had only recently split up. Sue had returned to Manchester with their two children, leaving John on the island by himself.

"I'm getting there," he replied. "Some days are better than others, but the kids have a half-term break coming up soon, so they'll be coming over for a week. I'm hoping to be in the new house by then."

Bessie had helped John do some house hunting the previous month. John had been delighted when the owners of the property he liked best, a recently renovated bungalow in the same neighbourhood where he was currently renting, dropped their price. His offer had been accepted almost immediately and Bessie knew he was happy to getting settled into his new home.

"I'm looking forward to seeing it once you've moved in," Bessie told him. The house, when they'd seen it, had been deliberately neutral in décor. John had shown Bessie various paint samples for the colours he was planning to use for each room. The end result promised to be quite interesting.

"Yes, well, we'll see how it all turns out," John said, flushing. "Sue always handled painting and decorating, so this is all new territory for me. I have a feeling some of the colours aren't going to work as well as I'd hoped."

Bessie hid a grin. She had the same feeling, but she wasn't going to share that with John. "You'll learn more through trial and error than from having others tell you what to do," she said.

Before John could reply, they heard a car pulling up outside. Bessie opened the door to Hugh Watterson and his girlfriend, Grace Christian.

"Hugh, you've grown again," Bessie exclaimed as she hugged the young policeman.

He blushed and shook his head. "I think it's just these boots," he muttered, glancing down at his feet.

Bessie looked at the stylish leather boots he was wearing and pressed her lips together. Under the circumstances, chuckling would be inappropriate, but she couldn't help but smile as she looked at the rest of Hugh's outfit. Bessie had known Hugh since he was a child, and now, in his mid-twenties, he still looked little more than fifteen. The fancy trousers and collared shirt didn't really do much to help with that, but it was something of a surprise, as Bessie was used to seeing Hugh in jeans and tattered T-shirts when he wasn't in uniform.

Grace now joined him in the doorway and Bessie stepped back to let them both inside, giving Grace a hug as the girl walked past. There was no doubt in Bessie's mind that the pretty young schoolteacher was responsible for the changes to Hugh's wardrobe. She'd seen other changes in the young man as well, as he became increasingly dedicated to his difficult job. Now she could only hope that Hugh would get around to proposing before Grace gave up on him.

The guests all brought food with them, and within half an hour Bessie's small cottage was filled to overflowing with friends from around the island.

"Honestly, you'd think we were moving away or something," she remarked to Doona as they both refilled their wine glasses in the kitchen.

"Everyone was just looking for an excuse to celebrate something," Doona replied. "Mid-October is a bit of a quiet time for parties."

Bessie couldn't argue with that. "Hop-tu-naa isn't far off," she did point out. "Although that's more for the little ones, I suppose."

The night was cool, but dry, and Bessie soon found herself in her favourite place in the world, standing on the beach behind her home. She breathed in the salty sea air and sighed deeply.

"You're going to miss this," Hugh suggested as he joined her.

"I will, but it's only for a week," Bessie replied. "And all of the cabins are meant to be able to see at least one of the lakes on the property, so I'll still have a water view."

"Doona was showing us all the brochure down at the station. Do you think it would be a good honeymoon destination?" Hugh asked.

Bessie shook her head. "Save it for when you have little ones," she said firmly. "Take Grace to Paris for your honeymoon. It's known as one of the most romantic cities in the world for a reason."

"I suppose you're right," he said with a chuckle.

"And when are you going to ask her?" Bessie demanded.

Hugh flushed. "I was thinking Christmas," he muttered. "I want it to be really special, you know?"

"What you're asking will make it special," Bessie told him. "I wouldn't wait if I were you. If you want to spend the rest of your life with her, why not start right now?"

"I don't know," Hugh said with a shrug. "I'll think about it."

Bessie sighed. "Men," she said, shaking her head. She didn't get to lecture Hugh any further, though, as Grace joined them on the beach.

"It's such a beautiful night," she said.

"There's a bit of a chill in the air," Hugh replied, looking at her with concern. "Are you sure you're warm enough?"

"I'm fine," Grace told him, smiling brightly. "Although I'd probably be better with your arm around me."

Hugh grinned and slid his arm around Grace. Bessie smiled at the pair.

"I'm going to miss you two," she said.

"It's only a week away," Hugh said. "You'll barely have time to miss anyone."

"I hope we'll be too busy to miss anyone," Doona said. Bessie hadn't noticed her friend's approach, but now she turned and smiled.

"I feel like a small child," Bessie confessed. "It's silly how excited I am about our holiday."

"I know what you mean," Doona agreed. "I haven't been away since my last honeymoon and that doesn't exactly bring back warm memories."

"I can't remember my last proper holiday," Bessie said thoughtfully. "Although as I've never worked and I live on the beach, I suppose my entire life has been a holiday."

Everyone laughed and then Bessie headed back inside to spend some time with her other guests. Quite a few of her friends from Manx National Heritage and the Manx Museum had come to wish her well and she didn't want any of them to feel neglected.

Two hours later, the last of the guests were leaving. Bessie hugged everyone as they left, grateful that they'd taken time out of their busy lives to celebrate her upcoming trip.

"Well, that was fun," she said to Doona as she shut the door behind Hugh and Grace. "And tiring."

Doona nodded. "It was at that," she agreed. "It's a good thing we're going on holiday tomorrow. We can get some extra rest."

"I thought you had us booked in for all sorts of activities," Bessie countered. "Don't tell me we're just going to sit around all week."

Doona laughed. "I've signed us up for just about everything that is only for adults," she told Bessie. "But we should still have plenty of time to rest, relax and recover from tonight."

"We should have had the party at my house," John said from his spot at the sink as he finished the last of the washing up. "I did offer."

"But you're trying to get packed up to move," Bessie replied. "Besides, it's easier to park down here and this way guests could take walks on the beach if they wanted to."

"The only guests I saw walking on the beach were Hugh and Grace," Doona said.

John laughed. "Ah, young love," he said. "I hope those two make it. They seem perfect for each other."

Doona and Bessie were quick to agree with the man. Everyone liked Grace and thought she and Hugh were well suited.

"It would have been nice if Mary could have come to the party," Bessie said almost to herself. Her friend, Mary Quayle, was still across while Mary's husband, George, was being investigated by the police. Bessie missed the quiet and shy woman who had become a good friend.

"I think the investigation should be finished some time next month," John told her. "But that's all I'm prepared to say on the subject."

Bessie smiled at him. "I'm glad it's finally wrapping up," she said. "Remember that I still have that painting in my spare room. I'd love to know what I should do with it."

John nodded. "I haven't forgotten," he assured her.

Bessie had been given a painting of Laxey Beach by a man who was currently on the run from the police. She'd been uncomfortable accepting it at the time and now she felt strange about keeping it. Once the police investigation into the man's business affairs was complete, she was hoping someone would advise her on what she should do with the painting that she loved, but didn't feel she should keep.

Now the women joined in the clearing up and they soon had Bessie's cottage back to its normal spotless state.

"I hope you both have a wonderful time," John said as he stood on Bessie's doorstep, ready to leave. "You know I'm only a phone call away if you need anything."

Bessie shook her head. "We're going to go and relax and maybe paint a picture or two. We won't need to bother you."

"I hope not," John told her. He gave them each a quick hug and then he drove away, leaving Bessie and Doona to head to bed.

"Thanks for suggesting I just stay here tonight," Doona said as she headed for the stairs. "This will be much easier in the morning and it means I can't oversleep."

Bessie laughed. "You're too excited to oversleep," she predicted.

At almost exactly six o'clock the next morning Bessie opened her eyes and smiled to herself. She felt like an eager five-year-old, giddy with anticipation. She went to wake Doona and found her friend already awake and sitting up in bed reading the holiday park brochure yet again.

"Have you memorised it yet?" she teased.

Doona laughed. "Only the good parts," she retorted. "I can name all of the restaurants and tell you exactly which pools are only open to adults. Those are the things that matter most to me."

Bessie nodded. "I'll let you be in charge of planning our days. I'm happy as long as I can eat and take a walk every day."

"Neither will be a problem," Doona said confidently.

But there was no time for a walk that morning. The two women took showers and got dressed and then finished packing their bags. Doona carried the bags down the stairs and out to her car. They didn't even bother with breakfast, agreeing that they would eat on the ferry instead.

The drive into Douglas seemed short as the pair chatted about their itinerary for the week.

"We'll go over it properly on the ferry," Doona said eventually. "I have a complete list of everything I've signed us up for. I tried to strike a balance between keeping us busy and letting us relax."

"That sounds just about right," Bessie said happily.

"Of course, we haven't had to pay for anything, so if we decide to skip things we're signed up for, it doesn't really matter."

"But we might be stopping other people from doing that activity," Bessie said with a frown.

"I doubt it," Doona said. "When I rang to make our bookings the woman at the park said that we could probably have just waited and booked on arrival. Apparently the activities for adults are never over-subscribed, especially in mid-October."

"Maybe the park will be lovely and quiet, then," Bessie said.

"We'll have to see," Doona replied. "First, though, we have to get there."

They'd reached central Douglas and Doona drove them to the Sea Terminal. She followed the signs for cars travelling on the ferry. They turned around a corner and found a long line of traffic in front of them.

"Oh dear, I didn't expect this," Bessie said.

"I was warned," Doona told her. "I haven't travelled by ferry in years, but Hugh told me all about his trip in August. Apparently there's lots of queuing."

"So I see. No one seems to be going anywhere, either," Bessie replied.

"They haven't started checking people in yet," Doona said, pointing to the two small booths at the front of the queue. "Once they do, it's supposed to go quite quickly."

A short time later they spotted several men walking towards the booths. It wasn't long after that the shutters on the booths were opened and the first cars were being checked in. Other men spread out and began directing the traffic, sending cars to each booth as the previous car pulled away. When it was finally Doona's turn, she handed their ticket to the man in the booth. He entered some information into the computer and then handed her a boarding card.

"Once you're on board you can get your cabin keys from the customer service desk," he told her. "Have a safe journey."

"Cabin?" Bessie asked as Doona drove away, following the slow-moving queue that was now snaking away from the check-in area and towards the ferry.

"It was part of the prize," Doona replied. "We get use of a cabin on board for the journey, both out and return."

"How very fancy," Bessie said. "I haven't been on the ferry in many years, but when I did travel across once in a while, I was always quite jealous of the people who'd booked cabins. In my imagination, the cabins were hugely better than the main seating area with the squalling children and the huddled masses."

"I've never been inside one," Doona told her. "But at least it's a bit of private space and they are all en-suite as well."

"What a nice surprise," Bessie said. "I didn't think this holiday could get any better, but it just has."

They'd reached the end of the new line of cars and Doona

switched off her engine again. "I suspect we'll be here for a while," she told Bessie in response to the question she hadn't yet asked. "I'm told they load the freight on first."

For close to an hour the pair watched as huge container lorries made their way into the belly of the ferry. Some minutes later the front end of the lorry would emerge, leaving its container behind.

"This is quite interesting," Bessie said after a while.

"It isn't bad," Doona replied. "And at least we don't have children with us."

Bessie exchanged glances with Doona. In between watching the lorries, they'd both noticed the woman in the car in front of theirs. She was travelling with three small children. After the first fifteen minutes or so, she'd climbed out of the car and tried taking a short walk with the trio, but the oldest child, a small boy of four or five, kept running off and dashing in between cars. When she finally caught up to him, dragging his two small sisters after her, she'd returned them all to the car and shut them up inside. For a moment, she stood outside the vehicle with the three children shouting inside it.

"Do you think she's imagining just running away?" Bessie had asked Doona.

"I would if I were her," Doona shot back.

Instead, the frazzled woman went into the boot of her vehicle and emerged with a box of biscuits. Bessie and Doona could hear the tears turn to shouts of joy as she showed them to the children. While Bessie and Doona didn't mind the long wait, it was clear to them that the poor woman in front of them couldn't wait to get on board the ship so that she could let the children run around.

"I'm even more grateful for that cabin now," Bessie remarked.

"Indeed," Doona replied.

Eventually the long line of cars began to move slowly towards the ferry. Doona followed the car in front, making her way onto the ferry's car decks. Bessie looked around.

"It's not very passenger friendly," she remarked as several men directed Doona down the narrow corridor. The cars were packed together tightly, with barely enough room between them for people to get through.

Doona and Bessie climbed out of the car carefully. Cars were still making their way onto the deck, so the women had to move cautiously towards the nearest stairs.

"Help me remember that we're on deck 5A," Doona told Bessie when they reached the stairs.

"I'll try," Bessie promised.

They climbed several long flights of metal stairs before finally arriving at a door that said "Passenger Deck."

"Let's find customer service," Doona suggested. "I'm ready for a bit of peace and quiet."

Bessie couldn't have agreed more. The main passenger lounge looked completely full as groups of people claimed tables and chairs for themselves. In the small children's play area, it seemed as if twenty small children were fighting over half a dozen plastic blocks. A small sign that read "Quiet Deck" was only just visible behind a man who was shouting for everyone in his party to follow him.

The women made their way towards the customer service desk. It was located next to a small gift shop where queues of people were waiting to buy fizzy drinks and bags of crisps for the journey. The woman behind the customer service desk looked as if she was already worn out by the demands of the day.

"But we were told that we could all sit together," a tall man was shouting at her.

"All seating in the main lounge is 'first-come, first-serve,'" the woman said. "I'm sorry that you can't find seats together, but there's nothing I can do about it. There might be more seating in the quiet lounge."

"So if anyone complains when my six-month old twins start crying in the quiet lounge, I can tell them that you told us to sit there?" he demanded.

"Sir, if you'd just like to wait a few minutes," she said, "once everyone is on board the seating tends to sort itself out. I might be able to get a few groups to share to allow you and your party some space. Unfortunately I can't do anything right now, though. I have to take care of our guests who've booked cabins or have other special requests."

"Oh sure, take care of them. They've paid extra for special treatment. Don't worry about the rest of us!" he yelled.

"Sir, as I said, once the ship is fully loaded, I'm sure we can do something, but you'll just have to be patient."

The man opened his mouth to shout again, but he was interrupted by the arrival of a very pretty young woman.

"Dan, come on, stop shouting at the poor woman. Your mother and I found some lovely people who are happy to share their space with us. It's all good," she said.

"I won't forget this," he said crossly to the woman behind the desk. "Next time we'll fly."

"I sincerely hope you do," the young woman behind the desk muttered as he stormed away.

The pretty blonde flushed. "I'm so sorry," she said. "Dan needs a holiday very badly. We both do, really. The twins haven't slept through the night once in the last six months and we're both exhausted. He shouldn't have taken it out on you, though. I'm terribly sorry."

"If you need anything, just let me know," the woman told her. "I hope you enjoy your holiday."

"We're going to spend a fortnight with my parents," she replied. "I intend to hand the twins to my mother and sleep for the first week."

"Good luck," the woman told her with a chuckle. "What can I do for you ladies?" she asked as she turned to Bessie and Doona.

Doona handed over their ticket and the woman gave her two keys to cabin 319. "You just need to go up the stairs on either side of the shop," she told them. "There are lots of signs, you can't get lost."

Having climbed what felt like five hundred steps to get out of the car decks, neither woman was excited by the idea of more stairs, but this was a much shorter flight and the stairs here were carpeted. The woman at customer service was right, there was no way to get lost. They followed signs down first one corridor and then another before they found cabin 319. Doona inserted the key and glanced at Bessie.

"I hope this isn't a disappointment," she said.

"I'd be happy with a small room with two chairs in it," Bessie told her.

"There is that," Doona agreed.

The cabin wasn't exactly a disappointment, but it wasn't quite as luxurious as Bessie had always imagined. There were four berths, with the top two folded against the walls. Doona folded them down and then found the small ladder that allowed easy access.

"I can't resist," she told Bessie. "I'm going to climb up."

She couldn't actually sit upright on the top bunk, but she laid down and put the small hard pillow provided under her head. "I suppose I could sleep if I had to," she said eventually.

Bessie had made herself at home on the bunk on the opposite side of the cabin. There was less than two feet between the two bunks and now she tucked her feet under her to allow Doona the necessary space to climb down.

"I imagine you don't want to climb up?" Doona asked.

"Not even a little bit," Bessie replied tranquilly.

As Bessie dug out a book and settled back into the cushions, Doona explored.

"The loo is nice," she announced when she returned from inspecting it. "There's even a shower if you feel as if you'd like one."

"I can't imagine why I would," Bessie replied.

"There are tea and coffee making things," Doona told her. She'd made her way between the bunks and was inspecting the small table at the end of the cabin. "And a few biscuits, as well."

"As it's your holiday, you should have them," Bessie said generously.

"We can share them, as it's our holiday," Doona replied. She tore open the wrapper and passed Bessie a biscuit.

"What can you see out the porthole?" Bessie asked before she took a bite.

Doona looked out the tiny window and shook her head. "Nothing much," she replied. "There are ropes and things hanging in the way. I can just about make out a bit of Douglas. Maybe, when we're underway, we'll be able to see the sea."

"I'm more interested in seeing Heysham," Bessie replied, referring to their destination port.

"Only four hours or so of sailing time," Doona told her cheerfully. "I'm sure you brought enough books to last that long."

Bessie patted her large handbag. "Of course I did," she answered. "And a few snacks, as well."

CHAPTER 2

A few minutes later, however, both women couldn't resist the temptation to go and stand on one of the outside decks. The ferry sounded its horn and began to move slowly away from Douglas. Bessie and Doona stood for a time watching the town behind them getting smaller and smaller.

"It's too cold to stay out here," Doona said eventually. "I should have brought a jacket."

"It's the wind," Bessie replied. As they'd made their way out of Douglas Bay the wind suddenly seemed to start coming at them from every direction.

"I think we should go back inside and have tea," Doona suggested.

A strong breeze blew Bessie's reply away. Instead of bothering to try speaking again, she simply nodded. The friends were settled back in their cabin a minute later.

"I brought the list of everything I signed us up for," Doona told Bessie as they waited for the kettle to boil. "I think we're doing everything we agreed on when we had our planning session last week."

The pair had both been busy for several days with packing and making all of the little arrangements that have to be made before a holiday. They'd done little more than chat briefly on the phone for almost a week.

"That was a week ago," Bessie said with a laugh. "I can't remember what we agreed. Tell me what we're doing, then."

Doona dug around in her handbag, eventually pulling out a small notebook.

"That looks like one of John's little books," Bessie remarked. The police inspector always had a similar writing pad to hand for taking notes when he talked to people.

"He keeps giving them out to everyone at the station," Doona told her. "He's trying to get us all to be more organised."

"Is it helping?" Bessie asked.

Doona shrugged. "It was useful for planning our trip, anyway," she said.

"Maybe I should get one," Bessie mused. "I could keep track of all the books I've read and the series I enjoy. I read so much these days that I tend to forget titles as soon as I've finished a book."

"I have about a dozen of them at home," Doona replied. "I'll bring you a couple once we're back."

"I'd appreciate that."

"Anyway," Doona said, flipping back the cover of the notepad, "I thought we'd have a quiet night tonight. Maybe have dinner at one of the restaurants, or, if we're too tired from the journey, get some take-away or something."

"That sounds good," Bessie agreed. "Although I can't see us being tired. All we're doing is sitting around and drinking tea."

The kettle picked that exact moment to boil, which made both women laugh. Bessie quickly made them each a cup of tea before the conversation continued.

"Tomorrow I've signed us up for an early morning walk in the woods. Their specialist forest rangers do a number of different walking tours, but the early morning one is the only one that is exclusively for adults. He or she will be taking us through the forest and talking about conservation and wildlife protection and what they do at the park in both those areas."

18

"That sounds a little serious for a holiday, but at least we get to enjoy a walk in the woods," Bessie commented.

"The woman who took our booking said that it's actually a really fun way to see the park and learn about the different things they do to make the park a good place for people and for the animals who live in the area. We could see badgers, squirrels, rabbits and any number of birds."

"How long is the walk?" Bessie asked.

"It's meant to take two hours, but guests are welcome to stop at any time if they decide it isn't for them," Doona told her. "The only real downside is that it starts at eight, which is awfully early for the first day of our holiday."

"I'll be up," Bessie said with a laugh. She woke up right around six every morning without an alarm. Her body clock paid no attention to things like weekends or holidays.

"I thought you would be," Doona said with a grin. "But I do plan to have some very lazy mornings while we're there."

"Just not tomorrow morning."

"Yeah, just not tomorrow morning," Doona agreed. "Anyway, that's the only thing on the schedule for tomorrow. I thought we could explore the park and maybe try out the pools, if we get bored."

"Do we get busier then, later in the week?" Bessie asked.

"We have at least one activity booked for just about every day," Doona replied. "Tuesday afternoon we're trying pencil sketching. On Wednesday we get to attempt watercolour painting. Thursday I've left free so we can splash in the pool or even try crazy golf. I thought by then we might need a break from everyone and everything. We could always go out and do some sightseeing around the Lake District, if you want."

"Let's not plan anything now," Bessie suggested. "Let's see how we feel as the week goes on."

"Perfect," Doona replied. "On Friday we're doing the second half of the watercolour workshop in the afternoon and then, in the evening, we're taking that tour of Torver Castle that we discussed."

"I'm glad we could fit that in," Bessie said happily. "I'm looking forward to seeing it."

"I've booked us for something on Saturday that you don't know about," Doona said now. She flipped her notebook shut and sipped her tea.

"Really? What?"

"The woman I spoke to told me that they've just added a book club to their schedule, especially for adults."

"How on earth does that work?" Bessie asked.

"Apparently, when we check in we'll each be given the set of books, usually four or five titles. The book club doesn't meet until Saturday, to give everyone time to read at least one of the books."

"What about the people who arrive later in the week?"

"They only have check-in on Sundays and Fridays. The book club is only open to guests who come for an entire week, not shorter breaks. It runs on Saturdays for guests who arrived the previous Sunday and on Thursdays for guests who arrived on the previous Friday."

"It sounds complicated," Bessie said.

"They just started it a few weeks ago, and apparently it's proving very successful. Some of the books are classics, so most guests will probably have already read at least one of the titles. She told me that Jane Austen is featured quite heavily, although they do try to include at least one book that is more modern, maybe a mystery or a romance."

"What if I don't want to read any of the books?" Bessie had to ask.

"You don't have to go to the club," Doona said promptly. "From what I was told, that hasn't ever happened. Apparently the sorts of guests who are interested in attending are also the sorts of guests who love to read and will happily read and discuss just about anything."

Bessie laughed. "That sort of sounds like me," she admitted. "Although as I've grown older I have less patience with books. I used to force myself to read all of every book I picked up. Now I'm quite happy to abandon a title after the first three chapters if it doesn't interest me."

"I read everything Jane Austen wrote when I was a teenager. If at least one of the books is by her, I won't have to read anything else," Doona said.

"I'm pretty sure I've read all of her books as well," Bessie replied. "I hope they might be able to introduce me to someone new, though. I love discovering new authors."

"We'll just have to wait and see," Doona said. "Anyway, that's our week. I'm hoping we can have a lovely and very fancy meal on Saturday night. Sunday we have to be out of our accommodation by midday if we're going to make it back to the ferry on time."

Bessie nodded. "Let's not talk about Sunday," she said. "I don't want to think about going home yet. We've not even gone very far away."

Doona stood up and looked out the porthole. "I can't see the island anymore," she said. "So we've gone some distance, anyway."

"But we still have at least three hours of sailing time," Bessie pointed out. "You did bring a book, didn't you?"

Doona shook her head. "I didn't think about the ferry journey," she said sheepishly. "I knew we were going to get the books for the book club once we arrived at Lakeview, so I assumed I didn't need to bring reading material. I think I'll go down and grab a few magazines from the gift shop."

Bessie thought for a moment. "I'll come as well," she said as Doona swallowed the last of her tea. "I brought several books, but right now a magazine sounds good. Something that doesn't require a great deal of mental effort."

"So a glossy celebrity gossip magazine," Doona suggested.

"Exactly," Bessie said with a laugh. She rarely bought those sorts of magazines, but lately she'd found herself picking them up a bit more often. They were the perfect things to waste an afternoon with when her mind was preoccupied with other matters. Today she just felt like indulging herself by whiling away the long sailing by reading about the over the top wedding celebrations and extravagant parties that minor celebrities seemed to live for.

The ship's main deck was still cacophonously noisy and chaotic.

The two women didn't waste much time selecting a few titles each and heading for the tills. They waited patiently behind a harassed-looking couple who were each holding a small wailing child. The woman who joined the queue behind Doona and Bessie had a crying baby of her own. She also had a toddler who was covered in something sticky attached to her leg. The girl behind the till rang them up on autopilot, muttering meaninglessly at Bessie when Bessie tried to start a quick conversation. Back in their cabin, the two women couldn't help but laugh.

"Now I know why I never had children," Doona said, wiping at the purplish mark the toddler had left on her trousers as he fell into her.

"Is it jam?" Bessie asked.

"I have no idea, but I'm hoping so," Doona replied. "To think I actually applied for a job with the ferry company a few years back. I wouldn't have lasted through my first sailing."

"School's in session, so nearly all of the families who are travelling are the ones with very small children," Bessie remarked. "Children are very noisy when they're small."

"And sticky," Doona added, shaking her head at the stain the little boy had made. "At least I was sensible enough to travel in old clothes," she told Bessie.

"I didn't even think about it," Bessie admitted. She'd worn a pair of trousers and a light jumper, nothing different from her normal attire.

"I was a little bit worried about being seasick," Doona told her. "I wanted to be as comfortable as possible."

"I didn't think about that, either," Bessie replied. "It's been years since I went anywhere on the ferry, but I never used to get seasick. The idea never even crossed my mind."

"I took a tablet before we left this morning," Doona said. "Although with all the waiting around we did before we boarded the ship, it's probably worn off by now anyway."

"Are you feeling okay?"

"Yeah," Doona answered, sounding surprised. "Actually, I feel pretty good."

The pair curled up with their magazines for a while, trading titles back and forth as they went. The only sound was pages turning for some time and then, suddenly, Doona's tummy rumbled loudly.

"Oh, good heavens, I am sorry," she exclaimed.

"I'm surprised mine hasn't replied in kind," Bessie replied. "We were going to get breakfast when we boarded and we never did."

"I can't believe I forgot about a meal," Doona said, laughing. "Should we go and see what they do for lunch?"

"Yes, let's," Bessie agreed quickly. "We still have over an hour of sailing time and I feel as if I'll starve if I don't eat until we dock."

Back down on the passenger deck, the pair wound their way through the crowd, heading to the small café in the back corner of the ship. There were only a few tables, and they were all full of large family groups.

"Let's take something back to the cabin," Doona suggested, nearly shouting over the noise.

"Definitely," Bessie agreed.

They studied the menu board for a moment and then Bessie shook her head. "Hot food sounds too heavy," she told Doona. "I'm just going to get a sandwich and a bag of crisps for now."

"That works for me," Doona replied.

The pair walked over to the large cooler and each selected a sandwich. Bessie added an apple and a bag of crisps to her tray and then selected a cold bottle of fizzy drink. Doona opted for a banana, crisps and a bottle of apple juice. They paid for their selections and walked as quickly as they could back through the throng.

The cabin felt blissfully quiet in spite of the noises of the ship's engines that hummed constantly in the background. Once they'd finished eating, Doona decided to take a walk on the outside deck.

"We aren't that far from Heysham," she told Bessie. "I want to see if I can see it yet."

While she was gone, Bessie tidied up the tea things from earlier, neatly stacking the dirty cups and spoons on one of the trays from the café. She set the tray outside their door, adding all of the rubbish from their lunch to it. Then she settled back in with her magazines.

"I would have helped with the tidying up," Doona told her when she returned a short time later.

"It only took a minute," Bessie said. "But what could you see?"

"Nothing much yet," Doona said with a sigh. "I'm starting to get bored."

Bessie laughed. "It is rather tedious," she agreed. "Did you explore the whole ship?"

"No, but I think I might if you don't mind being on your own for a while longer," she replied.

"Oh no, you go," Bessie said emphatically. She was quite used to entertaining herself and had plenty to keep herself busy with.

This time Doona didn't return until after an announcement had come over the tannoy.

Ladies and gentlemen, we are approaching Heysham and should be docking in about ten minutes. At that time, we will ask all car passengers to make their way to the rear staircases and return to their vehicles for unloading. I repeat, we will be asking all car passengers to return to their vehicles in approximately ten minutes. All foot passengers are asked to remain in their seats in the passenger lounge until further notice. Our guests who are occupying cabins are asked to prepare to vacate them as soon as we dock. Thank you.

Bessie was just gathering up all of her things when Doona opened the cabin door. She quickly packed up her own belongings and then sat down on her bunk opposite Bessie.

"We only have a few minutes before we have to join the masses," she said.

"But we're here," Bessie replied, feeling a bit silly for being so excited.

"We are indeed," Doona said. "It will be nice to be on dry land again."

"You aren't feeling poorly, are you?" Bessie asked.

"No, I'm fine," Doona answered.

"Did you have a chance to see the whole ship?"

Doona flushed. "I saw the bridge," she told Bessie. "Passengers are allowed to walk around the front of the ship, and from there you can see into the bridge."

"That sounds interesting. Maybe I'll take a look on the way home."

"You should," Doona replied.

"Why are you blushing?" Bessie had to ask.

"I met the captain," Doona replied, not quite meeting Bessie's eyes. "He was, well, a bit overwhelming."

"In what way?"

"He's Italian," Doona said dryly.

Bessie laughed. While she hated stereotypes, some of them were well deserved, and she often thought that Italian men took great pride in living up to the reputation they had around the world.

"Did he show you around the bridge?" she asked her friend.

"He did, and then he offered to show me the captain's quarters," Doona replied.

Bessie laughed again. "That seems very direct."

"I think he was just being friendly," Doona said. "I'm pretty sure it wasn't actually a proposition."

"But you turned it down anyway."

"I would have, but we ran out of time," Doona told her. "It was time to start the docking procedures and he had to get back to work."

"How fortuitous," Bessie said.

"He's going to be captaining our return journey," Doona told her. "He wants me to join him on the bridge once we're underway."

"Well, you have an entire week to think about whether you want to do that or not," Bessie told her. "For now, let's get out of here and try to find your car."

Doona laughed. "Oh, I don't have to think too hard," she said. "The man is gorgeous and his accent is very sexy. I think I'll happily let him flirt with me all the way home."

The two women were in the best of spirits as they dropped off the cabin keys at the customer service desk and made their way back to Doona's car. Then they waited patiently while the long and slow process of unloading the ship began. Eventually it was their turn to drive carefully off the ferry and back onto dry land. Doona had given

Bessie a map before they'd left; now Bessie did her best to follow it and direct her friend.

The route wasn't particularly difficult and once they'd reached the motorway the signs for the Lake District were easy to follow. They'd barely entered the Lake District when they saw their first sign for Lakeview Holiday Park.

"According to the sign, we have about twenty miles to go on the motorway," Bessie told Doona.

Once they'd exited the motorway, there was a further sign for Lakeview. Bessie pointed it out to Doona as they waited at the roundabout at the exit.

"So we go straight across here and then take the next right?" Doona checked.

"That's what their sign says," Bessie told her.

It was only about an hour after they'd left the ferry when they turned into the entrance road for the park. As they made their way into the woods, Doona had to brake suddenly as a squirrel dashed across the road. A moment later Bessie spotted two rabbits chasing one another through the trees.

"How nice of the animals to come and greet us," Bessie said with a laugh, as another squirrel seemed to try to race alongside them for a few yards.

"I'm just worried about running something over," Doona grumbled. "I'd feel terrible if I killed a rabbit or a squirrel."

They drove around a bend and suddenly found that they weren't alone in the forest after all. Ahead of them a long queue of cars stretched for what looked like miles. Doona stopped at the end of the line and looked at Bessie.

"I suppose we can't run anything over if we aren't moving," she said.

"But why are there so many cars on the road?" Bessie asked. "I was expecting to find a car park, actually."

"From what the brochure said, the check-in is a drive-through, much like the ferry was this morning. Check-in time is two o'clock and it isn't much past that now, probably everyone has turned up at the same time."

Bessie dug into her bag and pulled out a small box of chocolate-covered biscuits. "As long as we're waiting, we might as well have a little treat," she told her friend.

They moved forward more quickly than they had expected and it wasn't long before they could see the long row of drive-through windows where people were being checked in. Several members of the park's staff were busily directing people to each window, much like they'd seen at the ferry terminal earlier, but on a larger scale.

A tall man in the holiday park's uniform was walking along and chatting with each driver on the road. At one point he directed a car to leave the line and move to the front. Bessie and Doona exchanged glances.

"VIPs?" Doona wondered.

"It looks like an expensive car," Bessie remarked. "So maybe they've paid extra to get through faster."

"I can't blame them," Doona said. "If I had small children in here, I think I'd be willing to pay just about anything to get through check-in and out of the car."

Bessie handed her another biscuit. "It shouldn't be too long now," she said encouragingly. "You're next to talk to the man on foot anyway, even if we are still about thirty cars from check-in."

Doona grinned. "Maybe I can charm him into letting us move up," she suggested.

Before Bessie could reply, the man was tapping on Doona's window. She lowered it and smiled.

"Welcome to Lakeview Holiday Park," he said cheerfully. "I'm Pete, a reservation specialist. Do you have your reservation letter handy?"

Doona pulled the paperwork from her bag and handed it to the man. He scanned through it and then smiled at her.

"Ms. Moore, we've been expecting you." He glanced into the car and gave Bessie a smile as well. "And your guest. Please follow me."

Doona looked over at Bessie and shrugged before she put the car into gear and drove very slowly behind the man. He led her around the long queue and up to the entrance gates. There were three gates, but only one was actually open. Now he unlocked a second one and waved Doona through it. As soon as she'd driven through, he pushed it shut and locked it behind her.

"We're getting a lot of angry looks," Bessie murmured.

"I'm just doing what I'm told," Doona replied.

Both women stared straight ahead, unwilling to make eye contact with any of the long line of people they'd just cut in front of. Pete now walked back to Doona's window.

"If you'll just drive over to window number one, they'll take good care of you," he told her.

Doona looked over at the row of windows. Window one was shut up tightly. Pete had now walked away, heading back up the road. Doona shrugged and looked at Bessie.

"Maybe it will be magically open when we get there?" she said doubtfully.

Before they'd gone more than a few feet, there was a sudden flurry of activity at the first window. It wasn't magic so much as three flustered-looking girls rushing about to unlock the doors and get the shutters on the small booth open before Doona drove across.

"Ms. Moore, welcome to Lakeview Holiday Park," one of the girls called as Doona approached. As soon as Doona stopped the car, the girl began to speak.

"Congratulations on winning a week's holiday here. I'm Mai Stratton, the guest services manager, and I'll be coordinating your stay. I know you've already pre-booked a number of activities, but if you want to change anything or add anything or just want questions answered, please don't hesitate to ring me directly."

She handed Doona a business card. "My mobile number is on the back. I'm at your service twenty-four hours a day while you're here."

Doona and Bessie exchanged looks again. This sort of VIP treatment felt strange to Bessie.

"I have the keys to your lodge just here," the young woman continued. While she passed keys, maps and brochures to Doona, Bessie studied her.

As far as Bessie was concerned, Mai didn't look old enough to be the guest services manager. In her Lakeview Park uniform, with her long blonde hair and bright blue eyes, she looked like a teenager getting her first work experience. She couldn't have been any taller than Bessie herself, only a few inches over five feet, and she was almost unhealthily thin. Bessie couldn't imagine the girl dealing with irate customers like the man they'd seen on the ferry.

"If you'd like to move your car into the car park, I'll have your bags taken to your accommodation for you," she told Doona.

The car park was behind the check-in area and Doona quickly found a space near the park entrance. It seemed as if everyone else was driving into the park rather than parking.

"I thought cars weren't allow inside the park," Bessie commented as they got out of the car.

"They aren't," Mai told her as she joined them. "Except for a short time on check-in days. Everyone drives to their accommodation to unload their belongings and then returns their car to the car parks for the rest of their stay," she explained.

"I see," Bessie said.

"They'll be driving back in at the end of their break as well, to pack everything back into their vehicles, but we'll arrange to collect your cases for you and deliver them to your car," she added.

"That's very kind of you," Doona said. Bessie could tell that her friend was feeling a bit overwhelmed by all of the special treatment.

"Do you treat all of your contest winners this well?" Bessie couldn't help but ask.

Mai shook her head. "Every contest is different," she said, not meeting Bessie's eyes.

Doona pulled their suitcases from the boot of her car and set them on the ground. A young man in a golf cart pulled up next to them and quickly loaded the cases into the cart.

"They'll be waiting for you in your lodge," he said before he quickly drove away.

"Most guests rent bicycles," Mai told them as they headed down the path to the park entrance. "They're an easy way to get around the park quickly."

"I don't think so," Doona replied. "I haven't been on a bike in years."

"I'm definitely not interested," Bessie chimed in. "I'm quite happy to walk everywhere."

Mai nodded. "Well, bicycle rental is, of course, included in your prize. If you change your mind, just stop at the bike centre any time and they'll sort you out. We do have adult-sized three-wheeled cycles if that sounds more tempting."

"I'll keep that in mind," Doona replied.

"So I'll just walk you to your lodge, then," Mai said. "You're at number eight, Foxglove Close, one of our premium accommodation areas. I want to make sure everything is suitable for you."

"I'm sure it will be fine," Doona told her. "And I'm sure you have other things you could be doing."

Mai flushed. "Check-in day is always busy," she said vaguely.

"We have a map," Doona said. "I'm sure we won't have any trouble finding our way."

"Well, if you're sure," Mai said hesitantly.

"We have your card," Bessie pointed out. "We can always ring you if we need something."

Mai looked relieved. "Thank you," she said. "But please do ring if you think of anything I can do to improve your stay."

"We will," Doona told her.

"There's a special champagne reception at five o'clock in our premier restaurant, *L'Expérience Anglaise*," Mai added. "All of our VIP guests are invited. The reception is at five and then a special five-course welcome meal will be served. I do hope you'll be able to attend."

Doona turned to Bessie. "Champagne and a five-course dinner? How does that sound?"

"Lovely," Bessie replied.

"We'll see you around five," Doona told the young woman.

"Excellent," Mai beamed at them. "Have a wonderful afternoon."

The two women watched the girl as she hurried away.

"I didn't realise you'd won a full VIP package," Bessie remarked.

"No, I didn't either," Doona replied. "And all this attention is making me quite uncomfortable."

"I promise I won't give you any special treatment," Bessie told her with a wink.

"I hope not. It already seems like it might be a long week."

The pair made their way down a long path through the woods. They could hear the steady stream of cars making their way into the park, but they couldn't actually see them. After several minutes they came to a crossroads.

"It's very well signposted," Bessie remarked. They turned, following the direction of the arrow that pointed towards the small cul-de-sac where their cabin was located.

"It's such a lovely day for walking," Doona said, after a second crossroads that was equally well marked.

"It really is," Bessie agreed. For the middle of October, it was surprisingly mild, but not at all hot. The skies were somewhat over-cast, but it didn't feel as if it was going to rain.

A few minutes later they emerged from the woods into a small clearing. In front of them was a small lake with a few kayaks tied up on one side. A path led around the lake, with several short roads, dotted with cottages of different shapes and sizes, coming off of the path.

Bessie and Doona walked slowly towards their accommodation, enjoying the views. Beyond the lake, at some distance away, they could see the huge indoor swimming complex and several groups of small shops and restaurants. The buildings were centred around a large grassy area filled with tables and chairs.

As they got closer to the cabins, they could see the road that ran behind them. There were dozens of cars parked along it and people seemed to be rushing about in every direction, unloading their things and chasing after children.

Bessie and Doona were grateful that they'd been able to avoid that part of the experience as they found Foxglove Court between Daisy Drive and Heather Lane.

As they approached number eight, Doona had a key in hand and she quickly unlocked their door. "Ta-da," she announced as she pushed the door open with a flourish. Bessie walked inside and Doona followed quickly behind, pushing the door shut on the noise and commotion outside.

The door opened into a short corridor and Bessie was quick to open every door she came to. The first door revealed a small closet, where Bessie found that their bags had been tucked away. The next, on the opposite wall, opened into a large bedroom. The windows gave her her first look at the much larger lake that was just past the road that ran behind them. A number of sailboats were making their way around the lake and Bessie stood and watched for a moment while Doona kept exploring.

"The kitchen is pretty well stocked," Doona told Bessie, when Bessie joined her a moment later in the large and comfortably furnished sitting room. Bessie looked out more windows that show-cased the lake. Sliding glass doors led out to a spacious patio that was furnished with a table and six chairs.

Now Bessie peeked into the kitchen. There were biscuits and snacks in the cupboards and not only cans of fizzy drinks, but also several bottles of wine in the refrigerator.

"Did you order the wine?" Bessie asked.

"No, but it's my favourite white and one of my favourite reds," Doona told her. "And there's a bottle of very expensive champagne in there as well."

"They really are giving you the VIP treatment," Bessie said.

On the other side of the sitting room was the second, much larger bedroom. The en-suite had a jetted tub and a huge shower.

"This one should be yours," Bessie told her friend.

"Are you sure?" Doona asked.

"The other bedroom is lovely," Bessie answered. "And the last thing I intend to do while I'm here is have a bath in a jetted tub. You'll enjoy it, though, won't you?"

"I'd really like to try it out," Doona admitted. "I've never been in one and they always look so lovely on telly."

"So I'll suffer in silence in the bedroom that's twice the size of my room at home, and put up with only having a shower that could accommodate three of me comfortably."

Doona laughed. "It is all very luxurious, isn't it? I'm not sure I'll ever want to leave."

They opened a bottle of wine and sipped glasses of it while they unpacked. Then they sat on their patio and finished the bottle while they watched the other new arrivals. Their boxes of books for the book club sat unopened on the dining table. Bessie was curious what they had been given to read, but not curious enough to interrupt her people watching. It didn't seem long before they needed to get ready for the reception.

"What do we wear?" Bessie wondered.

"I'm just going to wear nice trousers and a light jumper," Doona told her. "Sort of exactly like what you're already wearing."

Bessie laughed. "I think I'll change into more of the same, then. Having travelled a long way in this outfit, I'll feel fresher if I do."

The walk to the centre of the park, where the shops and restaurants were clustered, took only a few minutes. Bikes whizzed past them occasionally, carrying their riders back and forth around the site.

"I think walking is much better," Bessie said after a large group pedaled past them. "It isn't far and it's the perfect night to take things slowly."

"I agree totally," Doona replied. "Besides which, I never learned to ride a bike. I certainly don't intend to start now."

The large French-style restaurant was at the end of a row that included a toy shop and a shop that seemed to sell nothing but bathing suits.

"I think 'The English Experience' is a strange name for a French restaurant," Bessie said as Doona pulled open the large glass door.

"It is rather," Doona agreed.

Mai was standing at the front desk and she rushed over to greet them. "I hope your accommodation is everything you were expecting," she gushed as she ushered them into the large and empty dining room.

"It's really lovely," Doona replied.

"Let me get you some champagne," she said, dashing away.

"It looks as if we're first," Bessie murmured.

"Ah, Doona, there you are," a loud voice shouted from the back of the restaurant.

Bessie stared at the man who was now hurrying towards them. He was tall and almost plump, with brown hair that was definitely thinning on top. His face was lit up with a broad and welcoming smile. Beside her, Doona griped her arm tightly.

"It's Charles," Doona whispered.

"Charles?"

"My second husband."

CHAPTER 3

"*A*h, Doona, it's so good to see you again," the man said as he grabbed Doona's hands. "I've missed you so very much. You can't imagine."

"No, I probably can't," Doona replied dryly. She pulled her hands away and took a step backwards. "I think we'll be leaving now," she said.

The man's face fell. "Oh, darling Doona, don't be like that," he said imploringly. "I invited you here so that I could apologise and we could start again. At least give me a chance to explain."

"Explain?" Doona echoed. "You cheated on me. You really only married me in a pathetic attempt to hide your affair with a married woman. We've been apart for over two years. There's nothing for you to explain."

Charles chuckled. "There, you see, it's all so black and white with you." He turned to Bessie. "That was part of our problem," he said in a confiding tone. "Doona never saw the little grey areas."

"I hardly think there are grey areas when it comes to cheating," Bessie said coolly. She knew too much about how the man had treated her dear friend to be anything more than barely civil to him.

He flushed. "You could be right," he said, giving Bessie a sad smile.

"All I really want is two minutes of your time, though. Surely you can give me two minutes?" he appealed to Doona.

"Two minutes," Doona said, holding up her watch and staring at the second hand.

"I don't even know what happened," Charles began. "I mean, one day I was working hard and looking forward to the weekend, when I would fly over and get to see you, and then out of the blue, your solicitor rang me up and told me we were through."

"I received a letter," Doona said, her voice icy cold.

"Accusing me of cheating, I assume," he said. "And you believed it, without even taking the time to discuss it with me."

"There were photos," Doona told him.

"They could have been old photos," Charles defended himself.

"You were wearing the wedding ring I gave you in the pictures," Doona replied.

Charles flushed and shook his head. "You should have given me a chance to explain," he argued. "I loved you. I haven't stopped loving you. Do you know how hard I worked to get you here today?"

"I didn't win a contest, did I?" Doona demanded. "You set this all up."

"I did," Charles said proudly. "I'm managing the holiday park now and I just knew if I could get you here I could win you back."

He took a step forward and grabbed Doona's hands again. When her eyes met his, his face became pleading. "Give me a chance, please. It isn't what you thought it was."

Doona pulled her hands away. "You've had over two years to make your explanations," she said tightly. "I don't know what your game is, but I'm not playing it."

Charles shook his head. "It isn't like that at all. I was so hurt when your solicitor told me you wanted a divorce that I threw myself into my work. I got myself sent away to manage some new properties on the continent and I was there for over eighteen months. Once I got back I realised that I can't keep running away. You were the best thing that I ever happened to me. I know I made some mistakes, but I can explain, truly I can. Just give me a chance."

"No," Doona said a bit too loudly.

"Look, we can't really talk here," he said, almost whispering now. He glanced around and then back at Doona. "I was set up," he hissed at her. "Herbert Howe set me up so that he could sue for divorce and get away from Jessica without paying out a fortune. I was as much a victim as you were."

"Really?" Doona asked. "You poor thing. No wonder you've come rushing back to me only a few years after I dumped you."

"This isn't the place for this conversation," Charles said now.

Bessie looked around and realised the room was slowly filling with people. She'd been so intent on the conversation between Doona and Charles that she hadn't noticed earlier.

"After the reception is dinner and then I'll be here all night talking to guests. Have breakfast with me in the morning," he suggested to Doona. "I'll be in my office any time after six. Come and find me and I'll explain everything."

"I don't think so," Doona said.

"You won't be sorry," Charles promised. He took Doona's hands in his again. "Please, breakfast."

He turned and headed off towards the back of the restaurant before Doona could reply. When he walked through the door marked "kitchen" Doona blew out a long breath.

"Are you okay?" Bessie asked her friend.

"Not so much," Doona replied, her voice shaking.

"We should go back to the cabin," Bessie said, taking Doona's arm.

"And miss out on the champagne reception and VIP dinner? I don't think so," Doona said firmly. "I just need a minute to pull myself together."

"And some champagne," Bessie said, taking two glasses of the bubbly drink from a passing waiter. She handed one to Doona, who took a large sip.

"Ah, that's better," she said, giving Bessie a smile that looked almost genuine.

"So that was Charles," Bessie said in a conversational tone.

Doona laughed. "It was indeed," she agreed. "I'm sorry I didn't introduce you. Next time."

"Is there going to be a next time?"

"Not if I can help it," Doona said. "If I'd known he was here, I wouldn't have come. But I don't have to tell you that."

Bessie nodded. She'd been Doona's shoulder to cry on during the difficult divorce. She knew how badly Charles had hurt her.

"Do you suppose Charles is paying for our stay out of his own pocket?" Doona asked.

"I don't know," Bessie replied. "I don't know how such things work."

"Well, I intend to find out," Doona said.

"Does it really matter?" Bessie asked.

"Yes, or maybe no," Doona said with a deep sigh. "I don't want to feel as if I owe him anything. And I will, if he's paying for this, even though I didn't know he was here when we came."

"Well, I can certainly pay for my half of the holiday if we have to," Bessie told her. "Why do you think he brought you here?"

"I have no idea," Doona told her. "But I know one thing. It isn't because he suddenly realised how much he loves and misses me."

"You never did tell me the whole story about how you found out he was cheating," Bessie said. "Was it an anonymous letter?"

"We'll talk later," Doona assured her. "For now, I intend to have fun."

She drained her glass of champagne and then looked around for the waiter. Several were now circulating with drinks as well as trays full of starters. Bessie and Doona both helped themselves to several of the choices.

"The food is delicious," Bessie said after she'd finished her own glass of champagne.

"I can't wait to see what's for dinner," Doona told her.

"It's a tasting menu," a voice from behind them said.

The pair turned around and smiled at Mai. They'd seen her circulating around the room, but hadn't noticed her joining them.

"That sounds interesting," Bessie said.

"It's basically several small courses that give you a sample of some of the most popular items on the restaurant's menu. We're hoping you'll want to come back to dine here again and again while you're staying with us," Mai told them.

"If the rest of the food is as good as the starters, we'll definitely be back," Doona told her.

"Mai, where have you gone?" a loud voice shouted from the kitchen doorway.

"Oh, please excuse me," the girl said, blushing. "Duty calls."

"I wonder who that is," Bessie murmured as they watched Mai join the man in the doorway. He looked to be somewhere in his fifties, with short grey hair. He was fit and trim and wearing an immaculate suit that Bessie was certain had been very expensive.

"That's Lawrence Jenkins," a voice from Bessie's left said.

The two women looked at the man who had joined them. He was tall, with brown hair and eyes. To Bessie he looked no more than forty and his smile lit up his entire face.

"Should I recognise the name?" Bessie asked.

The man laughed lightly. "Oh, goodness no," he exclaimed. "He's a business colleague of some sort to our illustrious leader, Charles Adams. I'm not sure exactly what his connection with Lakeview is, but he seems to be quite happy to give orders to the staff."

"I didn't know Charles's surname was Adams," Bessie said, trying to process too much information too quickly.

"I kept my maiden name," Doona said quietly. "Anyway, I don't believe we've met," she said to the man who was listening intently to their conversation.

"I'm Harold Butler," the man said, bowing deeply. "I'm, well, I'm the assistant general manager or something like that. Titles don't really interest me. Let's just say that if you need anything while you're here, I'm happy to help, shall we?"

"That's very kind of you," Bessie said.

"Keeping guests happy is the best part of my job," he replied. "Really, if I can help, just ring me."

He handed them each a business card. "My mobile number is on the card," he said. "You can reach me any time."

Before the women could reply, he was looking past them. "Must dash," he said apologetically. "But do ring me if you need anything."

He was swallowed up by the growing crowd before Bessie and Doona could reply.

"He seemed very nice," Bessie remarked.

"Don't be fooled by appearances," a voice hissed from behind her.

Bessie spun around, beginning to feel disoriented by all the people who kept interrupting their conversations.

Again, it was Mai Stratton who was smiling at her. "Harold is very nice," she said. "But he's not a fan of Charles Adams. Just be careful what you say around him."

"Why doesn't he like Charles?" Bessie had to ask.

"Harold was our general manager until about three or four months ago," Mai said, keeping her voice low. She glanced around before she continued. "Charles just turned up one day with orders from central office to take over. No one seems to know why."

"Poor Harold," Bessie said. "Was he a good general manager?"

Mai shrugged. "He was doing okay," she said. "But he's really too nice to do the job. He wants everyone to like him, but a lot of the staff took advantage of that. Charles is better at keeping everyone in line."

A sudden buzzing noise startled Bessie. "What was that?"

"Time for dinner," Mai said loudly and brightly. "Come on."

Bessie looked at the tables as she followed Mai. They were all set with linen tablecloths covered with what looked like expensive flatware and glasses. Crystal chandeliers sparkled above them.

"You two are over here," Mai told them, showing them to a small table for two in a quiet corner. "Enjoy your meal."

Doona picked up the small card that was leaning against her plate. "Mrs. Doona Moore Adams" had been printed on it. She stared at it for a moment and then shook her head. Bessie sat down in her seat and watched as Doona very carefully tore the word "Adams" off the card.

"That's better," she said as she sat down opposite Bessie. There was a candle burning in the centre of the table and Bessie grinned as Doona dropped the piece she'd ripped off the card onto the flame.

Bessie watched as the dining room filled with guests. When everyone was seated, waiters began to move around the space, carrying trays full of the first course and pouring glasses of wine.

For several minutes the pair ate and drank silently, letting the background noise of the room wash over them. Bessie watched as Mai and Harold moved from table to table, presumably making sure everyone was happy.

They had just started on the second course when a tall blonde woman appeared in the doorway. She looked around the room as if she was trying to find someone. To Bessie it seemed as if her eyes stopped on Doona for a short while, before moving on. The room grew quiet as everyone noticed the new arrival.

Bessie looked over at her friend. "Someone you know?" she whispered.

"Jessica Howe," Doona whispered back. "The woman Charles was seeing behind my back."

"What's she doing here?" Bessie asked the obvious question.

"I've no idea," Doona hissed.

"Ah, Mai, there you are," the woman called from the doorway. "Do us a favour and tell Charles I'm here, would you?"

"Certainly, Ms. Howe," Mai said, turning and heading towards the kitchen door.

The room remained silent while Mai was gone. Bessie used the time to study Jessica Howe. She would have put the woman somewhere in her thirties, but it was hard to be certain, as she was wearing a great deal of makeup. Her hair was platinum blonde and it looked dry and brittle, even from across the room. Her eyes were a luminous blue that Bessie suspected came from coloured contact lenses. She had generous curves that were being showcased in a very tight dress that was not only cut low at the front, but had a very short skirt.

"Charles is really busy in the kitchen," Mai announced when she returned. "He said to tell you he'll see you later. In the meantime, you're welcome to enjoy the dinner."

"Oh, am I?" Jessica asked, her voice rising in pitch with every word. "Busy in the kitchen, is he? Tell him to get out here right now or he'll regret it," she shouted shrilly. "I won't be treated like this, not after everything he's put me through."

"Calm down, Jess," Charles said as he walked in behind Mai. "There's no need for a scene. Have some dinner and we'll talk later."

"I don't want to talk," Jessica shouted. "I want to kill you."

It seemed as if everyone in the room gasped at the same time.

"Surely you'll do a better job on a full stomach," Charles suggested. "I'm not going anywhere. I'm working."

"I think we've had quite enough of this little drama," another voice chimed in. Lawrence Jenkins walked in behind Charles and nodded tightly at him. "Ms. Howe, if you'd like to come with me, we can have a chat while you wait for Charles to finish here."

"Charles is finished here," she replied. "In every possible way."

"Yes, well, that's something we can better discuss elsewhere," Lawrence said smoothly. He walked over to her and took her arm. "Let's go somewhere a little more comfortable. I'm sure we'll find lots to talk about."

For a moment it looked as if the woman was going to argue, but Lawrence turned her around and led her out of the room. It seemed as if everyone sighed with relief together as the front door shut behind the pair.

"Well, that was interesting," Bessie said brightly to Doona.

"Do you think we can change our return ferry booking?" Doona asked.

"If not, we can always just drive down to Heysham and stay in a hotel there," Bessie suggested.

The waiters were busily refilling wine glasses and serving the next course. Doona took a bite of chicken in a white wine sauce and sighed. "We can't leave," she said. "The food is too good."

Bessie laughed. "The rest of the holiday will probably feel quite dull after tonight's excitement," she said.

"I certainly hope so," Doona said emphatically.

The rest of the evening went more smoothly. Various courses were served as the wine flowed continually. By the time the puddings were being distributed, Bessie was feeling very full and rather sleepy.

"I think I ate too much," she said as she finished the last bite of her crème caramel.

"I know I ate too much," Doona replied. "And I drank too much as well, but at least I haven't thought about Charles for at least five minutes." She giggled. "Oooops, I just thought about him," she told Bessie.

"I do hope you aren't thinking fondly of him," Bessie said.

"No, I was thinking about stabbing him with this spoon," Doona said, holding up her spoon.

"I'm not sure you could do much damage with a spoon."

"I'm pretty sure I'm mad enough to kill him with a spoon," Doona countered.

"If I could have everyone's attention," Mai said loudly from the centre of the room. "I want everyone to meet Nathan Beck, our chef. He's responsible for all of the gorgeous food you've enjoyed tonight."

Mai gestured towards the thirty-something man who was standing beside her. His long dirty-blond hair was tied in a ponytail down his back. He smiled vaguely at the tables full of people who were applauding politely. When the applause stopped, Mai nudged him.

"Oh, um, well, thank you for coming. I hoped you enjoyed the meal and I hope to see all of you back again during your stay," he said. He glanced around, then focussed his gaze on one of the waitresses.

"And, of course, my thanks to all the hardworking wait staff, especially my beautiful wife, Monique."

Bessie watched the pretty brunette blush brightly.

"Yes, well, of course, everyone has worked hard tonight," Mai said, sounding annoyed. "Anyway, thanks again to Nathan."

The guests clapped again, with somewhat less enthusiasm. That seemed to mark the end of the evening. Guests began to gather up jackets and handbags and depart back to their cabins and cottages.

Bessie looked at Doona. "Ready to head back to our temporary home?" she asked her.

"That's probably a good idea," Doona replied. "If I stay here I might just tell Charles a few things."

"We should definitely go, then," Bessie said.

The pair stood up and picked up their bags. They were nearly to the door when Mai caught up to them.

"I do hope you enjoyed your evening," she said brightly.

"The food was delicious," Bessie replied.

"And the entertainment was definitely interesting," Doona added dryly.

"Ms. Howe was a bit overwrought," Mai said. "She and her husband have been having difficulties."

"I'm sure her affair with Charles hasn't helped," Doona shot back.

Mai flushed. "I don't know anything about that," she said.

"I know far too much about that," Doona told her. "But what did Charles tell you about me?"

"Oh, but, that is, I mean," she looked confused. "He said, but, well, I don't think, I mean, maybe I should let you get back to your accommodation. Do ring me if you need anything."

The girl hurried away before Doona could do anything more than shake her head. "What has Charles been telling them about me?" she demanded of Bessie.

"I'm sure I don't know," Bessie replied. "And I'm also sure that Mai isn't going to tell you."

"We're here for a week," Doona said grimly. "She'll tell me before we leave."

The pair headed for the door, and this time they weren't stopped. Outside, it was a perfect autumn evening. The air was crisp, but not cold, and both women inhaled deeply.

"It smells like autumn," Bessie said.

"It does," Doona agreed.

"It seems strange not to smell the sea, though," Bessie remarked as they started along the path that would take them back to Foxglove Close.

They walked in silence, both lost in their own thoughts. Bessie wanted to ask Doona hundreds of questions, but she didn't want to upset her friend. Back at their cul-de-sac, people were still arriving and dashing about with suitcases and boxes. Bessie and Doona quickly made their way into number eight. As soon as they got inside, Doona went into the kitchen and came out with a bottle of wine and two glasses.

"I've probably had enough for tonight," Bessie said.

"Let me pour you a glass anyway," Doona replied. "You don't have to drink it, but it will keep me from drinking the entire bottle."

They took their wine out onto their small patio and sat down.

"What a mess," Doona said after a few minutes.

"Why would Charles bring you here?" Bessie asked the first question that popped into her head.

"I haven't the foggiest idea," Doona replied. "We haven't spoken in over two years. Once I found out he'd cheated, my advocate and his solicitor handled all contact between us. I didn't even think he knew I'd moved to Laxey."

"You've told me some things about your marriage, but certainly not everything. I didn't know you found out he was cheating from a letter," Bessie said. "I don't want you to talk about anything that you'll find upsetting, but I'd love to hear the whole story."

Doona nodded. "It might do me some good to talk it all through," she said. "Maybe we can work out what Charles really wants, as well."

She topped up both of their wine glasses and then sat back in her chair and closed her eyes. "We met at a party," she began in a low voice. "I was leaving just as he was coming in. He was gorgeous and so very charming. I fell in love with him when our eyes met for the first time."

Bessie took a sip of wine, wondering what she could possibly say to make this easier on her dear friend. "I'm sorry," she finally muttered as the silence stretched between them.

"He was incredible," Doona continued now. "He'd travelled all over the world as an important manager for a major hotel chain. They were opening a new hotel on the island and he'd come for the grand opening. Within minutes he'd invited me to join him at the big party the next evening. The party itself was full of minor celebrities and the very cream of the island's social crop, and I was completely overwhelmed, but Charles made me feel as if I were the only woman in the room, or at least the only one who mattered to him."

She paused for a sip of wine. Bessie leaned over and patted her arm. "If this is too painful, we can talk about the weather," she suggested.

Doona laughed. "I'm fine," she insisted. "I've had two years to recover, after all."

"And you've had no contact with the man in all that time?" Bessie checked.

"None, but let me get back to the story," Doona said. She sat back again and took a deep breath. "Charles had to head back to London after that weekend, but we talked on the phone all the time until he could visit again. We got engaged on that next visit and married about two weeks later. It was all such a whirlwind, and I was the happiest I'd ever been on our month-long honeymoon."

"Didn't you tell me that you travelled around Europe for the month?" Bessie asked.

"We did," Doona confirmed. "We visited many of the company's finest properties and were treated like VIPs everywhere we went."

"Sort of like now," Bessie muttered.

"Exactly like now," Doona said. "I didn't think about it before, but maybe I should have suspected something."

"You thought you'd won a very special prize," Bessie reminded her.

"Yeah, but all the fussing over us is extreme. I wish I knew what Charles was up to."

"What happened after the honeymoon?" Bessie had to ask.

"Charles suggested that I stay on the island, as he travelled so much he was never in his London flat anyway. He used to fly across to visit whenever he could, or at least that's what he told me. Then one day, about two months after our honeymoon, I got a letter. Well, it was more like a package. Inside was a letter telling me exactly why Charles had married me, along with photos, copies of restaurant receipts and telephone bills and a lot of other things."

Bessie reached over and squeezed Doona's hand. "I can't imagine how awful that must have been," she said.

"It hit me really hard," Doona admitted. "According to the letter, Charles was involved with Jessica Howe, the blonde we saw earlier. The letter said that her husband, Herbert, was starting to get suspicious, so Charles had quickly married me to try to hide the affair."

"And there were photos and things that proved that?"

"There were photos of them together, including some where he was wearing his wedding ring," Doona told her. "But I didn't believe the letter, or rather, I didn't want to believe the letter. I didn't tell Charles I was coming, but I took a few days off work and flew across to Leeds, where he was working at the time. I checked into a room at the hotel where he was and then I went into the bar to wait for him."

Bessie quickly poured some more wine into Doona's glass. "You don't have to tell me all the horrible details," she said.

"I can't believe I never told you them before," Doona countered. "All those weeks and months I spent crying on your shoulder and I never told you the whole story."

"In the early days you weren't always all that coherent," Bessie teased. "And once you started to recover, I wasn't going to drag it all up."

Doona laughed and took a drink. "It all feels rather long ago now," she said. "Even with seeing Charles again tonight. Or maybe I'm just comfortably numb from too much champagne and wine."

"You'll have a headache in the morning," Bessie predicted.

"It's worth it," Doona told her. "Anyway, I sat in the bar and then this blonde woman walked in. I knew who she was from the photos, but she didn't seem to have any idea who I was. As we were the only two people in the place, she sat down next to me and we started talking."

"Jessica Howe?"

"Indeed. We started out chatting about life in general, but after a few drinks she told me all about her husband, who is much older than she is and very wealthy. She was his trophy wife. His first wife had given him three children, and he didn't want any more as he was still paying a fortune in child support. At least that's how she saw it. Anyway, she was bored with him and their life together but she didn't want to divorce him and lose out on all the wonderful things his money could buy."

"Yikes, what a lovely woman," Bessie muttered sarcastically.

"After another round of drinks, she told me all about her lover," Doona said tartly.

"Charles?"

"Exactly. It seems the pair had met at a party about a year earlier. Now she spent her time travelling around the world, staying wherever Charles was currently working. She knew her husband was suspicious, but she was sure they were discreet enough that he couldn't prove anything."

"And all the while, you'd seen the proof," Bessie said.

"Yeah, I might not have mentioned that to the lovely Jessica, though," Doona said dryly. "Anyway, she even told me how incredibly clever her lover was. He'd recently married some stupid woman who had no idea what her husband was up to behind her back."

"Oh dear," Bessie gasped.

"A few minutes later Charles himself came in. He didn't recognise me from behind in the dark bar. He simply called to Jessica and she rushed over to him. I watched the whole thing in the mirror behind the bar. They hugged and then hurried out of the room together, clearly heading to bed. I told the bartender that my drinks were meant to be on Jessica's tab and then went up to my room and cried until morning."

"I wish I'd known all of this earlier," Bessie said. "I wouldn't have been nearly as polite to that man."

"Thanks, Bessie," Doona said with a sad smile. "Anyway, I flew home the next day and made an appointment with my advocate. Charles rang repeatedly until I changed my number. I don't know what his game is now, but I don't trust him, not even a little bit."

"I don't blame you," Bessie replied. "I think we should just ignore him and enjoy our holiday."

"I'm going to go and see him tomorrow morning," Doona told her.

"Our woodland walk starts at eight, so we were going to have an early breakfast anyway. It won't take me five minutes to explain to him exactly how I feel now that the shock of seeing him has worn off. Once I'm done with him, he'll leave us alone for the rest of the week."

Bessie could only hope that her friend was right. But Charles had gone to a lot of trouble to get Doona to Lakeview. He must have some reason for having done so, and he might not be as easily deterred as Doona seemed to think.

"We never opened our books," Doona said, gesturing towards the two boxes on the small dining table, just inside the door.

Bessie grinned. "I was just thinking that I need something to curl up with tonight," she told her friend.

"I'll go get the boxes," Doona said. She was in and out of the cabin in a moment, returning to the table with the two small boxes. "They've taped them shut," she told Bessie. "I wonder if there are scissors in the kitchen?"

"There's just about everything else," Bessie told her.

Doona disappeared into the kitchen while Bessie tugged uselessly on one of the box lids. Whoever had sealed them had done a good job. Doona was back only a moment later.

"Did you find scissors?"

"Nope, but I found a knife," Doona replied, holding up a kitchen knife with a long blade.

"Do be careful," Bessie said as her friend waved the knife in the air. "It looks really sharp."

"It isn't, actually," Doona replied with a laugh. "Although it's very fancy, with our address engraved on the handle." She'd tried slicing at the packaging tape with the blade, but it didn't seem to cut through it.

"Let me try," Bessie suggested.

Doona turned the blade sideways and slipped it under the lid. Now she could slide it along the seal, slicing through the tape as she went. It only took her a few seconds to open both boxes.

"So, what do we have?" Bessie asked.

They opened their boxes together and Bessie read out the titles.

"Jane Austen's *Emma*, Helen Fielding's *Bridget Jones's Diary*, Bill

Bryon's *Notes from a Small Island,* and Agatha Christie's *The Murder of Roger Ackroyd.* It's an interesting collection," she said.

"I know I read *Emma* when I was at school," Doona replied. "But I've not read the others."

"I've read *Emma* and absolutely everything by Agatha Christie, but the other two are new to me," Bessie told her. "I think I'll try one of them tonight and see how it goes."

Doona yawned. "I'm too tired to read tonight," she said. "I was thinking about trying out that fabulous bathtub, but I think I'm just going to go to bed. I'll see you in the morning."

Bessie gave her friend a hug and then they went into their bedrooms, each carrying their own box of books. Bessie got ready for bed and then read a chapter of the Helen Fielding book. When she found herself dropping off to sleep over the pages, she gave up and switched off the light.

It seemed a long night for Bessie in the strange place. The sound of doors opening and closing woke her repeatedly as their neighbours made their way in and out. By five, Bessie was ready to give up on sleep and start her day, even though she felt more tired than she had when she'd gone to bed.

CHAPTER 4

*B*essie took a shower and then got dressed. As she patted on her rose-scented dusting powder, she took a moment to think about Matthew Saunders, the man she'd once loved. He never would have cheated on me, she told herself firmly. Her reflection looked uncertain, so Bessie turned her back on it. In the kitchen, she filled the kettle and found the jar of instant coffee. She needed the caffeine this morning after her restless night.

A short time later, Doona joined her. "Ah, coffee," she muttered, stumbling into the kitchen. "I could smell it from my room."

Bessie handed her the mug she'd just filled and then made a second cup for herself. She didn't try to speak to her friend, who was still in her robe and slippers. Doona sank down in a chair and sighed deeply.

"I shouldn't have finished that last bottle of wine," she said, resting her head in her hands.

"Do you need headache tablets?" Bessie asked sympathetically.

"Yes, please," Doona replied "I thought I had some, but I can't find them in my bag."

Bessie passed her the bottle of tablets. Doona was quick to shake two into her hand, then wash them down with a sip of coffee.

"We don't have to be at breakfast for at least an hour, right?" Doona asked.

"That should be about right," Bessie answered.

"I'm going to take a long, hot shower," Doona told her. "I'll be out when my headache is gone."

Bessie nodded. Doona shuffled off slowly, leaving Bessie to wash the two mugs and then tidy up the small kitchen. With nothing else to do, Bessie took her book out onto the small patio. There were walls on either side of the patio that were tall enough to give them privacy. A shorter wall, maybe three or four feet high, across the front of the patio was presumably meant to keep guests from walking across the grass to get to the path below them. It also made the small patio feel cosy and Bessie settled in happily.

She made it through the second chapter and then gave up. Bridget Jones's life just wasn't something Bessie could relate to and she set the book to one side. Bessie sat back and watched the wildlife moving around behind their cabin. She saw a few rabbits and an abundance of squirrels dashing about. As time moved forward, they began to be replaced by people.

People watching was one of Bessie's favourite activities. She often sat on the rock behind her cottage and watched the families and individuals on Laxey beach. Those people were nearly always holiday-makers, no different from the groups that now surrounded her here. Several large groups went by on their bikes, weaving in and out around one another. Small children pedaled hard, their stabilisers keeping them from crashing to the ground.

A very large group stopped on the road right behind Bessie and began to wave. Bessie wondered if she should wave back, but luckily stopped herself just before one of the men shouted.

"Granddad, come down and join us."

A voice came from the patio next to Bessie's. "I'll be down when I'm ready," it called. "I'm having a quiet cuppa by myself. We said we'd meet for breakfast at seven. I'll see you then."

The adult members of the group exchanged glances and then they all moved away, heading towards the centre of the village.

"Ten minutes' peace and quiet," the voice on the next patio muttered. "Is that too much to ask?"

Bessie smiled to herself. The man was only just out of sight from where she was sitting. He sounded quite fed up with the large group, who were presumably his family. While she sometimes wondered what her life might have been like if she'd married Matthew and had children, she never really felt as if she'd missed out by not having a family of her own. Now, as she sat back in her seat, she was content with the knowledge that she could have as much peace and quiet as she liked on her holiday. A few minutes later, Doona joined her.

"You're looking much better," Bessie told her.

Doona had obviously taken some time over her appearance. Her highlighted brown hair had been washed and brushed until it shone. She was wearing more makeup than Bessie was used to seeing on her, and her green eyes seemed to sparkle. There was no hint now of the hangover that Bessie knew Doona was suffering from.

"I feel better," Doona replied. "The tablets have kicked in, and the shower helped as well. I'm feeling weirdly confident, so let's get over to the centre before I lose my nerve."

Bessie nodded and rose to her feet. She quickly picked up her handbag from where she'd left it by the door and followed Doona out the front door. A man of maybe seventy was just emerging from the cabin next to theirs. Bessie smiled at the man, whose bearing was almost military in spite of his age. He was completely bald and his brown eyes gave both women a quick once-over that left Bessie feeling as if she'd been thoroughly inspected.

"Good morning," she said brightly. The man had no way of knowing that she'd overheard his early morning conversation with his family.

"Good morning," he replied curtly.

The trio all turned and began to walk silently towards the village. After a moment, Doona spoke to the man.

"I'm Doona Moore," she said. "And this my friend Bessie Cubbon. It seems as if we're neighbours, so it seems silly not to at least introduce ourselves."

The man smiled and then paused and gave them a small bow. "I'm Andrew Cheatham," he replied. "It's a great pleasure to make your acquaintance."

Before the conversation could continue, a huge crowd of people suddenly hastened towards them.

"Granddad, I fell off my bike," a small boy shouted.

"Granddad, are you going to sit with me at breakfast?" a little girl asked.

"Gwandda," a tiny toddler shouted from her mother's arms.

Bessie smiled at Andrew. "You seem to be very much in demand," she remarked.

"It was nice to meet you," Doona said.

Andrew smiled vaguely in their direction as he was swallowed up in the crowd. Bessie and Doona continued on their way without him.

"Have you worked out what you're going to say to Charles?" Bessie asked as they reached the door to the main building, called the Squirrel's Drey. It contained a large food court with a spacious area with seating in the middle. It also housed the swimming complex and the ten-pin bowling centre.

"Nope, but I'm sure it will be interesting," Doona said grimly.

Charles had told Doona that the executive offices were next to the food court, so Bessie got herself a full English breakfast and sat down at one of the tables.

"I'll be back in ten minutes or less," Doona told her.

"If you aren't, I'll come in after you," Bessie replied.

Doona nodded and then marched resolutely towards the door marked "Staff." She knocked once and then pushed it open. Bessie glanced at her watch and then started to eat. She was startled less than a minute later when her mobile phone buzzed.

It seemed to take her forever to find the phone, which had, as ever, found its way to the very bottom of her bag. She frowned when she pulled it out and saw that it was Doona who was ringing her.

"Hello?"

"Bessie? Could you come back here, please?" Doona's voice sounded odd.

Bessie was on her feet at once. "I'm on my way," she told her friend. Her breakfast forgotten, Bessie knocked once on the door and then pushed it open exactly as Doona had done. She found herself in a long corridor. Doona was waving to her from the end of it. She hurried towards her friend, feeling dread in every step. When she reached Doona, she hugged her tightly.

"What's wrong?" she asked, looking at Doona's pale face and frightened eyes.

"Charles has been murdered," Doona whispered.

Later Bessie would wonder why she wasn't shocked by Doona's announcement, but at the time it never occurred to her.

"Did you ring the police?" she asked her friend.

"I did," Doona replied. "They're on their way."

"Ladies, I really don't think you're meant to be back here," a friendly voice called down the hall to them.

Bessie smiled at Harold Butler as he joined them. "Good morning. How are you this morning?" she asked.

"I'm fine. Thank you so much for asking," he replied. "But really, this area is for staff only. If you need to talk to Charles, I can let him know that when I next see him. There's no point in standing around here waiting for him. He could be anywhere."

"He's in his office," Doona told the man.

"Oh? Did he tell you to wait out here?" Harold asked.

"No, he's, well," Doona sighed and then shook her head. "He's dead," she said flatly. "I'm just waiting here for the police."

"Dead? The police? But what on earth?" he took a deep breath. "Sorry, I'm rather flummoxed. I'd better ring Lawrence."

Harold walked back down the corridor and disappeared into one of the offices along it. Bessie and Doona exchanged glances.

"Are you okay?" Bessie asked her friend as Doona leaned back against the wall.

"No, really I'm not," Doona replied. "I'm upset and angry and frustrated and I'm still hung over and I feel like hel, er, miserable."

Before Bessie could reply, the door at the end of the hall swung open and Lawrence Jenkins came rushing towards them.

55

"What's this nonsense about Charles, then?" he demanded harshly.

"He's dead," Doona said.

"I didn't realise you were a doctor," Lawrence said in an aggressive tone.

"Now, Lawrence," Harold muttered from where he had just arrived behind the other man.

"I think I'd better check on Charles," Lawrence said. He tried to push past Doona, but she stood firmly in front of the office door.

"We don't want to disturb the crime scene," she said sharply.

"Crime scene?" Lawrence shouted. "Look, lady, I don't know what's going on in there or what your game is, but you need to get out of my way. It sounds as if Charles needs some help."

Doona shook her head. "He's well beyond that," she told him. "And I've assured the police that I've secured the crime scene."

"Except it isn't a crime scene. If Charles did suddenly pass, well, that's sad, but it isn't a crime. Now move out of the way," he said.

"I work for the Isle of Man Constabulary and I think I know a crime scene when I see one," Doona explained. "If I'm wrong, I'll apologise to the police when they get here."

"You've already rung them?" Lawrence asked. He shook his head. "Stupid, crazy, hysterical women, who needs them?" he muttered under his breath.

Bessie was about to give him an earful, but Harold interrupted.

"I've rung Joe. He's on his way," he said.

"Excellent," Lawrence said. "Joe Klein is our head of security. When he arrives, he will escort you and your friend out of the staff area, and, if I have anything to say about it, off Lakeside Holiday Park property altogether," Lawrence told Doona haughtily.

Doona rolled her eyes at Bessie and then leaned back against the wall again. Bessie felt as if she might go mad listening to the large clock on the wall as it ticked off the minutes while they waited. Each tick seemed reluctant to follow on from the previous one and Bessie was certain at one point that several minutes went by before she heard another reluctant tick.

When the hallway door opened again, Bessie was eager to inspect the new arrival. The man who walked towards them had the look of a career policeman. His eyes were cool and assessing as he took in the scene. Bessie would have guessed that he was probably in his sixties. He was wearing a brown uniform and carrying an extra twenty pounds, mostly around his waist.

"Is there a problem?" he asked, his voice low.

"These ladies need to be escorted out of this area," Lawrence said loudly. "They aren't meant to be back here."

"I'm sorry, ladies, but Mr. Jenkins is correct. This is a staff area. If you'll just come along with me," the man said.

"I told the police that I would stay here and make sure no one entered the crime scene," Doona told him. Bessie was surprised at how steady her friend's voice sounded.

"Crime scene?" the man repeated. "I'm Joe Klein, the head of security at Lakeview Holiday Park, so if there's a crime, I suppose I ought to know about it."

"Charles Adams has been murdered," Doona told him. "I found the body when I went to meet with him a short time ago."

"Murdered? That's a pretty serious accusation. Maybe I better check it out," Joe said.

"The police aren't going want the scene compromised," Doona said.

"I was a cop for nearly forty years," he told Doona. "I think I know what I'm doing."

Bessie could tell that Doona was reluctant to let the man look into the office. If only the police would hurry up and get there, Bessie thought.

"Joe, get them out of here," Lawrence said tightly. "We can sort out whatever has happened to Charles once they've gone."

The security officer shook his head. "I think I'd better see what she's talking about before I chase anyone away," he told Lawrence.

Doona stepped back reluctantly and let Joe open the office door. Bessie was standing in just the right place to see far more than she wanted to see.

Joe glanced into the room and then looked hard at Lawrence.

"We'll all be waiting nice and patiently for the police to get here," he told him.

"Ridiculous," Lawrence snapped. He pushed Bessie to the side, heading towards the still open office door.

Joe put out his arm to stop him. "You can have a look if you really want to," Joe said. "But I think you'll be sorry you did."

Harold also appeared to take that as an invitation and he quickly crowded forward as well. The two men stared into the small office and then both spun around.

"Can't you take care of this?" Lawrence asked Joe. "I mean, you were with the police. Surely you can handle something like this."

Joe shook his head. "Murder is well outside of the remit of our security team," he said firmly. "You know as well as I do that we have to notify the local constabulary for serious issues. I can't think of anything more serious than this."

"There could be sensitive documents on the desk in there," Lawrence said. "At least let me go in and collect the papers that Charles was working with."

"I think just about everything on the desk is covered in blood," Joe told him. "Anyway, the police aren't interested in how he was running Lakeview. All they'll want to do is work out who killed him."

"But he wasn't just managing this site," Lawrence argued. "We were working on purchasing some other properties. I can't have news of that leaking out before we're ready."

"You aren't going in there," Joe said firmly. "Maybe you and Harold should go and sit in his office for a while. You did say that the police are on their way, right?" he asked Doona.

"That's what they said, but it seems to be taking a long time for them to get here," Doona replied.

Joe nodded and then pulled out his mobile phone. He took a few steps away from the group and spoke quietly into it for several minutes. Bessie couldn't make out what he was saying, but at least the noise covered up the incessant slow ticking of the hallway clock.

As Joe spoke, he walked further back up the corridor. Bessie was startled when Lawrence suddenly ran towards Charles's office door.

Doona grabbed his arm, but he pushed her backwards, hard. As she fell to the ground, Joe managed to get his hand on Lawrence's shoulder.

"Trying to hide the evidence?" A cool voice that sounded amused floated down the corridor.

Bessie turned and looked at the pretty, fifty-something woman who was walking towards them. She was wearing a blue suit and her brown hair, caught up in a tidy bun, was streaked with grey. Her eyes were the same colour as the streaks in her hair. Now she looked at each of them in turn, a faint smile on her face. Doona climbed back to her feet as Lawrence spoke.

"I was just hoping to retrieve some important papers," he said, clearly frustrated.

The new arrival glanced into the office and then shook her head. "You should know better," she said sternly. "We shouldn't have to keep talking about what your security team can and can't do."

"I'm more worried about keeping my business confidential than in arguing over jurisdiction," Lawrence said.

"And I'm more interested in finding out who murdered Charles Adams than I am in your business," the woman shot back.

The hallway was now becoming crowded with men and women, some in police uniforms and others who must have been crime scene team members. The woman glanced at all the new arrivals and then took a deep breath.

"Right, I'm Inspector Margaret Hopkins, for those of you who don't know me," she said, addressing her comment towards Bessie and Doona. "Those of you who do know me," she said, looking directly at Lawrence, "will know I take the job of investigating very seriously. This is murder and my job doesn't get more serious than that."

She pointed to someone in the crowd of new arrivals and a man came forward. After a quiet conversation, he disappeared back into the crowd.

"Margaret, please, I know that finding out what happened to Charles is important, but if I could just have five minutes in his office, I'd really appreciate it," Lawrence said.

"Call me Inspector Hopkins," she said. "And no, you may not have five minutes in the office. In fact, I think it's probably in everyone's best interest if you go down to my office and wait there. I'm sure we'll have plenty to discuss once I've had a chance to inspect the scene."

"Your office? I don't think so," Lawrence said stiffly. "I have a holiday park to look after."

"What exactly is your title here?" the inspector asked, voicing the very question that Bessie was thinking.

"I'm, well, that is, I'm a business associate of the park's general manager," he said.

"So you don't actually work for Lakeview Holiday Park?" the woman asked.

Lawrence flushed. "No, not as such," he muttered.

"Then I can't imagine anyone will miss you if you're not here," the woman said with a satisfied smile. "And as it's your partner who's been brutally murdered, I'm sure you'll want to do everything you can to help us find the man or woman responsible for such a horrific crime."

"Well, yes, but, I mean...."

Inspector Hopkins held up her hand. "I think you need to gather your thoughts," she said in a kindly voice. "I'm going to have someone take you down into town. I'll be there in a few hours and we can talk then."

Lawrence opened his mouth, presumably to protest, but she deliberately turned her back on him and began a whispered conversation with one of the men in a white lab coat. A uniformed constable stepped forward and smiled nervously.

"Sir, if you'd like to come with me," he said to Lawrence.

"I'd rather not," Lawrence told him. "But your bi, er, boss, doesn't seem to have given me much choice."

"No, sir, she hasn't," he agreed.

Bessie and Doona exchanged glances and Bessie quickly looked down to hide a smile. It was nice to see the unpleasant man being dealt with. When Lawrence and his escort had disappeared through the door at the top of the corridor, Margaret Hopkins turned back to them.

"Joe, thanks for keeping him under control until I got here," she said to the security chief. "Goodness knows what evidence he would have trampled all over in order to find whatever he's after."

"Just doing my job," Joe said with a shrug. "I'd still be doing your job under other circumstances."

The woman smiled. "Most days you could have it," she told him.

He laughed. "Yeah, well, maybe not," he replied.

"Do you have anything to report before I start?" she asked him now.

"Nothing that needs discussing before you've gone through the scene," he told her.

"Great. If you have other things to do, you're welcome to leave. I'll find you when I'm ready for a full report. If you want to stay and help, that's okay, too," she said.

"I'll stay and work the scene, if I may," he replied. "It's been a while, but I think I still remember how."

The inspector nodded and then turned her attention to Harold Butler. "Mr. Butler, it looks as if you just got your old job back," she said.

Harold blushed and then turned pale. "I hope you aren't hinting that I had anything to do with, well, that," he said hotly, gesturing towards the open office door.

"I wasn't hinting anything," she replied in a measured tone. "Merely making an observation. If you'd like to wait in your office, I'm sure I'll have a great many questions for you shortly."

"Yes, of course," he said sulkily. He stomped off down the corridor, eventually turning into one of the offices. A moment later that office door swung noisily shut.

"That just leaves you two," the inspector said, her eyes moving from Bessie to Doona and back again. "I assume one of you is the woman who found the body."

"That would be me," Doona admitted.

"How far into the room did you walk?" the inspector asked.

"Not very far at all," Doona replied. "I knocked but didn't get a reply. I was just going to leave, but then I decided I'd leave Charles a note if the office wasn't locked. I tried the handle and it wasn't locked, so I pushed the door open and, well, you know what I saw."

The other woman nodded. "And you immediately rang the police?"

"I did. I work for the Isle of Man Constabulary. I'm just civilian front desk staff, but I know enough about criminal investigations to know what to do in such situations, which is ring 999 and keep everyone out of the way."

"Precisely," the woman agreed. "So I'm left with just you," she said, turning to Bessie. "Can you tell me, in ten words or less, what you're doing here?"

"Doona rang me for moral support after she rang you," Bessie replied.

"Exactly ten, very good," the woman said. "I can tell we're going to have an interesting conversation later."

She turned away and motioned for one of the uniformed men to join her. "Jack, please take these ladies out into the food court and sit with them until I'm free. They can get something to eat or drink if they want, but I'd rather they didn't chat with one another or anyone else."

"Yes, inspector," he replied.

Bessie and Doona followed Jack out of the crowded hallway and back into the large food court. Bessie blinked in surprise at the sheer number of people who were now packed into the space. It felt to her as if everyone around stopped to stare as the uniformed constable escorted her and Doona to one of the very few empty tables.

Bessie sank down into a seat. She was surprised to find that she suddenly felt like crying. It was probably more to do with shock and tiredness than anything else, she decided. The only things she knew about Charles Adams were not things that would make her mourn his passing.

"Did you ladies want tea or something to eat?" the constable asked.

"I'm fine," Doona said blandly.

"Me, too," Bessie replied. She sat back in her seat and shut her eyes.

Her brain immediately flashed up an image of what she'd seen in Charles Adams's office. The body had been lying across the desk and there had been blood seemingly everywhere. Bessie sat up straight and opened her eyes.

"Then again, tea might be nice," she said loudly.

The constable looked around and then caught the eye of one of the women who was clearing tables. He gestured to her to come over.

"Could you possibly get some tea for these two ladies?" he asked her.

"There isn't any table service in here," the woman told him. "You have to go to the counter."

"Yes, well, that's rather difficult," the man said. He leaned closer to the woman and whispered. "They're under police guard, you see," he hissed. "I can't leave them alone and I can't let them go wandering off."

The woman looked at Bessie and Doona and then back at Jack. "Really? Did they have something to do with all the excitement in the offices, then? Someone said there was a robbery or something."

"Or something," Jack said. "I can't tell you anything and I can't let them talk to anyone, you see. But they're really nice ladies and they've had a rough morning. They could use a cup of tea and a biscuit each."

The woman nodded. "I'll get them something," she said.

"Thank you," Bessie told the man. "I really could use a cuppa."

"I thought as much," the man replied. "I can't imagine you're used to finding dead bodies."

Bessie glanced at Doona and then had to swallow hard to suppress the rueful chuckle that bubbled up inside of her. Finding dead bodies seemed to be her latest hobby, but that was the last thing she wanted to tell the young policeman. He might get altogether the wrong idea about her.

Three cups of tea and a generous plate full of biscuits were delivered only moments later. Bessie took a sip of the hot liquid and then sat back in her chair with a chocolate digestive. She nibbled it slowly, letting her thoughts wander. Charles was dead and there seemed no shortage of likely suspects for his murder.

"I'm sorry," Doona said after a moment. "I shouldn't have dragged you into the corridor. We've missed our walk."

"I wouldn't have gone without you," Bessie replied. "And you shouldn't have been alone there with the body."

"Ladies, please," the young policeman interrupted. "Inspector Hopkins did ask that you not speak to one another while you wait."

"Sorry," Doona said. "It's been a tough morning and sitting here in silence is hard."

"Maybe we should have a little chat, then," a voice said from behind Doona.

"Inspector Hopkins," the policeman jumped up. "I, er, I got them some tea and biscuits, for while they were waiting."

"So I see," she said. "And a cup for yourself."

"I didn't ask for it," he said nervously. "The lady just brought three cups."

"And several dozen biscuits," the inspector remarked. She leaned over and grabbed herself several. "Harold is allowing us to use an empty office for our interviews," she said now. "I'd like to start with you, as you found the body," she told Doona.

"Yes, of course," Doona said, her face pale.

Bessie watched as Doona stood up shakily and then slowly followed the senior policewoman back through the "Staff" door.

"Is she your daughter?" the policeman asked, sounding sympathetic.

"No, just a very dear friend," Bessie replied.

Whenever Bessie found herself spending time with a stranger, she usually engaged him or her in conversation. She was fascinated by people and loved hearing all about their lives and their families. Today, though, she simply couldn't find the energy to start a discussion with the young man sitting with her. Instead, she sat back and watched the crowd, steadily eating her way through several biscuits.

She noticed Andrew Cheatham, their next-door neighbour, as he walked through the large space. He had two small children with him, one holding on to each of his hands. Bessie smiled as the little trio joined the short queue for ice cream. After they'd gone, Bessie looked at her watch. She was surprised to find that Doona had only been gone for around half an hour.

"Is this the first murder you've had to investigate at Lakeview?" Bessie asked the man sitting across from her.

He looked startled for a moment before he replied. "Murder doesn't happen often anywhere," he said.

Bessie didn't argue. "I suppose the park's own security handles pretty much everything else," she said.

"They do," he agreed. "Although we have been called out for the occasional thing. Sometimes guests prefer to deal with us rather than rely on the park's security team."

"Mr. Klein seemed to know what he was doing," Bessie suggested.

"Oh, Joe's great," the man agreed. "But there are certain rules about what has to be reported to us."

"I see," Bessie replied. "What sorts of things...."

Bessie stopped herself when she spotted the inspector walking towards them. The constable jumped to his feet again.

"Oh, good, there are few left," the woman muttered as she scooped up the last of the biscuits. "This is breakfast," she told Bessie, "and probably lunch as well."

"Surely, with all this food around, you'll be able to get a proper lunch," Bessie said.

The woman shrugged. "We'll see. Lots to do before lunchtime, anyway. I'm ready to interview you now."

Bessie stood up slowly. "Where's Doona gone?" she asked. She hadn't seen her friend come back out of the staff area.

"She said to tell you she'd meet you back at your cabin when I've finished with you," the woman told her. "Shall we?"

Bessie forced herself to smile and nod.

CHAPTER 5

*T*he inspector spent a moment giving the young policeman his new orders before she led Bessie to the small office she was using for interviews.

"Have a seat," she said, waving Bessie into an uncomfortable-looking wooden chair.

Bessie sat down and frowned. The seat was hard and she was tired of sitting anyway.

"I know it's not the most comfortable chair around, but I'll try to keep this brief," the inspector told her. "Let's start with your name and go from there."

"I'm Miss Elizabeth Cubbon, but everyone calls me Bessie."

The woman made a note in a small book and then smiled. "If you don't mind, then, I'll call you Bessie as well," she said. "And you can call me Margaret."

"Thank you," Bessie said, feeling slightly uncomfortable with the informality, but not about to argue.

"So, what brings you to Lakeview?" Margaret asked, leaning back in her chair. The casual pose didn't fool Bessie. The woman wasn't going to miss a thing.

"My friend, Doona Moore, won a week here in some contest," Bessie replied. "She invited me to join her."

"Lakeview is a family holiday park. You didn't mind being two single ladies surrounded by large family groups?"

"Not at all. There are a number of activities for the adults, including art classes and a book club," Bessie told her. "There's plenty for us to do."

"And Mrs. Moore didn't mind coming to the park where her ex-husband was general manager?"

"Doona didn't know Charles was here," Bessie replied, working hard to keep her voice under control.

"Do you think she still would have come if she had known?"

"I doubt it. Charles broke her heart and it took her a long time to recover. I don't think she ever wanted to see the man again."

Margaret nodded. "Take me through your day, yesterday, please."

Bessie took a deep breath and then launched into as succinct an account of her Sunday as she could manage. Margaret didn't interrupt as Bessie told her about their journey, the champagne reception and the dinner that followed. When she'd concluded, Bessie sat back in the miserable chair and waited for the questions that would follow.

"Did either of you leave your accommodation during the night?" Was the not unexpected first question.

"I certainly didn't," Bessie replied. "I assume Doona didn't either, but I was in my room with the door shut, so I suppose she could have."

Bessie felt as if she'd just betrayed her friend, but she wanted to be sure to be scrupulously honest with the inspector.

Margaret raised an eyebrow and then made another note. "Is there anyone else here that you knew before your arrival yesterday?" she asked now.

Bessie shrugged. "Not as far as I know," she replied. "I suppose there could be, though. It's a very large park and we've only been here, well, less than twenty-four hours."

"What about Mrs. Moore? Did she know anyone here other than her ex-husband?"

"You'd have to ask her that," Bessie replied. "She didn't mention anything like that to me, aside from recognising Jessica Howe, as I told you earlier."

Margaret nodded. "Neither of you knew Lawrence Jenkins or Harold Butler before your arrival?"

"I certainly didn't," Bessie said. "I suppose Doona might have had contact with one or the other when she was booking the holiday, but she didn't mention it to me if she had."

"Mr. Jenkins was Charles Adams's business partner and had been for at least ten years. I find it surprising that Mrs. Moore was married to Charles and yet never met the man," Margaret said.

"They weren't married for long," Bessie said dryly.

"Actually, they may have been married for longer than you think," the woman replied.

Before Bessie could question that remark, she continued.

"I think that's all I need from you today," Margaret said, standing up. "I'd just like to have one of my staff take your fingerprints, if you don't mind."

"Fingerprints? Why?"

"Elimination purposes," the woman explained. "In case you touched anything in or around Charles's office. We'll be trying to get prints from the door frame, the handle, anything and everything."

"I was very careful not to touch anything," Bessie countered.

"So are you refusing to let us take your fingerprints?" Margaret asked, her tone suddenly frosty.

Bessie sighed and shook her head. "No, of course not. But you won't find them at your crime scene."

"Mrs. Moore suggested that I contact her supervisor, Inspector John Rockwell, on the Isle of Man if I needed any background information about her. Can you suggest someone on the island that I could talk to about you?"

"John Rockwell is a friend of mine," Bessie told her. "I'm sure he'd be happy to answer any questions you might have about my character."

"Did you meet the inspector through your friendship with Mrs. Moore?" the woman asked.

"Not at all," Bessie said with a grin. "I met him over a dead body."

The inspector gave Bessie a long hard stare and then smiled tightly. "Now I'm really looking forward to having a chat with Inspector Rockwell," she said.

Bessie chided herself for her rather offhand words. "It's a long story," she said, ready to launch into it.

Margaret held up a hand. "I think I'd rather hear it from the inspector, thanks," she said. "I'd like you to keep your focus on the body we have here."

"I'm trying not think about that," Bessie replied. "There was an awful lot of blood."

"Yes, well, I'd rather you didn't repeat that little detail. In fact, I don't want you talking about the murder at all. If anyone asks, tell them you aren't allowed to answer any questions, please. I have a long list of people I need to interview and I'd like to be the one breaking the news of Charles's demise to them all."

"I won't say anything," Bessie assured her. "But there are already rumours starting. The woman who served our tea thought there was a robbery."

Margaret smiled. "That's the sort of rumour I would like to see encouraged," she said. "Feel free to tell people that if you like."

Bessie shook her head. "I'd rather just say nothing," she replied. "I don't feel comfortable lying."

"Well, thank you for your time," the inspector said, opening the office door. "I know where to find you if I have any more questions. In the meantime, I hope you enjoy your holiday."

"I'm not sure how enjoyable it's going to be now," Bessie said with a sigh. "I hope Doona is okay."

"I'll just ask that you remain on site until further notice," Margaret added. "I'm hoping we'll have this worked out in a day or two, but if I have further questions, I'll want to be able to find you."

"We're meant to be here through Sunday," Bessie told her. "We have signed up for an excursion to Torver Castle. I hope we can still do that on Friday."

"As long as it's all been arranged through the park, I won't argue," the woman replied. "But I'd rather you and your friend didn't go off on any sightseeing trips by yourselves. You told me yourself that you had plenty to do here. You enjoy that and then I can find you if I need you."

"I just hope we won't get bored," Bessie muttered, feeling as if she were suddenly trapped. She and Doona hadn't actually planned to leave the park during their week-long stay, but now, having been told they couldn't, Bessie was contrarily seized with a desire to explore the local countryside.

Margaret didn't reply, she simply took Bessie into another office so that one of her staff could take Bessie's fingerprints. Once that was done, Bessie was told that she could leave. The staff loo was closed while several police officers were examining it, so Bessie headed back out to the food court to try to find somewhere to wash her hands. The fingerprint ink that covered every finger made her feel vaguely as if she were guilty of something.

As she scrubbed her hands in the nearest ladies' loo, Bessie was aware that a couple of women were staring at her with undisguised curiosity. Bessie decided she was too old to care what they thought and merely kept scrubbing. Eventually, before the ink was completely gone, the pair left, whispering loudly about the various things they'd heard about why the police were in the park. As she was all too aware of the real reason for their presence, Bessie didn't even bother to listen to their gossip.

With her hands clean, Bessie pulled out her mobile and rang Doona. The call wasn't answered. As she had no idea where her friend might be, Bessie decided to head back to their lodge. If Doona wasn't there, maybe she'd left Bessie a note. Barring that, at least Bessie could read a book and wait for her there.

She walked as quickly as she could through the crowded food court area. It was getting close to lunchtime and the tables were filling up. As Bessie reached the doors to the outside, she heard her name.

"Mrs. Cubbon? Wait for me." Bessie looked around and spotted the gentleman from the cabin next to theirs walking rapidly towards her.

She could see a table full of his family behind him and several of the members were watching his progress.

"Mrs. Cubbon? I hope I've remembered that correctly," he said as he reached her side.

"It's Miss Cubbon, actually," she replied. "And you're Mr. Cheatham, I believe?"

"You have a good memory, Miss Cubbon," the man replied. "If you're heading back to Foxglove Close, I'll walk with you, if I may."

"But what about your family?" Bessie asked, gesturing towards the table near the centre of the room. It seemed to her as if most of the men and women sitting at it were frowning at Bessie.

The man glanced over at them and then shook his head. He gave them a cheery wave and then offered Bessie his arm. "They'll survive without me for one meal," he told her.

They walked out into a warm autumn midday. Bessie took a deep breath and then sighed. "It's a beautiful day," she said.

"It's quite warm for October," the man replied. "Perfect for a holiday in the woods, wouldn't you say, Miss Cubbon?"

"Oh, please call me Bessie," she said. "Everyone does."

"And I'm Andrew," he answered. "Although no one calls me that. It seems like everyone calls me 'dad' or 'granddad,' and sometimes I quite forget my Christian name."

Bessie smiled. "There does seem to be rather a lot of them," she said.

Andrew laughed. "Three children with their spouses, seven grand-children, with two spouses there as well, and two great- grandchil-dren. That makes eighteen of us when we're all together."

"Good heavens," Bessie gasped. "I can't imagine organising all those people to get you all here at the same time."

They'd reached a narrow bridge that crossed a small stream and Andrew paused to watch the water flowing for a moment. "My daughter, Helen, was in charge of that. I'm sure she sold it to her brothers as probably our last chance to have a family holiday before I die."

Bessie wasn't sure if he was serious or not. "I'm sorry, are you ill?" she asked after an awkward silence.

Andrew chuckled. "I'm perfectly fine and in great shape, but Helen has been predicting my imminent demise since her mother died in nineteen-seventy-three. One of these days she'll be right, I suppose."

"But not for many years," Bessie said.

"You never know," Andrew said. "Anyway, I love them all, especially the little ones, but they wear me out quite a bit and I sometimes I need a break. We've all been together since breakfast, so I thought I'd head back to my little oasis and have a quiet lunch on my own."

The man didn't seem to be in any hurry now though, as he stood and watched the stream.

"When did you last play Poohsticks?" he asked Bessie after a moment.

"Oh, goodness, I never have," Bessie replied. "The stories weren't a part of my childhood and I never had children of my own. I read the books, as an adult, but I never tried playing the game."

"Well, there's a first time for everything," the man said. He turned from the bridge railings and looked around. "Sticks," he said, pointing towards a small tree nearby. A few small sticks were visible on the ground around the trunk.

"There's a skill to picking the best sticks," Andrew told her. "I always look for sticks that are quite streamlined, that will slide through the water the fastest."

Again, Bessie wasn't sure if he was serious or not. She picked up the nearest stick, a short one that still had a small leaf attached to it. "It might not be streamlined, but at least I'll be able to tell it's mine," she told the man.

Andrew picked up and then discarded several sticks before selecting one. "Now we must find our spots on the bridge," he told her. As they walked back towards the bridge, a large crowd of bicycles rode past. Bessie stepped backwards quickly, nearly knocking Andrew over.

"Steady there," he said, his hands settling on her waist for a moment while he regained his balance.

Bessie caught her breath and flushed at the unexpected contact. She took a step forward as soon as it was safe to do so.

"Right, I'm going to stand here," he said, moving back onto the bridge. "I think the current is fastest right about here."

Bessie took a moment to study the stream. Andrew was probably correct, she decided. The stream did look to be moving faster right under where he was standing than anywhere else.

"Of course, as this is your first game, you get first choice of bridge position," he said, taking a step away from the railing.

Bessie chuckled. "I think I'll have that space, then," she said.

Andrew nodded. "You'd be foolish not to," he said.

She took his place at the railing and he moved a few steps to her left. "I shall count to three and then say 'drop.' At that point you may drop your stick."

Bessie held her stick at arm's length over the water. Andrew held his at the same height.

"One, two, three, drop," Andrew said.

They both let go of their sticks and then walked quickly to the other side of the bridge. For several seconds they both watched anxiously for any sign of their sticks. Bessie was starting to think the sticks had become stuck under the bridge when she noticed something in the water.

"I think that's my stick," she said excitedly.

"It may just be," Andrew said.

A moment later Bessie was certain that it was her stick that she could see. "But where has yours gone?" she asked.

"It's just there," Andrew pointed. "Coming out from under the bridge now."

Bessie could just see it as it meandered past them.

"My leaf made mine easier to see," she said.

"They always seem to take longer than I expect to come out," Andrew told her. "But you were the clear winner. Congratulations."

"Thank you," Bessie replied, feeling only a little bit silly.

"But I'm sure you're eager to get back to your friend. I mustn't keep you, especially after your rather eventful morning," he said.

"I just hope Doona's at the lodge," Bessie replied as they continued their walk.

"There are all sorts of rumours flying around the park as to what happened this morning," Andrew said in a conversational tone.

"I'm sure there are," Bessie said levelly.

Andrew chuckled. "And you aren't going to answer any questions," he said.

Bessie shrugged. "I really can't," she told him.

They'd reached the entrance to Foxglove Close.

Andrew slowed his pace. "I won't try to change your mind," he said. "But I was a cop for a great many years and I know a murder investigation when I see one unfolding. I hope you and your friend aren't caught up in it. If you ever need anyone to talk to, I'm right next door."

Bessie was so busy processing his words that she barely remembered to mutter "good-bye" to him as he disappeared into number seven. She turned her key and pushed open her door, hoping her friend would be there.

She found Doona on their patio, pretending to read one of the book club books. Bessie could tell that Doona had been crying and she quickly sat down in the chair next to her. After putting an arm around her friend, Bessie waited for Doona to speak.

"It doesn't feel real," Doona said after a moment.

"I can't imagine how you must be feeling," Bessie replied.

Doona pulled back from Bessie and took a deep breath. "I really don't want to talk about it," she said firmly.

Bessie opened her mouth to argue, but the look on Doona's face had her snapping it shut again.

"We're meant to be on holiday and I don't intend to let Charles's death spoil that," Doona said tightly. "I've already rung and rescheduled our woodland walk for tomorrow morning at eight. We didn't have anything else scheduled for today, so I thought maybe, after lunch, we could go to the pool."

"I suppose we could," Bessie said slowly, her mind racing. She couldn't help but feel as if they had a lot discuss, but she understood Doona wanting to put the whole thing out of her mind as well.

"They took my fingerprints," Doona said, her eyes staring out towards the lake behind the building. "I couldn't really argue, as they're already on file somewhere from when I was hired by the constabulary back home."

"They took mine as well," Bessie told her.

"Why would they take yours?" Doona demanded. "You didn't even go near the door."

"Inspector Hopkins said it was in case I'd touched the door or the door frame at all," Bessie replied.

"You never even got close," Doona said.

"But she doesn't know that for sure," Bessie replied.

"I think she's going to compare our fingerprints to any they can get off the murder weapon," Doona said bleakly.

"Of course she is," Bessie said. "Did you see a weapon?"

"No, but it must have been a knife of some sort, I think."

"It doesn't matter, really. We were both fast asleep in our beds when Charles was killed. I'm sure the good inspector will find the culprit very quickly."

"I went out for a walk in the middle of the night," Doona said quietly.

"Oh, dear. You should have woken me if you couldn't sleep. I would have kept you company," Bessie said.

"I didn't want to disturb you, and I needed some fresh air and space to think," Doona replied. "I just wanted to be alone."

"Where did you go?"

"That's just it," Doona said with a sigh. "I walked into the little village and then beyond it. It was so peaceful and quiet that I just kept walking and walking for over an hour."

"Did you see anyone?"

"Sure, there were a few people working at places all over the site. I even saw Charles, at a distance, and then hid in the shadows until he went inside the Squirrel's Drey."

"He didn't see you?"

"No, he was on his mobile, shouting and waving his arms around. I don't think he'd have noticed me even if I hadn't hidden."

"Do you have any idea who he was talking to?" Bessie asked.

Doona shook her head. "I was too far away to hear him clearly, even though he was yelling," she replied. "I was just thinking about trying to get closer when he disconnected and went inside."

"Was that on your way out or back to the cabin?"

"It was on my way out. But I walked around the perimeter of the entire park after that, so I didn't actually come back past the Squirrel's Drey."

"And you didn't notice anyone skulking in the shadows and then following Charles back inside?" Bessie asked.

"I wish I had, but no, as far as I could tell, Charles was alone. Everything was all locked up everywhere, and I saw Charles lock the door behind himself when he went back inside as well. Either the killer was already in the building, or he or she had a key."

"Or Charles let him or her in later," Bessie added.

"Or some other random person with a key opened the door for the killer," Doona sighed. "I'm glad this is all Margaret's problem and not mine."

"I'm just glad she's the one who has to deal with Lawrence Jenkins. He seems thoroughly unpleasant," Bessie said.

"The inspector was quite surprised that I'd never met him," Doona told her. "Apparently he and Charles were partners in a number of different ventures over many years."

"Do we know anything about the man?"

"Charles never mentioned him to me," Doona replied. "I didn't know about Charles's business ventures, either. And, I still don't have any idea what they might entail."

"Maybe you were entitled to more in the divorce," Bessie suggested. "You should ring your advocate."

Doona flushed. "I'm not going to think about that right now," she said firmly. "I'm more worried about needing my advocate because I've been arrested for murder."

Bessie laughed and then stopped abruptly when she realised that

Doona was serious. "I know you didn't kill Charles," she said. "I'm sure the inspector will work it out quickly."

"But I'm a suspect," Doona said sadly. "And I don't have any alibi."

"You'd need means and motive, even if you had the opportunity," Bessie replied, feeling as if she were quoting John Rockwell.

"As I said, I think he was stabbed. Knives aren't hard to come by, especially in a building with that many restaurants in it."

Bessie nodded. "I suppose that's true," she said reluctantly.

"As for motive, I didn't exactly keep quiet about my dislike for the man."

"Margaret Hopkins seemed to know what she was doing," Bessie said. "I'll bet she'll have the whole thing wrapped up by bedtime."

"I wish I had your confidence," Doona replied gloomily. "I just hope she has it solved before it's time to head home. I have to be back at work a week from today."

"John won't fire you if you get held up," Bessie said. "But what does this do to our holiday? If Charles was paying for it, are we going to have to pay now ourselves?"

"I talked to Mai when I rang to reschedule our walk. She didn't know about Charles yet, so I pretended I didn't either. Instead, I asked about how I'd come to win the contest. It sounds like Charles set it up so that as far as everyone here knows, I did actually win the week's holiday. I gather the park gives away similar packages several times a year. Unless something changes, I'm guessing we'll be fine. If we have to stay after our week is up, that's another matter, of course."

"I can't imagine they'd be able to accommodate us," Bessie said. "Do you think they'd have a place for us to stay?"

"I didn't ask Mai that," Doona replied. "We'll cross that bridge when we come to it."

"Fair enough," Bessie agreed.

"Margaret did tell me that I'm not to leave the site without her permission," Doona said with a sigh. "I'm not sure what that does to our trip to Torver Castle on Friday."

"Friday is a long way off," Bessie said airily. "Besides, I asked her and she said we could go as long as it's all been arranged by the park."

"Oh, good. I know you're looking forward to that."

"Aren't you?"

Doona shrugged. "After today, I'm not sure I'm up to meeting any ghosts," she replied.

"I don't think anyone has seen the ghosts at Torver Castle since the turn of the century," Bessie told her. "No one lives there now and there are all sorts of reports of lights going on and off and mysterious noises from behind the walls after hours, but there's never been a confirmed sighting of anything."

"Do you believe in ghosts?" Doona demanded.

"I believe in unexplained phenomena," Bessie replied. "The island has its own set of ghost stories and I've spoken to people who swear they've seen ghosts over the years. Some of them are very convincing." She shrugged. "I suppose I'm willing to keep an open mind, even though I've never seen a ghost myself. What about you?"

"I know people who claim to have seen Charlotte," Doona replied, referring to Charlotte de la Tremouille, the wife of the Seventh Earl of Derby. "But we all dragged our boyfriends down to Castle Rushen when we were teenagers, hoping to see her. I never did."

Bessie nodded. She was familiar with the legend. Charlotte had been staying at Castle Rushen while her husband travelled to England to fight on behalf of the king during the English Civil War. It was there that she received the news that he'd been captured and beheaded by the Parliamentarian forces. According to island folklore, Charlotte haunted Castle Rushen's throne room, waiting there anxiously for her husband to return from the war.

Local tradition had it that when a man takes you to the castle for a visit, the countess will tell you whether he's your perfect match or not. Charlotte's marriage, unusually for her social class at the time, had been a love match, which made her story all the more tragic and was meant to give her the ability to recognise true love matches in castle visitors. Women visiting with their dates were advised to leave their suitors behind and enter the throne room on their own. When Charlotte appeared, if she was crying, you were with the wrong man, but if she was smiling, you'd found your soul mate.

The story had been around for hundreds of years. Bessie herself had never tried it, but she knew others of her generation who had, one or two of whom claimed they'd seen the ghost. Over the decades, the story seemed to go in and out of favour.

"It's been years since I heard of anyone visiting Charlotte before they agreed to get engaged," Bessie remarked. "At one time, everyone seemed to be doing it."

"Well, I wish she'd have popped out and let me know not to marry Charles," Doona said. "Although I never actually visited Castle Rushen with him, so maybe that's my fault. She didn't warn me about my first husband though, either, and I visited the castle with him many times."

Bessie shivered. "All this talk about ghosts is making me feel uncomfortable," she told Doona.

"I'm mostly feeling hungry," Doona replied. "I never did get any breakfast, aside from an odd biscuit while we waited to be questioned. It must be time for some lunch, right?"

"It's well past that," Bessie exclaimed when she checked her watch. "It's nearly two o'clock." It felt as if the morning had been very long, as she'd spent most of it doing nothing much, but it also didn't seem as if it should be two o'clock already.

"In that case, let's go and find something to eat before the restaurants shut," Doona suggested.

"Did you have anywhere special in mind?" Bessie asked.

"Not really. Did you?"

Bessie smiled. "I thought maybe we should go to *L'Expérience Anglaise*," she said. "The food was delicious last night and I was thinking that another visit might help me remember more of what happened yesterday."

"We are not snooping," Doona said sternly. "Margaret Hopkins is quite capable of solving this murder."

"I didn't suggest any such thing," Bessie said in a hurt tone. "You have to admit the food was wonderful there."

Doona nodded. "It really was," she agreed.

"So, let's go," Bessie said. "I'm starving as well."

CHAPTER 6

*B*oth women took a minute to freshen up. Bessie ran a comb through her hair, making faces at her reflection as she did so. She brushed some powder across her nose and added a slick of lipstick before heading out to meet Doona in the sitting room. Doona took a few minutes longer to wash her tear-stained face and reapply her makeup.

"If we eat a big meal now, maybe we should just stop in the little grocery shop after we're done and get a few things in for an evening meal in our lodge," Doona suggested as they walked to the door.

"That sounds good," Bessie replied.

"I stuck my head in earlier and they have a nice selection," Doona told her. "They even have their own bakery, so we can get some bread and cheese and meat and just curl up with some wine and the telly, if you want."

"I think I'll have a book instead of the telly," Bessie told her. "But otherwise it sounds wonderful."

They walked back to the village slowly. Bessie smiled to herself as they crossed the small bridge. She'd have to remember to tell Doona that their neighbour used to be with the police. Now didn't seem like the time to mention that, though.

The restaurant was mostly empty when they arrived.

"Table for two?" the girl at the front desk asked.

Bessie recognised her as Monique Beck, the chef's wife.

"Yes, please," she replied.

The girl led them to a small table in the back of the room. It wasn't far from where they'd sat the previous evening. Monique handed them menus and took their drink order. Both women stuck to soft drinks.

"Everything sounds wonderful," Bessie said as she read through the menu.

"I'm going to have that fish dish that we had a tiny portion of last night," Doona said.

"That was good, but I think I'd prefer the chicken," Bessie said as she remembered their feast from the previous evening.

A loud crashing noise interrupted their discussion. The door to the kitchen swung open, and as Monique emerged, they could hear another crash from behind the door.

"Is everything okay?" Bessie asked the girl as she delivered their drinks.

"We're all just a little on edge," Monique answered in her lilting French accent. "We don't know what's going on in the main building and that has upset Nathan. Good chefs are very sensitive."

Another noise from the kitchen, less a crash than a bang, had Monique turning pale. "I'll be right back to get your order," she said quickly before she headed back into the kitchen.

Bessie looked at Doona. "I wonder what will happen in the kitchen when Nathan finds out what's actually going on," she whispered.

"Unless he already knows," Doona replied.

"You suspect the chef of murdering Charles?"

"I suspect everyone," Doona replied in a tired voice.

Monique was back a moment later. She took their order, but it was obvious that she was distracted and Bessie had to ask her twice about side dishes before Monique answered. Finally, after writing everything down, Monique turned back towards the kitchen. She was stopped by another customer.

"This isn't what I ordered," the man said angrily. "We waited nearly an hour for our food and most of it is wrong."

Monique flushed. "I'm so sorry," she said. "I'll get it taken care of right away."

She took the plate of food and walked back to the kitchen. Bessie shook her head.

"Monique is at least as upset as her husband," Bessie remarked.

Harold Butler walked into the restaurant and headed straight for the kitchen. Bessie thought about speaking to him, but he dashed past so quickly she didn't really get a chance. A moment later there was another loud noise from the kitchen. After a few minutes, Harold emerged.

"I'm very sorry, ladies and gentlemen," he said in a loud voice. "We've had a very difficult morning here at the park and it's causing troubles with everything throughout Lakeview. All of your meals are on the house and I'm going to work with Monique to get you what you ordered as quickly as possible."

He began moving from table to table, talking to each of the small groups that were there, making notes of everyone's complaints. As so few tables were occupied, it wasn't long before he reached Bessie and Doona.

"Have you been waiting terribly long?" he asked, his usually cheery tone absent.

"We just arrived a few minutes ago and Monique just took our order," Bessie answered. "We're fine."

"Excellent," he said. "I would like a chance to talk to you two, but first I have to sort out this mess." He was gone before Bessie or Doona could respond.

"I wonder what he wants," Bessie said.

"I don't want to know," Doona replied sourly.

Monique was back a minute later with a sliced baguette and butter. She dropped them on the table and left without saying a word.

Bessie and Doona ate their bread and watched as Harold worked the room. Wine began to flow at several tables and Monique was suddenly busy delivering food all around the room. It was only a couple of minutes before she was at their table, delivering their order.

"Let me know if you need anything else," she muttered as she walked away.

Bessie looked down at her plate. "It doesn't look as good as it did last night," she said. She poked at the chicken breast. "It's not as tender, either."

Doona was inspecting her own lunch. "This doesn't smell the same as last night," she said quietly. She took a bite and made a face. "It isn't the same and it isn't very good," she said.

Bessie was shaking her head. "Mine isn't very nice, either," she said. "I imagine Nathan is very distracted."

The door to the restaurant suddenly swung open. Bessie froze as Jessica Howe strode into the room.

"Where is he?" she demanded in a loud voice.

Harold walked quickly over from where he'd been placating customers and grabbed Jessica's arm. "Please don't shout," he hissed at her.

"I won't shout if you tell me where that slimy, lying, cheating...." She trailed off when she spotted Doona.

"You, I knew I recognised you last night. We got drunk together once, about two years ago. What are you doing here?"

Harold glanced at Doona and then back at Jessica. "Let's not bother the other guests," he said nervously.

"Where's Charles?" she demanded. "He's hiding from me somewhere because he knows I'm going to kill him when I find him. Tell me where he is."

"I don't know," Harold said, shrugging. "I'm just doing my job."

Jessica's eyes narrowed. "You're lying," she said fiercely. "Before I kill Charles, I'm going to have him fire you."

Harold laughed, a strangely nasty sound. "Surely you realise that if Charles could fire me, he would have done so before now. He may have my old job, but he can't get rid of me."

"Jessica? What's going on?" The man standing behind Jessica looked about sixty. He was wearing the sort of very expensive casual wear that suggested he'd have been much more comfortable in a business suit. His eyes, as he scanned the room, were cold. They settled on Doona for a moment before glancing at Bessie. Bessie felt a chill as her eyes met his.

"I was just thinking about getting some lunch," Jessica said. "But they're done serving lunch for today."

"Really? I thought perhaps you were looking for your lover," the man said. "I know where he ought to be, hell. And if I find him before you do, I'll be happy to put him there."

The crashing noise came from inside the dining room this time. Bessie was surprised to see that Monique had dropped a tray full of dishes. The girl looked pale and exhausted as she bent down and started cleaning up the mess.

"Jessica, we're leaving," the man announced, taking her arm.

Bessie braced herself for the argument that was sure to follow, but Jessica's reaction surprised her.

"Of course, darling. Let's go," she cooed at the man. "I can make us both some nice lunch back at our chalet."

The pair left arm in arm, which had Bessie shaking her head.

"What a strange couple," she murmured to Doona.

"Indeed," Doona replied.

They both looked down at their half-eaten lunches and then sighed at the same time.

"Was it that bad?" a voice asked at Bessie's elbow.

Bessie glanced up and then smiled at Nathan, the chef. "It wasn't quite the same as last night," she said.

"I'm so sorry," he said. "We had a very late night, with the party and the dinner, and then a very disturbed morning. I'm simply not myself."

"Sit down," Bessie invited.

The man pulled an empty chair from the next table over and sank into it. "Thank you," he said. "I do hope you'll try eating here again later in your stay. I'm sure tomorrow will be a better day."

"What's going on that's causing all this trouble?" Bessie asked, hoping the man didn't know she'd been involved in what had happened next door.

Nathan shook his head. "That's part of the problem," he said in a confiding tone. "No one is telling us anything."

He looked around the restaurant, which was slowly emptying. Monique had finished picking up broken plates and glasses and had gone into the kitchen. Harold was talking to four people at a table on the opposite side of the room.

Nathan leaned in towards Bessie and spoke very quietly. "The police have been here all morning. They took Lawrence away, but no one has seen any sign of Charles Adams since they arrived. I think Charles and Lawrence were involved in something criminal and they got caught red-handed."

"What sort of thing?" Bessie asked.

Nathan shrugged. "I don't know, maybe stealing money from the park? Whatever is going on, they've kept Charles tucked away all morning. Monique has been ringing him constantly to find out what's happening and he hasn't answered."

Bessie glanced at Doona, but her friend was busy studying her fingernails and pretending that she wasn't interested in the conversation.

"Harold was questioned by the police, so he has to know what's going on, but he won't tell us anything," Nathan continued.

"Did you need Charles for something this morning?" Bessie asked, her mind racing through a dozen questions she'd like to ask.

"He always comes in first thing in the morning to go over the specials with me," Nathan explained. "Then Monique types them up and makes copies of the sheet. When he didn't arrive, Monique and I had to work it all out for ourselves, which took a lot longer than normal and threw off our entire day."

"When did you see him last?" Doona threw in.

"He left while we were clearing away the last of the dinner plates last night," Nathan replied. "Monique walked over to his office with him. He had some new recipes that he wanted me to take a look at, so she went with him to collect them."

"What sort of new recipes?" Bessie asked. "Anything we can look forward to during our stay?"

"I don't think so," Nathan said, shaking his head. "There were one or two that we might be able to adapt for here, but most of them were not what I would consider appropriate."

He leaned forward and lowered his voice again. "Charles is always looking for ways to cut costs, but I'm a chef and I won't change out high quality menu items for cheaper ones just to increase profits."

Monique approached the table now. "Shall I clear these plates?" she asked hesitantly.

"Yes, thank you," Bessie said with a smile.

"I'm sorry the food wasn't more to your liking," she said as she piled the plates onto an empty tray.

"Your husband was just telling us about all of the upheaval this morning," Doona said. "Perhaps you shouldn't have even opened."

"Oh, but we can't shut," Monique said in a shocked voice. "Lakeview's guests would be very disappointed. Ours is the premier restaurant here."

"It won't be if you keep making a mess of things like today," Harold said harshly as he approached. "I've had nothing but complaints about the food here today."

"Charles wasn't here to do the specials," Monique said defensively. "That meant Nathan and I had to do them all by ourselves, which took ages. We were hours behind before the doors even opened."

"I'm not much interested in your excuses," Harold said. "Lunch is finished. You have two hours to get yourselves sorted before dinner service begins. I expect a dramatic improvement."

He swept out of the restaurant after that, not allowing anyone time to reply. Monique looked around to make sure that all of the other guests had left and then put her tray down on an empty table. She walked to the door and turned the lock before she slid the sign on the door to read "closed."

"Sit down and take a break," Nathan urged his wife. "You've been on your feet for hours."

"There's so much to do before dinner," she argued.

"Not that much," Nathan disagreed. "Unless Charles turns up to tell us otherwise, we'll just do the same specials for dinner that we had for lunch. That saves us a lot of time. Sit with me for ten minutes and then we'll both get back to work."

"But what about our guests?" Monique asked, looking pointedly at Doona and Bessie.

"I want to talk to our guests," Nathan told her.

Monique pulled up another chair and then looked at her husband. "I don't think...." she began.

He held up a hand. "I'll probably get fired for this," he told Bessie and Doona, "but with everything else going on, I just have to ask. Who are you?"

"What do you mean?" Bessie asked after glancing at Doona, who wouldn't meet her eyes.

"Charles was very excited about your coming," he told them. "He'd been talking about it for weeks and yesterday he was shouting at everyone, insisting that everything had to be perfect for you. Then, last night, you barely spoke to him and today he's nowhere to be found. We're all confused about the two of you and why you're here."

"We won a week's holiday in a contest," Bessie said. "That's all."

Nathan shook his head. "We have contest winners here all the time. If you don't want to tell us what's really going on, just say so, but please don't lie to us."

"We aren't lying," Doona said after a short pause. "We really did just win the week here as a prize. Charles and I were, well, let's just say I knew him years ago. We had no idea he was working here now or I wouldn't have come, free holiday or not."

Nathan chuckled. "So many people seem to dislike the man," he said thoughtfully. "I suppose it's good that I'm not the only one."

"Nathan, that isn't fair," Monique scolded. "Charles works very hard and he's kind and he's a good boss. Much better than Harold, anyway. You know that Lakeview has been doing really well since he's been here."

"I thought it was doing fine under Harold's management," Nathan replied. "And I didn't have to get approval for everything I did or deal with constant 'budgetary adjustments.'"

The man made air quotation marks around the last two words, finishing his remarks by making a face.

Monique flushed. "Charles wants to increase the park's profits. Surely there isn't anything wrong with that? We wouldn't have jobs if Harold ran the place out of business."

"How long have you two been working here?" Bessie interrupted their argument to ask.

"About a year," Nathan replied.

"Did you meet here or somewhere else?" Bessie questioned.

"We met in Paris," Monique replied. "I was waiting tables in my family's restaurant."

"And I was studying to be a chef," Nathan picked up the story. "I used to eat at a different restaurant every day, trying out different things and seeing how different chefs plated their meals."

"But then he started eating at our restaurant every day," Monique said, giving her husband a smile.

He took her hand and squeezed it. "It didn't help with my chef training, but I had a good reason for wanting to eat there all the time," he said.

"That seems a long time ago," Monique said, staring out of the window at the front of the restaurant. "And I'm not quite sure how we ended up here, in this place."

"I was offered the job of head chef at a famous London hotel," Nathan said. "We got married and moved to London, but the job didn't work out. They expected too much and paid too little. After that, we moved around quite a bit, seemingly always moving north, for some reason. We got here about a year ago, and for the most part, working at the holiday park suits us."

Monique opened her mouth and then snapped it shut again. Someone knocked on the door, startling them all.

"It's just Mai," Nathan said as he walked to the door. "Harold probably sent her over to shout at us in the nicest possible way."

Monique giggled. "Probably," she agreed.

Nathan unlocked the door to let Mai in, quickly locking it behind her once she was inside.

"Ah, Ms. Cubbon and Mrs. Moore, I was wondering where you two were," Mai said as she spotted the trio at the small table.

"We were just taking our time over lunch," Bessie replied. "Mr. and Mrs. Beck were kind enough to let us stay for a bit after they'd closed."

"Yes, well, anything we can do to improve your holiday, just ask," the girl replied brightly. "I just wanted to check in on Nathan, really. I heard there were some problems at lunch?"

"Charles never showed up to do the specials," Nathan said in a tired voice. "That put us behind schedule and sort of messed everything up."

"Are you okay now?" she asked, putting a hand on his arm.

He smiled at her, but it was Monique who answered. "We're fine," she said, getting up from her seat. She crossed the room and slipped her arm around her husband. "We'll have everything sorted for dinner, no problem."

"Good," Mai said briskly. "I hate getting complaints about the food here. I know Nathan is better than that."

"We certainly are," Monique replied haughtily.

"But what's on your schedule for the rest of the day?" Mai asked Bessie and Doona. "Surely you have activities booked?"

"We were meant to be going on the woodland walk this morning, but we, er, missed it," Doona told her. "That was all that we had on the schedule for today, but I suppose we ought to be reading our books for the book club on Saturday."

"Oh, you should save those for a rainy day," Mai suggested. "It's beautiful out today." She pulled a folded piece of paper from her pocket.

"Let's see, there's a family squirrel walk in half an hour," she said. "I suspect that will be full of small children, though. Have you thought about trying out kayaking? Or we could see if there's a tennis court free?"

Doona and Bessie exchanged glances. "I don't think so," Bessie said after a moment. "I think maybe a nice long walk around the village is what we need after our lunch."

"I can ring the ranger station and see if there's a ranger available to give you a tour," Mai said brightly.

"We've already rescheduled our woodland walk for tomorrow morning," Doona said. "I think Bessie was suggesting just wandering around and seeing the park."

"Yes, well, of course you're welcome to do that," Mai said with doubt in her voice. "But I'm happy to arrange something special for you."

"I'm sure we'll be fine on our own," Doona said firmly. "I really don't like people making a fuss over me."

Mai flushed. "Charles insisted, that is, he suggested that we treat you like our most important guests ever. I don't want him to think that I'm neglecting you."

"You have nothing to worry about there," Doona said dryly.

Bessie turned an inappropriate chuckle into a cough. "Maybe we should get out of everyone's way," she said, rising to her feet.

"Yes, I know you all have a lot to do before dinner," Doona said.

"Thanks," Nathan replied. "Please do give us another try later in your stay. I promise you won't be sorry."

"We'll definitely be back," Doona assured him. "But I do want to try some of the other options as well, so it may be a while."

Nathan unlocked the door for them and pulled it open. Before the women could leave, however, two people walked in through the door.

"Miss Cubbon, Mrs. Moore, this is a surprise," Margaret Hopkins said, her eyes moving back and forth between the two women.

"We just finished lunch," Bessie replied, feeling guilty of something as the woman's cool eyes appraised her.

"Joe, what's going on?" Nathan asked the man who'd entered with the inspector.

Joe Klein shook his head. "Ask the boss," he said, nodding towards Margaret.

She smiled. "I'm hardly that," she murmured. "As for what's going on, I'd like to ask everyone a few questions. It will be easiest if we lock up here and move across to the main building where I have an office set up."

"This is about Charles, isn't it?" Nathan asked. "He's done something and he's been arrested."

"I said I needed to ask you questions," the woman replied. "I won't be answering any."

"But what about dinner?" Monique asked. "We have to start the dinner preparations now."

"I'm afraid my investigation takes precedence," Margaret told her. "I'll try to keep my questioning as brief as possible."

"But what about…." Monique began again, but Joe interrupted.

"The longer we argue, the more time this will take," he said firmly. "Let's go over to the other building and get it over with. Then you can get back and get started on dinner."

No one looked happy, but when Joe held open the door, Monique and Mai walked through it. Nathan held up the keys.

"I'll just lock up after everyone's out," he said.

Bessie and Doona followed the others, with Joe and Margaret at the rear. Nathan was last out and once he'd locked the door, he was quick to follow Joe and his wife. Bessie and Doona started to walk away, but didn't get far.

"Mrs. Moore, Miss Cubbon? Can I have a quick word with you, please?" Margaret Hopkins called.

Bessie and Doona stopped and turned back towards her. The policewoman waited until Joe had escorted the other three into the large building before she spoke.

"Thank you for not talking about what happened this morning," she said quietly. "I want to be able to question people about their interactions with Charles before they know he's dead, but it's very hard work keeping something like that quiet at a place like this."

"I'm amazed you've managed it so far," Doona said bluntly.

"Quite frankly, I am as well," the woman replied. "I'm glad Lawrence is tucked away in my office. I'm sure he wouldn't have kept his mouth shut. Harold seems to be doing a good job dealing with things and so far as I can tell, he hasn't said anything. My staff knows better than to talk, of course. In a little while we'll have to bring out the body, though, at which point we won't be able to pretend to be investigating a robbery any longer. I'd appreciate your cooperation until that time, though."

"Not a problem," Doona assured her.

Margaret nodded and then turned and strode quickly back to the main building. Bessie and Doona watched until she was out of sight.

"A stroll around the park, then?" Doona asked.

"Why not?"

The weather was just about perfect for October and the two women walked in silence for some time, following trails through the woods and around the various cabins and lodges.

"Wow, these look fancy," Bessie said as they rounded a corner and spotted a handful of very large, two-storey buildings.

"I saw them in the brochure," Doona told her. "They have their own saunas and four bedrooms, each with its own en-suite. I'm sure they're designed for multiple families to book together, because they're very, very expensive."

A man walked out of one of the large lodges now, talking on his mobile phone. His face was red and he was clearly upset. "I said I want to have a meeting on Monday about this," he was shouting. "Can you hear me now? I'm breaking up? Reception is terrible out here. Why I ever let Janet talk me into this holiday is beyond me. I'll ring you back from a proper phone." He stomped back into the cabin, slamming the front door as he went.

"Someone needs a holiday," Bessie whispered.

"I feel sorry for Janet, whoever she is," Doona replied.

The rest of the walk was fairly uneventful, aside from a few near misses with small children on bicycles and one close encounter with a squirrel who seemed to think they wanted to play with him. An hour later they were back at the centre of the village.

"So, shall we get some groceries in for our evening meal and then go back to our cottage and relax?" Doona asked.

"That sounds perfect," Bessie agreed.

Inside the Squirrel's Drey they found the small grocery shop. It was well stocked with more than enough options for their evening meal. Bessie found herself selecting biscuits and fairy cakes from the bakery, along with a loaf of fresh bread to go with the cheeses and meats she'd already selected.

"Those look amazing," Doona said as she pointed out the selection of French-style pastries. "Maybe I'll just try a few profiteroles and that little apple tart, oh, and...."

Bessie laughed as her friend trailed off. The selection was large and everything looked good after their disappointing lunch. "We are here for the rest of the week," she pointed out as Doona was having the shop assistant box up her selections. "You can always try some of the others tomorrow."

"I'm sure I'll leave some for tomorrow," Doona said. "But right now I'm starving. I didn't get enough lunch."

"No, me either," Bessie agreed, adding one of the apple tarts to her selections as well.

At the checkout, they billed everything to their cabin, as they'd been told they could do.

"It's going to be a huge shock if we get the bill for all of this at the end of the week," Doona whispered as they headed out of the shop.

"We'll sort it out if it happens," Bessie said. She wasn't going to let the uncertainty spoil her holiday. If they had to pay for everything themselves, well, she could afford it, and she would pay for Doona's share as well if Doona needed her to. Bessie had always been very careful with money, and the clever investments that her advocate had made on her behalf over the years meant that she had more than enough to meet her modest needs. Paying for the holiday wouldn't make more than a tiny dent in her bank account.

They made their way through the building towards the exit doors. Bessie felt her eyes being drawn towards the door to the staff offices, even as she tried not to look.

"Everyone is focussed on those doors," Doona hissed. "I wonder why?"

Bessie glanced around and saw that Doona was right. The usually bustling food court area was strangely quiet and all eyes seemed to be fixed on the door marked "staff." A moment later, the door swung open and Bessie understood why.

A man walked out backwards, followed by the sort of wheeled stretcher that is found in ambulances. A second man was pushing the stretcher. They both kept their heads down and headed straight out of the building where Bessie could now see an ambulance was parked near the doors. The body on the stretcher was covered with a sheet from head to toe, and the two men loaded it into the back of the vehicle. No one in the food court moved as the ambulance drove slowly away.

Bessie and Doona followed the men to the doors as the room began to return to normal. Outside, Bessie took a deep breath, feeling sadder than she thought she should. She was surprised to see Mai, Monique and Nathan all standing in front of the French restaurant.

"Who did they put in the ambulance?" Mai demanded, her face pale.

"And why did they drive away so slowly? Why no flashing lights? Is someone dead?" Monique threw out the questions so quickly that Bessie didn't know where to start with answering them.

"I'm sorry to inform you that Charles Adams is dead," Margaret said in a cool voice from behind Bessie. "I'm sure you understand that I have a few more questions for each of you now."

Monique gasped and then swooned. Nathan caught her just before she crashed to the ground. While he looked around helplessly, Mai began to scream.

CHAPTER 7

$\mathcal{J}$oe Klein was quick to deal with the screaming Mai. Nathan managed to get Monique into a sitting position on the ground, and the colour slowly began to return to her face. Before anyone could speak, someone behind Bessie began to laugh. She spun around and was surprised to find Herbert Howe standing to one side, watching the scene as it unfolded.

"Best news I've heard in a long time," he said loudly when he realised everyone was looking at him. "I can't wait to tell Jessica."

"Tell me what?" Jessica walked into the middle of the space. She looked from her husband to Monique, who was still sitting on the ground, and then back around again. Her eyes narrowed as she spotted Doona, but she didn't speak.

"He got what was coming to him," Herbert said in a gleeful voice. "I hope it was a very painful heart attack or maybe he choked to death on his own arrogance? Come on, what happened to him?"

Margaret looked steadily at the man for a moment before she spoke. "You must be Herbert Howe. We've been looking for you. I have some questions I'd like to ask you about last night."

"What's going on?" Jessica demanded. "Herbert, what have you done?"

DIANA XARISSA

"And you're Jessica Howe," Margaret continued. "You're on my list as well. We wanted to find you before the body was removed, but no one seemed to know exactly where you were."

"What body?" Jessica snapped. "What is everyone talking about?"

"Charles!" Mai shouted, tears streaming down her face. "Charles is dead."

Jessica turned pale and one hand clutched her throat. Bessie watched as she swallowed hard and then turned towards her husband. "You killed him," she said in a shocked voice. "After all this time and all the threats, you actually killed him."

Herbert laughed harshly. "If I had, I'd have made sure no one ever found the body," he said.

"I think that's enough discussion out here," Margaret spoke loudly. "Joe, can you please bring everyone inside? They can all wait in the conference room while I speak to each person on his or her own."

"Dinner service starts in less than an hour," Nathan objected.

"I think you're going to have to cancel dinner for tonight," Margaret told him.

"But we can't," Monique said as she struggled to get up. "People have bookings. We can't disappoint them."

"I'm sure we'll be able to work something out," Harold said smoothly from the edge of the crowd. "I'll take charge of rebooking everyone into other restaurants. You need to do whatever Inspector Hopkins asks."

"Thank you, Mr. Butler," Margaret said. She spun on her heel and moved back into the main building. A pair of uniformed officers helped Joe Klein round up the five people the inspector wanted to interview and then escorted them into the building as well. Bessie and Doona exchanged glances.

"Let's get back to our cabin," Doona whispered. "I've had quite enough excitement for one day."

They were only a few steps away from the building when Andrew Cheatham fell into step beside Bessie.

"So, Charles Adams was murdered," he said in a conversational tone. "I don't know who any of the people back there were, but I sure am curious."

Bessie grinned. No doubt the former policeman was feeling left out on the sidelines. "Doona, did I mention that our new neighbour used to be a policeman?" she asked her friend.

"Did he now? Would you like to join us for an evening meal?" Doona asked the man.

"I'd be delighted," the man said, smiling brightly.

In number eight, the two women did a quick tidy up for their guest.

"He seems quite nice," Bessie remarked. "I hope we can talk to him about the case like we do with John."

"Except we aren't getting involved in this case," Doona said sharply. "I invited him so that we can get a different perspective on everything, but we are not getting involved in any investigation."

"Of course not," Bessie agreed. Unless Margaret Hopkins starts looking at you as a suspect, she added to herself.

When Andrew knocked on their door a short time later, the friends were relaxing with glasses of wine on their patio.

"Come and join us," Bessie invited him in. "Would you like a glass of wine?"

"I'm not much of a drinker," he said in an apologetic tone. "I'll have a fizzy drink if you have one. Otherwise, water is fine."

Bessie showed him out to the patio and then went back inside and got his drink. When she went back outside, he and Doona were silently watching the families on their bikes going past.

"Why aren't you out with your family?" Bessie asked the man. She flushed as she realised that the question sounded somewhat rude. "I mean, we're happy to have you here, but I would have thought you'd be having dinner with them."

"The children and their spouses are going out for a fancy meal tonight. They've left all of the grandchildren and great-grandchildren together in one of the cabins with a dozen pizzas and half the merchandise from the candy shop. I didn't really fancy joining either group," he replied.

Bessie laughed. "I'd take the fancy dinner over the pizza party any day."

"But if I'm there, they can't talk about me," Andrew retorted. "This way they can have a serious discussion about my physical and mental health. Someone, and I know exactly who, will suggest that it's time for me to move into a home and then they can all argue through five courses about what's best for me." He shook his head. "If I'm there, it spoils all their fun."

"And people wonder why I don't regret never having children," Bessie commented.

Andrew laughed. "Oh, I love my children and their respective spouses. And I know they do everything out of love and concern. I just don't enjoy being discussed as if I'm a small child. Anyway, I'd much rather talk about murder."

"But what makes you think we'll want to talk about it?" Bessie had to ask.

"I rang a few people this afternoon," Andrew told her. "Once I realised that the police were working a murder case and my lovely next-door neighbours were involved in some way, I rang a few connections to find out what was going on."

"You checked up on us?" Bessie asked.

"I'm a cop," he said flatly. "That doesn't change when you retire."

"What did you find out?" Doona demanded.

"I found out that you were from the Isle of Man," he replied. "As it happens, I'm passingly acquainted with your Lieutenant Governor. I rang him and he put me in touch with John Rockwell at the Laxey CID."

"How is John?" Bessie asked.

"He's doing well, although he admitted to missing you both. Anyway, he'd just finished talking with Margaret Hopkins about you two and he was happy to answer a few questions from me as well. I'm sure he didn't tell me nearly as much as he told Inspector Hopkins, but he did fill me in on some of the recent events in your lives and that made me suspect that you'd be happy to talk about the murder here with me. If I'm wrong, I'll finish my drink and go quietly, of course."

"You're not wrong," Doona said. "I'm hoping you can help us work out what's going on here. We can't very well invite Inspector Hopkins to dinner."

"I don't think she'd come," he replied. "I'm sure she doesn't socialise with suspects."

Doona looked surprised for a moment and then sighed. "I know I'm a suspect," she said sadly, "but I'd rather not think about it."

Andrew nodded. "I know what you mean, and I'll try not to mention it again. I'd rather hear about the other suspects. All those people shouting and carrying on in the village interest me. What can you tell me about them?"

"Let's get something to eat before we start," Bessie suggested. She could feel the wine going straight to her head, thanks to her empty stomach.

The trio quickly made themselves plates of meat, cheese and bread. Doona put all of the delicious pastries, fairy cakes and biscuits onto a plate and then put the plate in the centre of the table on the patio so that everyone could help themselves.

After a few bites, Bessie sighed. "I'll tell you what I can, but Doona probably knows more than I do," she said.

"I'm eating," Doona said, refusing to look up from her plate.

Bessie looked at Andrew and shrugged. He reached over and patted her hand. "Just tell me what you know and we'll go from there," he suggested. "This isn't a formal interrogation or anything. We're just friends having a chat."

About a rather strange subject, Bessie thought to herself. She took a sip of wine and then looked out at the lake.

"The pretty blonde who started screaming when the inspector told everyone that Charles was dead is called Mai Stratton," Bessie said. "She's the manager of guest services or something like that."

"She very young for such an important position," Andrew remarked. "Any idea if she's good at her job or not?"

Bessie shrugged. "She tried hard to make sure we were happy, but beyond that I've no idea."

Andrew nodded. "What about the young lady who swooned and the man who caught her?"

"Nathan and Monique Beck," Bessie said. "He's the chef at the French restaurant and she's a waitress there."

"She seemed very upset to hear that Charles had died," Andrew said.

"When we talked to them earlier, she seemed to really like Charles," Bessie said thoughtfully. "Nathan was less fond of the man."

"And the older gentleman who found it all funny?" he asked.

"Herbert Howe," Bessie replied. "I don't really know anything about him, except that the thirty-something blonde woman is his wife, Jessica. Herbert said, several times, that she was having an affair with Charles."

"She was," Doona said flatly.

Andrew raised an eyebrow. "So a motive appears for one suspect, at least. Or maybe even for both of them. Do we know if Charles was getting tired of the lady?"

Bessie shrugged. "Anything's possible," she said.

"And the man who swept in and started giving orders at the end?" Andrew asked.

"Harold Butler. He's the assistant general manager, although I understand he was the general manager before Charles arrived," Bessie said.

"Another possible motive, interesting," Andrew murmured.

"Don't forget about Lawrence," Doona interjected.

Andrew looked questioningly at Bessie, who replied.

"Lawrence Jenkins was Charles's business partner," Bessie explained. "I'm not quite sure what that means in this context, but he was there this morning when Doona found the body."

"But he wasn't around after that?" Andrew asked.

"Inspector Hopkins had him taken to her office in town," Bessie said. "She said she'd question him there when she had a chance."

"Interesting," the man said. "I'd almost guess that she suspects him of something, maybe not murder, but something, certainly."

"He was eager to get into the office where the body was to get some papers," Doona said. "He definitely seemed like someone with something to hide."

"Of course, that could have nothing to do with the murder," Andrew said thoughtfully.

The threesome ate their way through their meal and then tackled the plate of pastries. Between them, they managed to eat every last delicious bite.

"I appreciate your talking to me," the man said after he'd washed down the last of the final biscuit. "I hate being on the outside of this. I wonder of the good inspector would let me be a special consultant on the case?"

"You could ask," Bessie suggested.

"I just might do that," he told her. "But for now, I promised to meet everyone over the age of eighteen for a moonlight walk around the park. Let's hope my children have finished their meal and haven't drunk too much."

"That sounds lovely," Bessie said. "I hope you have fun."

"I'll see you both tomorrow," he said as the two women walked him to the door. "We haven't even begun to discuss how the two of you fit into this murder investigation."

He was gone before Bessie could reply. She looked at Doona, who was pale and looked exhausted.

"You need some sleep," Bessie said firmly.

"I wasn't very good company, was I?" Doona asked.

"You were very quiet, that's all," Bessie said. She put her arm around her friend. "Now I think you should get ready for bed. It's been a very stressful day for you, hasn't it?"

"I kept putting it all out of my mind," Doona said numbly. "The blood and the body and the fact that someone killed Charles. As long as we kept busy I felt okay, but once I sat down it all just came flooding back."

"I'm sure things will look brighter in the morning," Bessie said, even though she wasn't sure of any such thing. "Go and get ready for bed and I'll make you a cup of milky tea for you."

Doona nodded and then disappeared into her bedroom. Bessie made the tea, adding extra sugar as well as a great deal of milk. When Doona came into the kitchen in her pyjamas, robe and slippers, Bessie had it ready.

"Drink this and then straight to bed," Bessie said firmly. "And don't set an alarm. If we wake up in time for the woodland walk, we'll go, but if you can lie in, that's more important."

"If I don't get up, go without me," Doona told her. "I don't want you to miss out on everything just because of me."

"None of this is your fault," Bessie pointed out. "Anyway, we'll worry about it tomorrow."

Doona nodded and then headed back into her bedroom. Bessie washed up the plates and things from dinner and Doona's tea and then double-checked that the door to the patio was locked. She stood outside Doona's door for a moment, listening to see if her friend was asleep. When she heard Doona crying softly, Bessie wasn't sure what to do.

After pacing around the small lodge for several minutes, Bessie listened again. This time she heard nothing but silence. Satisfied that her friend had fallen asleep, Bessie headed into her own bedroom. Once she was ready for bed, she pulled out her mobile phone to plug it in to charge. She was surprised to see that she'd missed a call. It took her several minutes to work out how to retrieve the message that had been left. When she finally accessed it, the message was short and to the point.

"Ring me," Inspector Rockwell's voice demanded in his most senior policeman's voice.

Bessie settled back in bed and dialled the inspector's home number. It rang twice before he picked up.

"Bessie? What on earth is going on over there?"

At the sound of the kindly voice, Bessie felt tears begin to stream down her face. "Oh, John, it's just awful," she said sadly. "And Doona might even be a suspect."

"Slow down," John said calmly. "Tell me exactly what's going on."

Bessie slid down under the covers and walked John through her entire day, from the time she woke up until she'd climbed back in bed a few minutes earlier. John was silent throughout.

"Now you need to take me through yesterday," John told her when she'd finished.

Bessie frowned. "I didn't think about that," she said. "Of course I do."

Again, John was silent as Bessie spoke. When she was finished, he sighed.

"What a mess," he told her. "I'm going to ask you a few questions, and I want you to be totally honest and not get offended on Doona's behalf, okay?"

"I'll try," Bessie said cautiously.

"Is there any chance that she knew Charles was going to be there?" John asked.

"Absolutely not," Bessie said emphatically. "She wouldn't have come if she'd known."

"You mentioned him in passing, but what do you know about Andrew Cheatham?" John asked next.

"He's our next-door neighbour on the street where we're staying," Bessie replied. "But that's about all I know. Why?"

"He has some very important connections," John told her. "And he has a solid reputation as an excellent investigator. If Doona has anything she doesn't want him to know, she'll do well to stay away from him, but I would suggest he'll be a powerful ally if you can get him on your side."

"He seems like a very nice man," Bessie said. "We had dinner with him tonight and he told us he'd spoken to you."

"He did, and he asked very smart questions. So did Margaret Hopkins. I think the investigation is in good hands with her, at least so far."

"Doona will feel better when she hears that," Bessie said.

"Having said that," John added, "if you have any reason to believe that Doona is in any danger of being arrested or even seriously considered as a suspect, you must ring me right away. I can be on a flight across within a couple of hours if I have to be."

"Surely it won't come to that," Bessie argued. "She didn't have any reason to kill the man, after all."

"On the contrary, some would suggest she had several good reasons to kill him," John disagreed. "Luckily, she isn't the only one, and we both know for certain that she didn't do it."

The pair talked for several more minutes, but fairly pointlessly. John was too far away to properly assess the situation.

"Please ring me every night with an update," John told her. "I don't want to ask Doona to do so. She has enough to worry about."

"I'll ring," Bessie promised. "And I'll be careful what I say to our friendly neighbour in the meantime."

After the call ended, Bessie switched off the bedside light and slid further under the covers. The night had a definitely autumnal chill and she was grateful for the thick duvet. Convinced that she'd never manage to get to sleep, she was surprised when her internal alarm woke her at six. She felt as if she hadn't moved a muscle the entire night.

A hot shower did a lot to relax the tightness in her back and neck after so many hours of lying still. Bessie patted on her dusting powder and got dressed for the woodland walk she'd missed the day before. When she emerged from her room, she found Doona in the kitchen, nursing a cup of coffee.

"You look as if you didn't sleep much," Bessie said sympathetically.

"I didn't," Doona replied. "The shower helped a little bit and the coffee is trying hard. I'm hoping a brisk walk in the woods will wake me up even more."

"It certainly can't hurt," Bessie said with determined cheerfulness. She poured herself a bowl of cereal with milk and her own cup of coffee while she told Doona about her conversation with John Rockwell.

"At least he knows what's going on," was Doona's only response when Bessie was finished.

They put on their trainers and made their way into the village centre. A small sign outside the main doors of the Squirrel's Drey told them to assemble next to the ice cream stand just past the French restaurant. It was too early for either to be open, although there were people wandering in and out of the Squirrel's Drey. Bessie didn't even glance inside, not wanting to be reminded of the events from twenty-four hours earlier.

At the ice cream stand, a young man was on the ground doing press-ups.

"Ah, there you are," he said, leaping to his feet. "I'm Brett. Welcome to Lakeview Holiday Park and welcome to our woodland walk," he said enthusiastically.

"I'm Bessie and this is Doona," Bessie replied.

"It's so nice to meet you both," he responded. "Are you ready to learn about our woodland flora and fauna?"

Bessie felt as if he was disappointed with her somewhat muted reply, but she couldn't possibly imagine manufacturing his level of enthusiasm for any reason. Doona remained silent as Brett pulled a clipboard out of his backpack.

"I thought I was right," he said. "You two are the only ones that signed up for today's walk. You were the only ones signed up for yesterday as well, so I was very sorry when you had cancel."

"So were we," Bessie told him. "But we're here now. It's a shame it's just us, though. I'd have thought such walks would be popular."

"I'm busier in the summer," he told her. "But this time of year I suppose no one wants to get up this early when they're on their holidays."

"That makes sense," Doona muttered.

"Well, let's get started, shall we?" Brett asked, giving them both a dazzling smile.

For the next two hours, Bessie learned far more about the plants and animals of the Lake District than she'd ever wanted to know. Brett told them all about which plants were safe to eat and which ones to avoid. He showed them the nearly invisible signs that the various animals in the area left behind. Finally, he showed them around the ranger station that was tucked away in a quiet corner of the park.

There they nursed injured animals back to health, taught classes for groups of all sizes and ages, and monitored forest conditions.

"Thank you," Bessie said when Brett finished the tour. "It's been very interesting."

"I'm glad you enjoyed it," Brett replied. "I love what I do, working in the forest and looking after the animals. I have the coolest job in the world. We do a lot of other walks and experiences. If you're interested, I'm sure they'll be spaces left on most of them."

"We'll check the brochure," Bessie told him.

"Would you like some tea before you walk back to your accommodation?" he offered. "I brew my own from some of the areas grasses and weeds."

"Gosh, that sounds interesting," Bessie said, looking at Doona desperately. "But I think we'll have to decline for today. Maybe another time."

Doona took Bessie's arm. "Thank you so much," she said, speaking for almost the first time since they'd started the walk. "But we need to get back. I'm sure Bessie would like a rest. I know I would."

Brett showed them out of the small station, still burbling on about his tea and how they should sign up for more walks as they walked away. Bessie turned back after several paces and waved.

"Thank you again," she called back to the man who was still standing in the doorway of the ranger station.

"Any time," he shouted back.

"Walk faster," Doona hissed. "Or he'll be trying to force his weird tea on us again."

Bessie laughed. "I'm sure it's not that bad."

"I'm sure it's awful," Doona countered. "Anyway, I don't want to find out."

"So what did you think of the walk?" Bessie asked as they slowly made their way home. "You were very quiet the whole time," she added.

"I have a lot on my mind," Doona replied. "Besides, Brett was so enthusiastic about everything, I didn't feel as if there was anything I could add."

"He certainly loves what he does," Bessie agreed. "And his tea seems to be doing him a lot of good."

"If I were twenty years younger, I'd have been quite tempted," Doona told her. "He'd be perfect for young Mai, maybe."

"She doesn't seem like the grass and weed tea type," Bessie said thoughtfully. "I think she'd be more interested in champagne."

"You could be right," Doona said with a shrug. "As I've made such a huge mess of my own love life, I don't think I want to comment on other people's."

They'd reached a small sitting area that overlooked the smaller of the two lakes. "Let's sit for a minute," Bessie suggested. "The view is wonderful."

The picnic tables and benches were less spectacular than the view, but Bessie was happy to sit down for a short time, regardless.

"We've our pencil sketching class this afternoon," Doona reminded Bessie. "And we need to have some lunch before that. What sounds good?"

"I'm already hungry and it's only half ten," Bessie said. "Maybe we could get Chinese or Indian?"

"Indian sounds better to me," Doona replied. "Let's get take-away and eat in our cabin, though. I'm not sure I'm up to a public place right now."

"That sounds good. We can go back and decide what we want. I can walk over and collect it if you just want to stay at home."

"I think I can manage collecting some food," Doona told her. "I don't want anyone to think I'm hiding, anyway."

After several minutes, Bessie began to shift back and forth on the uncomfortable wooden seat.

"Time to head for home?" Doona asked.

"This bench is pretty hard," Bessie said, apologetically.

"That's fine. I quite fancy sitting on our patio and reading for a while," Doona told her. "The chairs there are much more comfortable than these and the view is just as nice."

In their cabin, both women took books from their book club pile and settled into seats on their patio. Bessie's tummy was rumbling by half eleven.

"Time to order some food," she said to Doona.

"Perfect," Doona answered.

When they gave their location to the man taking their order, he insisted that someone from the restaurant would deliver their lunch.

"So, our VIP treatment continues, in spite of Charles's death," Bessie remarked when Doona told her.

"So it seems," Doona replied. "Again, I just hope we don't get billed for it all."

"We'll cross that bridge when we come to it," Bessie said. "For now, we should enjoy being pampered."

The food, when it arrived, was hot and delicious. Bessie ate far more than she'd intended, but her light breakfast had been many hours earlier.

"That was much better than yesterday's lunch," Doona remarked as she and Bessie cleared away the dishes.

"It certainly was," Bessie agreed. "I wonder if *L'Expérience Anglaise* is even open today."

"We'll have to check if we go to the Squirrel's Drey later," Doona said.

"Where is our class?" Bessie asked.

"In the arts and crafts building," Doona told her. "It's called the Rainbow Arts Centre and it's on the opposite side of the lake from the Squirrel's Drey."

"We walked past it this morning," Bessie said, once she'd realised which building Doona was talking about. "I just didn't know that it was the arts and crafts building."

They walked slowly around the lake, arriving at the Rainbow Arts Centre with a few minutes to spare. An older couple were already sitting in the small lobby area, presumably waiting for their instructor to arrive. Bessie and Doona joined them and quickly introduced themselves.

"We're Jack and Nancy Strong," the woman told them. "Our children sent us here for a week as a wedding anniversary present. I can't imagine what they were thinking. I'd have much rather gone on a cruise. Anyway, we're making the best of it and trying out just about every activity on offer. So far we've been bored to bits, but I keep hoping."

"I'm sure they meant well," Bessie said.

"Of course they did," Jack told them. "And we're sure to find something we enjoy by the end of the week, even if it means we have to try everything."

"Oh, I do hope I'm not late," a voice said from the doorway.

Bessie looked up and then frowned. Andrew Cheatham was an unexpected addition to the class.

CHAPTER 8

"Good afternoon, ladies and gentleman," another voice chimed in from behind them all.

Bessie turned around and smiled at the young woman who was standing in a doorway that led further into the building.

"I'm Andrea. Welcome to pencil sketching," she said.

The girl, who looked not much older than twenty, was dressed all in black. Bessie took in the jet-black hair that was cut in a severe bob, the white foundation with black lipstick and the multiple piercings. Andrea didn't look at all like a typical Lakeview employee.

"Come on back to the classroom and let's get started," she suggested.

Bessie glanced at Doona and shrugged before she got to her feet and, with the others, followed the girl into a large and brightly lit room. One entire wall was nothing but windows, which gave them an uninterrupted view of the lake outside. There were several easels set up in front of the windows, but Andrea led them to the back of the room where a small circle of easels surrounded an empty table.

"The easels are at various heights, so choose one that suits you, whether you prefer to sit or stand," Andrea told them. "They can be adjusted later if you start standing and then want to sit for a while, as well."

Bessie found an easel that seemed just about right for her height and Doona quickly claimed the one next to her, which was set just slightly higher. Andrew settled in at the one on Bessie's other side, even though Bessie thought it seemed a bit low for him. Nancy and Jack Strong moved next to Doona to complete the circle.

Andrea walked into the middle of the group and smiled at each of them in turn. "I'm glad you're all here," she said with a small smile. "I just need to go over a few things before we start. First of all, I can't make you a professional artist in three hours, but I can help you to improve as an amateur artist. Please don't feel as if what you do isn't good enough or isn't right. Art is entirely subjective and it's about what you feel and express, not what other people see, or think they see, in your work."

Everyone laughed nervously. Bessie didn't have particularly high hopes for the next three hours. She'd never been any good at drawing, but she'd also never had any proper lessons. If nothing else, she was determined to enjoy the experience.

"We're going to start by drawing a circle," Andrea told them now. "And that sounds quite easy, but actually, it is really difficult to draw a circle freehand. So I don't want you to try to make it perfectly circular. Just draw something that is more or less round and we'll go from there."

Bessie picked up a pencil from the tray below her easel and took a deep breath. When she noticed her hand was shaking, she scolded herself. This is only a holiday park activity, she reminded herself. Stop being such a big baby.

After another deep breath, she drew a lopsided circle on her paper.

"Excellent," Andrea said as she walked around the group. "I promise you that was the hardest thing you'll do today. The very first mark on the page is always the most difficult."

For the next hour, Andrea showed them how to shade and colour their circles until they began to take on depth. Then she had them add a square and helped them turn the square into a box.

"Now I want you all to turn around," Andrea told them. "Take three steps away from your picture and then turn around again. Tell me what you think of your piece from a few steps away."

Bessie turned and then smiled. While her picture wasn't exactly great art, it looked much better than she'd ever imagined she could have done.

"It isn't bad, is it?" Bessie said.

"Now I want you all to walk around and look at what your classmates have done," Andrea instructed.

"They are all very different, even though we started with the same basic shapes," Bessie remarked. "And they're all really good."

After everyone had admired all of the pictures, Andrea had them tear them off their easels. "Now we're going to try something a little bit harder, using the same techniques we just learned," she told them.

She put a tennis ball, a golf ball and a large square box on the table in the middle of the group. "I want you to draw what you see," she instructed them. "Take it slow, start with the shapes and see how you do. I'm here to help with whatever you need."

Bessie pulled up a chair and lowered her easel before she began. Standing still seemed to take more energy than walking, for some reason.

"You can chat with one another if you like," Andrea added with a smile. "This isn't school."

"I'm concentrating too hard to chat," Bessie told her. But after a few minutes, once the basic shapes had been drawn and she was working on shading, Bessie felt herself relaxing a little bit.

"I wasn't expecting to see you here," she said to Andrew, glancing over to see him frowning at this paper.

"My oldest grandchild, who is twenty-six and ought to know better, signed me up for about a dozen activities," he replied. "I cancelled quite a few of them, but then his mother, my daughter, said that that hurt his feelings, so I agreed to try at least one or two of the less, um, well, let's just say I agreed to try a few."

"And are you having fun?" Bessie had to ask.

"It isn't as bad as I thought it would be," he said, grudgingly. "And the instruction is much better than I was expecting, as well."

Andrea had walked over during the conversation, and now she smiled at Andrew. "I'm not sure if I should take that as a compliment or not," she said. "What were you expecting?"

Andrew shrugged. "I think I thought there would be a bunch of flowers on a table and we'd be told to draw them. I didn't expect to be given any instruction, really."

"Lakeview is trying hard to encourage adults to visit without children. We've added a number of activities specifically for them, like this class. I also teach finger painting, collage making and cartoon drawing to the under ten set, of course," Andrea explained.

"Do you have any idea what happened yesterday up at the main building?" Nancy Strong asked from behind her easel. "The police were everywhere."

"Apparently our general manager had some sort of accident," Andrea replied.

"Oh, I do hope he's okay," the woman said.

"Unfortunately, he passed away," Andrea said sadly.

"Oh, I'm sorry to hear that," Nancy said.

"I hope his passing doesn't change anything here," Jack said. "I suspect our children will be sending us here again next year."

"I'm sure things will remain the same," Andrea assured him. "Charles was only here for a short time. The previous manager, Harold, has taken back over, at least for the time being."

"What was Charles like to work for?" Doona asked, her voice quiet.

"He was lovely," Andrea said. "Oh, he was a bit of a flirt, but he didn't mean anything by it. One of my friends, she's a waitress in the Italian restaurant, she flirted back once and he turned her down flat. Told her he was married, although we never saw any sign of a wife around here, that's for sure."

"Wasn't he a bit old to be flirting with you?" Bessie asked.

"Like I said, he didn't really mean anything by it. He just had a way of talking to you that made you feel as if you were the only person in the world." Andrea sighed. "If I were a bit older, I might have been tempted."

Bessie looked hard at Doona, whose eyes were now filling with tears. "I think I need a little break," she announced. "Can I get a glass of water or something?"

"Oh, goodness, I nearly forgot," Andrea exclaimed. "We're meant to break for tea and biscuits. Just give me a minute."

While the girl make the tea and dumped biscuits onto a plate, Bessie crossed to Doona. "Are you okay?" she whispered.

"Mostly," Doona answered. "Nothing a cuppa and a chocolate digestive can't fix, anyway."

Bessie shook her head. She knew Doona was being brave, but the hurt that her friend was feeling went far beyond what tea and a sugary treat could mend.

"Your golf ball actually looks like a ball," Andrew said from behind them.

Bessie looked at Doona's drawing and smiled. "He's right," she said. "Yours is much better than mine."

Doona glanced over at Bessie's sketch and then smiled an almost genuine smile. "I did better than I thought I could," she said.

"If you want to feel even better about yours, come and look at mine," Andrew offered. "My golf ball looks like a hand grenade."

Bessie and Doona took the three steps needed to get to Andrew's easel. Bessie looked at the picture and then looked at Doona. They both struggled not to laugh, as Andrew was exactly right. His golf ball did rather resemble a hand grenade.

"You can laugh. I know you want to," he said. "I never claimed to be able to draw, and I'm actually having fun, so I don't even mind."

"The tea's ready," Andrea called, saving Bessie from needing to find a polite reply to Andrew's comments.

"So where is everyone from?" Jack asked as everyone made their drinks and selected biscuits. On hearing that Doona and Bessie were from the Isle of Man, he and Nancy launched into a seemingly endless story about a long-ago holiday they'd had on the island. That filled in the tea break nicely. When it was time to get back to their drawings, Andrea had a new challenge for them.

"We've been working with fairly uniform shapes," she told them. "Let's see how you do with something slightly less geometric."

After taking away the balls and the box, she set a vase full of flowers on the table. "The key to this is to start with the shapes you can see," she said. "The flowers are round, the vase is rectangular. Work from there, using your shading techniques to give shape to the flowers."

Bessie tore off her previous sketch, folding it carefully so that she could take it with her, and then stared at the blank sheet of paper. She wasn't even sure where to begin with this new challenge.

"Start with the shapes," Andrea said from beside her. She had a small piece of blank paper in her hand and she held it against Bessie's easel. With her other hand, she quickly began to sketch. Bessie watched as the girl drew a large rectangle for the vase with several light circles above it.

"There's your starting point," Andrea said. "Now you just have to fill in the detail."

With that, the girl set to work and within minutes she'd turned the rough shapes into a beautiful sketch. Bessie shook her head. "I can't do that," she said firmly.

Andrea laughed. "I do it twice a week," she said. "If you did the same, you'd get good, too."

Bessie grabbed a pencil and started in on her picture. An hour later she had something that was just about recognisable as a vase of flowers, even if it was nowhere near as good as the very quick sketch Andrea had done.

"It's just about time to wrap this up for today," Andrea announced. "You're all welcome to stay for another half hour if you'd like to keep working, but after that I have a class of four and five-year-olds that I'm sure you'll want to miss."

Bessie looked over at Doona. "I'm ready to go, but I can walk back by myself if you want to stay a little bit longer."

"I think I'll stay for a short while," Doona told her. "I've just about done and I'd like to finish."

Bessie looked at her friend's picture. It was much better than Bessie's, and she could see why Doona wanted to stay. "If mine looked like that, I'd stay, too," she told Doona. "I'll see you back at the cabin."

"I'll walk back with you," Andrew offered. "I gave up on mine about twenty minutes ago anyway."

Bessie looked over at Andrew's board. His vase looked like a shoebox and his flowers didn't look very healthy at all.

"I had fun," he told Bessie with a wink. "And that's all that matters."

"I can't argue with that," Bessie told him. She tore her last picture off her easel and then carefully put all three of her sketches into her handbag.

"Thank you so much for coming," Andrea told them both. "I hope you enjoyed yourselves. You're more than welcome to take the class again. If you do, we can work on more advanced techniques."

"Once is enough for me," Andrew replied. "Although I think Bessie shows promise."

"I think Doona's the one with the talent," Bessie replied. "Anyway, we're trying watercolours next. Do you teach that as well?"

"Oh, no, sorry," Andrea said. "That's Mai's class now."

Something in her tone made Bessie curious. "Mai Stratton?" she asked. "I thought she was guest services manager."

"Oh, she is," Andrea replied. "But she wanted to teach the water-colour class too and, well, whatever Mai wants, she gets."

"Why?" Bessie had to ask.

Andrea shook her head. "Let's just say she was very close to the general manager, shall we?" she replied.

"She had an affair with Charles?" Doona asked.

Andrea shook her head. "It wasn't that," she said. "I always thought Mai knew something about him that he didn't want anyone else to know. But I mustn't speak ill of the dead."

Doona pressed her lips together and went back to her drawing. Bessie thought about staying.

"I can wait for you," she said tentatively to her friend.

"No, you go," Doona said. "I'm fine."

"Let's go, then," Andrew suggested, offering Bessie his arm.

"You haven't taken your last sketch," Andrea reminded him.

Andrew looked at his easel and shook his head. "I don't really think I need it."

"You should take it and give it to your grandson," Bessie suggested. "You could tell him how hard you worked on it and how you'd love it if he'd frame it and hang it in his house."

"What a splendid idea," Andrew said, laughing. He carefully tore the drawing off the easel and rolled it up.

"I have cardboard tubes if you would like one," Andrea offered.

"Oh, yes, definitely," Andrew said. "I might even wrap it up and give it to him as a special present."

With his sketch safely inside the cardboard tube, Andrew offered his arm to Bessie again. "Shall we?"

Bessie grinned. "Let's."

Nancy and Jack were still busily putting the finishing touches on their drawings, so Bessie and Andrew walked out by themselves.

"All kidding aside, that was much more enjoyable than I expected," he told Bessie as they walked slowly around the lake.

"Andrea is a very talented instructor," Bessie said. "I felt like I learned an awful lot in a very short time."

"She seemed quite sad about Charles's death as well," Andrew commented.

Bessie could feel his eyes on her, but she kept hers turned towards the lake. "I'm sure everyone is sad about that," she replied.

"I understand Doona was his wife," he said.

"Ex-wife," Bessie amended. "But she didn't know he was here and she wouldn't have come if she had known."

"Are you quite sure about all of that?" Andrew asked.

Bessie looked at him in surprise. "I'm very sure," she said firmly, trying to read the look on the man's face.

"Perhaps you should have a long talk with your friend," he said after an awkward pause.

DIANA XARISSA

Bessie was going to argue, but another thought crossed her mind. "Who's been telling you about Doona, then?" she asked.

"I have various connections," he answered vaguely. They were nearly at the village centre, having just reached the ice cream stand where their early morning walk had begun. Now, however, the stand was open and a short queue of families with small children was waiting patiently for frozen treats.

"Let's get ice cream," Andrew suggested.

"It's nearly dinner time," Bessie pointed out.

"So?"

"I don't want to spoil my dinner," Bessie replied.

"Why ever not?" Andrew demanded. "You're on holiday. You can have something light for dinner if you aren't properly hungry after the ice cream, or, more likely, you'll discover that you can still manage a proper meal after a small treat."

"I never have pudding first," Bessie said, feeling slightly ridiculous.

"Well, once in a while, you should," Andrew said firmly. He took her arm and led her to the end of the queue. Bessie spent the waiting time dithering back and forth as to whether she was actually going to get anything or not, but once it was their turn, she found she couldn't resist.

"Just a very small cone," she told the man behind the counter. "Vanilla, no, strawberry, no, vanilla." She sighed and looked at Andrew. "I love both flavours," she said apologetically.

"She'll have two scoops," he told the man. "One each of vanilla and strawberry. I'll have the same, but with vanilla and chocolate."

Bessie thought about arguing, but changed her mind. Andrew's solution was a sensible one and the ice cream looked really delicious when the man passed it over the counter to her. Andrew insisted on paying, and again Bessie didn't argue.

Bessie tried first one and then the other of her scoops and sighed happily. "They're both really good," she exclaimed.

"I thought they would be," Andrew replied. "We visited the stand after lunch this afternoon and I thought the ice cream was exceptionally good."

"You already had ice cream today?" Bessie asked.

"I did," Andrew told her, his eyes twinkling. "Am I in trouble for having too much fun on my holiday?"

Bessie flushed. "I'm sorry. Of course it isn't my place to tell you what to do. I was just surprised, that's all."

"I don't usually eat ice cream twice a day," he said. "But I do think holidays are for indulging oneself, don't you?"

"I suppose so," Bessie said. She lived on the beach, in what many considered the perfect holiday spot, and she'd never held a paying job. Therefore, Bessie rarely actually took holidays, feeling as if she had nothing that she needed to take a break from. The idea of indulging herself the way Andrew meant felt somewhat foreign to her.

"I've never really grown up properly," Andrew whispered to her. "In spite of serving in the armed forces and working my way up in the police, I still feel like a small child inside. If I can get away with ice cream twice a day, I'm going to take advantage."

"Good for you," Bessie said, feeling as if she could learn a lot from the man's attitude.

They'd reached the bridge when they'd played Poohsticks the previous day.

"Let's sit for a while," Andrew suggested, gesturing towards a bench that faced out towards the sea.

"I sat on one of these benches earlier today and it wasn't very comfortable," Bessie told him.

"Just a few minutes, then," he replied.

Bessie sat down and stretched her feet out. She hadn't realised how tired she was. She'd alternated between sitting and standing in the class, but she'd been on her feet more than she was used to. In spite of the uncomfortable bench, it felt really good to sit down.

The pair sat in silence for a short time, watching a few men and women in kayaks chasing one another around the small lake. Bessie finished her ice cream and crunched her way through the cone. Beside her, Andrew was doing the same.

"I love being around water," Andrew told her.

"I live on the sea," Bessie replied. "This lake doesn't feel quite right."

"I've always wanted to live on the sea," Andrew said wistfully. "We were in London, or rather the suburbs of London, for many years. I sold the house when my wife passed away and I bought a tiny flat in the city. I have a distant view of the Thames, which isn't exactly the same as a sea view."

"You should come and visit the Isle of Man," Bessie told him. "As the island is only thirteen miles across, you're never far from the sea."

"I was there many years ago," he said. "During the war, actually. I don't remember much about it. It was just another place I was briefly stationed. Perhaps I will visit one day."

"There are holiday cottages a short distance down the beach from my cottage," Bessie told him. "You could hire as many as you need and your whole family could come. You'd be right on the water."

"I'd like that," Andrew said, staring out at the lake. "Bessie, you seem like a good person. I've talked at length with John Rockwell and he can't say enough good things about you. Please, if you feel as if you need any help, let me know."

"I assume you mean with the murder investigation," Bessie said.

"With that and with anything else that might happen while you're here," he said. "The investigation is a worry, as Doona could be a suspect, but a bigger worry, as far as I'm concerned anyway, is the murderer."

"You think he or she might target Doona next?" Bessie asked, suddenly afraid for her friend.

"I don't know why Charles was killed," Andrew said. "It could have nothing whatsoever to do with Doona. Or she could be right in the middle of the whole mess. I just know I'll feel better when Inspector Hopkins has someone behind bars."

"As long as she gets the right person," Bessie said tartly.

"She struck me as a smart lady," he told her. "And this is a high profile case. She'll be under pressure to solve it quickly, but she'll be very careful as well."

"I hope you're right about that."

Andrew reached into a pocket and pulled out a scrap of paper. "My mobile number," he told Bessie as he handed her the sheet. "I meant what I said. Ring me if you need help."

Bessie nodded and stuck the slip of paper in her pocket. "I should give you my number as well," she said. She dug around in her handbag for a pen and a scrap of paper.

"Here," she said when she'd finished writing out a slip for him. "There's my mobile number as well as my address and phone number at home in case you want to get in touch about a holiday on the island."

Andrew smiled and slipped the paper into a pocket. "I think I'll need to recover from this holiday before I'm ready for another," he said quietly.

"You two didn't get very far," Doona called to them from the path around the lake.

"We just stopped here to admire the view," Bessie told her.

"And eat our ice cream," Andrew added.

"You had ice cream?" Doona asked, frowning. "I didn't get any ice cream."

"You should have stopped at the little stand by the village centre," Bessie told her. "They have excellent ice cream."

"Maybe I'll just go back over and get some now," Doona mused.

"It must be dinner time," Bessie argued. "Are we eating back there tonight?"

"I thought maybe Italian," Doona said.

"That sounds wonderful," Bessie agreed quickly.

"Andrew, you're welcome to join us," Doona told the man.

"I wish I could," he replied, sounding sincere. "But I haven't seen the family in a few hours. I'm going to have to have dinner with them."

Bessie and Doona both chuckled.

"I suppose we should stop back at the cabin and freshen up before dinner," Bessie said, getting slowly to her feet.

"I definitely need to do that," Doona agreed. "I think I'll change as well. I feel as if I'm covered in pencil dust."

"I'll walk back with you then, ladies," Andrew said, getting up from his bench. "I'm supposed to meet everyone in about half an hour at the Chinese restaurant, so I have time to freshen up as well."

He looked at Bessie and winked. "And by freshen up, I mean grab a quick shot of whiskey," he whispered.

Bessie laughed again and then the two joined Doona on the path back to their temporary home.

"How did your drawing come out in the end?" Bessie asked her friend.

"I'm really pleased with it," Doona told her. "It's much better than I expected to be able to do."

"Maybe I'll have more luck with watercolours," Bessie muttered.

"Maybe I should sign up for the watercolour class," Andrew said thoughtfully.

"It's all just a bit of fun," Doona said. "I won't be quitting my day job to become an artist or anything."

"I think you should take some classes at the college at home, though," Bessie told her. "You have real talent."

Doona shrugged. "I was thinking about taking some classes," she told her friend. "Although I was thinking about taking things that would be useful for work, rather than art classes."

"No reason why you can't do both," Andrew said.

"No, I suppose there isn't," Doona replied pensively.

"I have a class of my own coming up soon," Bessie said. "You're welcome to join in, but I'm not sure paleography is for you."

"Is that reading old handwriting?" Doona asked. "It isn't for me, although it would be useful if someone would offer a class in reading my own handwriting."

"I know what you mean," Bessie said with a laugh. "I write shopping lists all the time and then, when I get to ShopFast, I can't read what it was that I actually needed."

"When is the paleography class?" Doona asked. "I remember you mentioned it a while back."

"It's the weekend after we get back," Bessie told her. "It's just the one day, the Saturday, at the museum."

"May I ask why you need to read old handwriting?" Andrew asked.

"I do a lot of research for the Manx Museum," Bessie replied. "I'm strictly an amateur, but I enjoy it. I've been working on wills, and the museum has a large collection of them, but they'd really like someone to go through the very oldest ones. In order for me to be able to do that, I need some training in how to read the handwriting of the time."

By the time Bessie finished her explanation, they had arrived back at Foxglove Close. There was a small bench right on the corner of the road and Bessie was surprised to see people sitting on it. As the little group took a few steps forward, the two people on the bench stood up.

"Miss Cubbon, Mrs. Moore, I've been waiting for you," Margaret Hopkins said. "We need to talk."

CHAPTER 9

*B*essie felt her heart sink as she forced herself to smile at the woman. "We were just going to get some dinner," she said, aware that she sounded nervous. "Can it wait until after that?"

The inspector shook her head. "I'm sorry," she said, not sounding sorry in the slightest. "But it really can't. If you'd like to wait out here with Constable Smith, I'd like to start with Mrs. Moore."

Bessie looked at Doona, who shrugged. "I suppose we don't have a choice," Bessie muttered, crossing to the bench and sitting down.

"Mrs. Moore, we can talk in your lodge, if that's okay," the inspector said.

"Margaret, is there anything I can do to help?" Andrew asked.

"I don't think so, but thanks," the woman replied.

Bessie frowned at the friendly exchange. Andrew had said he would help her and Doona, but now he was offering to help Margaret instead. As Doona and Margaret disappeared towards the cabin, Andrew crossed to Bessie.

"I can stay with you, if you'd like," he offered, earning a frown from the young constable sitting next to Bessie.

"No, you go and have dinner with your family," Bessie told him. "I'm sure this is just more routine questioning."

Andrew looked as if he wanted to argue, but after a moment he nodded. "You have my number," he reminded her. "Ring me if you need me."

Bessie nodded and then watched him walk away, suddenly feeling very alone in a strange place. "So," she said to the young man opposite her. "What made you want to become a policeman?"

When Margaret came to collect Bessie an hour later, she and the young policeman had become very well acquainted.

"I really don't think going back to school is ever a bad idea," Bessie was telling him. "I'm sure I can't imagine how difficult it would be for you, with a full-time job and a baby at home, but even if you just take one class at a time, you'll end up with a degree eventually."

The young man nodded and then suddenly snapped to attention when he spotted the inspector. "We were just chatting," he said quickly.

"So I hear," Margaret said. "Now it's my turn for a chat with Miss Cubbon."

"Yes, inspector," the man said. He turned to Bessie. "Thank you," he said sincerely. "You've given me a lot to think about."

"Where's Doona?" Bessie asked as she and the inspector headed towards the cabin.

"She's lying down in her room," the woman told her. "I hope I won't need much of your time and then you two can go and get something to eat."

Bessie really wanted to check on her friend, but she didn't think the inspector would approve. Instead, once they were inside the building, she followed the other woman out onto the patio. Margaret slid the door into the cabin shut.

"That should prevent our disturbing Mrs. Moore," she said. She sat down and gestured to the chair opposite hers. "Do sit down."

Bessie slid into the chair and forced herself to sit back and try to get comfortable. Every instinct wanted her to perch on the very edge of her seat, but she didn't want the inspector to notice her disquiet.

"After some preliminary investigating, I have a series of new questions for you," Margaret said. "Some of my questions may lead you to certain conclusions about things that may or may not be correct. I have to ask you to not repeat any of the things we discuss or any conclusions you may draw from our conversation."

Bessie frowned. "I'm not sure I can agree," she said after a moment. "Doona is my best friend and she's clearly involved in this mess."

Margaret nodded. "I should have been more clear," she said. "You can discuss things with Doona, but no one else. I've raised the same issues with her already."

"That's fine, then," Bessie said, pushing thoughts of John Rockwell and Andrew out of her head. She could keep secrets from them if she needed to.

"You were coming to Lakeview for a self-catering holiday, weren't you?" the inspector asked.

Bessie shook her head, confused by the question. "We were coming for a holiday where the accommodation made self-catering an option," she replied. "But as all of our meals were included in the prize that Doona won, we didn't plan on doing much in the way of cooking."

"What did you bring with you to facilitate any cooking or food preparation that you might have wanted to do?"

"Nothing," Bessie said. "I brought clothes and toiletries and nothing else. I'm pretty sure that Doona didn't bring anything, either. We simply didn't need to."

"So neither of you brought a knife of any kind?" Margaret asked.

Bessie took a deep breath. So that was what the questions were about, the murder weapon. "I didn't bring anything of the kind and I'm fairly certain that Doona didn't either," Bessie said. "We were told that our accommodation would have everything we could possibly need for food preparation, so even if we'd planned to cook, we wouldn't have needed to bring a knife."

Margaret nodded. "So, did your accommodation come with any knives?"

"I suppose so," Bessie said, thinking hard. "We had meat and cheese and bread for lunch the other day. We used knives for that, of course."

"And that was the only time you or Mrs. Moore used any knives for anything?" Margaret asked.

Bessie sat back and closed her eyes. The question felt important and she didn't want to get the answer wrong. "Give me a minute," she muttered as she took herself backwards through their stay. She couldn't recall anything other than the meal the previous day and was just about to say so when the memory suddenly flooded back.

"The boxes of books," she exclaimed, sitting up suddenly.

Margaret smiled. "What boxes of books?" she asked, looking as if she already knew the answer.

"We signed up for the book club session on Saturday," Bessie explained. "When we arrived, we each had a box of books for us to read before the session. The boxes were taped shut and Doona had to cut them open."

"And she used a knife from the kitchen here to do so?"

"Yes, one she found in the drawer, I imagine," Bessie said. "She cut through the tape on both boxes for us."

"And what did she do with the knife after she was done opening the boxes?"

Bessie shook her head. "I don't remember her doing anything with it," she said after a moment. "We were both tired after the reception and dinner. I think she may have just left it on the table out here."

"So who moved it next, and where did they put it?" Margaret asked.

"I don't know," Bessie said. "Or rather, I didn't move it. Now that I think about it, the knife wasn't on the table out here the next morning, but at the time, I didn't even give it a thought."

"Did you ever touch the knife?"

Bessie thought for moment. "I don't think so, but I may have. It simply didn't matter, you see."

"I want you to look at some photos," Margaret said now. "See if you can pick out the knife that Mrs. Moore used to open the boxes."

She handed Bessie a pile of photos. Bessie shuffled through them quickly and pulled out three. Those three she studied for a short while, and then she sighed. "I'm sorry," she said. "I think it's one of these three, but I can't be sure. I didn't pay that much attention to it at the time. I didn't think it was important."

"You're an excellent witness," Margaret said. "Most people would simply choose the one they thought was closest rather than admit they weren't sure."

"I'm not sure a murder investigation is any place for guessing," Bessie replied.

"I would have to agree with that," Margaret said. "But now I'm going to ask you to do just that. If you had to pick one of those three, which one would you choose?"

Bessie went back through the three pictures a third time. "This one," she said eventually. "But it's only a guess. The actual knife had our cottage address on it, of course."

"That's fine," Margaret assured her. "And it's very helpful."

"Was there anything else?" Bessie asked.

"Did you hear anyone moving around inside or just outside the cabin after you went to bed that first night?" the woman asked.

"I heard all sorts of strange noises," Bessie told her. "I can't tell you for sure whether they were inside the cabin or outside. I was asleep off and on, of course, as well. Doona told me she went out for a walk and I didn't realise that at the time. There seemed to be doors opening and closing most of the night, somewhere in the neighbourhood, but I can't tell you where. The lodges are much closer together than my nearest neighbours at home and I'm not used to hearing other people coming and going."

"I'm surprised it's so noisy out here. I would have thought it would be peaceful and quiet in the woods."

Bessie shrugged. "It's either been a lot quieter since that first night or I've slept much better. I certainly haven't heard as much coming and going since then."

Margaret nodded. "I'm going to stop there for tonight," she said. "I'll remind you that you and Mrs. Moore are not to leave Lakeview for any reason. Your Torver Castle excursion is fine, but that's not until Friday and I hope to have everything wrapped up by then, anyway."

"I hope you do," Bessie said fervently. She walked the inspector to the door.

"Thank you for your time tonight. Enjoy your evening," Margaret said in the doorway.

Bessie watched her walk away, a sick feeling in the pit of her stomach. Everything the inspector had said seemed to suggest that the knife from their cabin had been used to kill Charles. The only way that was possible was if the murderer was on their patio while Bessie was sleeping. She shuddered. Right now all she wanted to do was go home.

She shut the door and then walked over to Doona's bedroom. She tapped lightly, and then, when she didn't get a response, more loudly. When there was still no reply, Bessie tried the handle. The door opened and she cautiously peeked inside. Her friend was lying on the bed.

"Doona? Are you okay?"

"Has the inspector gone?" Doona asked in a low voice.

"She has."

"I thought she was going to arrest me," Doona told Bessie.

Bessie walked into the room and sat down on the edge of the bed. "I wouldn't have let her," she said.

"You couldn't have stopped her," Doona replied sadly. "I think the murderer used the knife from our cabin to kill Charles. They must have found my fingerprints on it. I can't imagine why I haven't been arrested, actually."

"Clearly the inspector is smart enough to know you didn't do it," Bessie said.

Doona smiled weakly. "Thank you, but I don't think the inspector has as much faith in me as you do."

Bessie shrugged. "Let's not worry about it for tonight," she suggested. "I'm starving."

"Strangely for me, I'm not even a little bit hungry," Doona replied.

"Isn't there a pizza delivery place?" Bessie asked. "Let's get pizza and garlic bread and just have a quiet night in."

"This is supposed to be a holiday, and we're missing out on all the delicious food," Doona complained.

"We have lots more days for delicious food," Bessie said. "Once the murderer is behind bars, we'll both feel more like fine dining."

Doona nodded. She sat up and the stretched. "She was very kind, under the circumstances," she remarked as she got out of bed.

"Inspector Hopkins?" Bessie asked. "I thought she was quite nice, but I do wish she'd be more forthcoming. I'd love to know what's really going on."

"I hardly think she's going to share anything with us. Especially when I'm her number one suspect."

Bessie didn't take the time to argue with her friend. She was far too hungry to think about much more than food. Doona insisted she didn't want anything, but Bessie made sure to order enough for two. When the food arrived a short time later, Doona changed her mind.

"That was really good," Bessie said as she finished her last slice of pizza.

"It was," Doona agreed. "I didn't want to eat, but I'm glad I did. I'm feeling much better."

"Excellent," Bessie said. "Now, how about that ice cream?"

Doona shook her head and then frowned. "Oh, why not?" she exclaimed. "This is a holiday."

"Exactly," Bessie agreed. "Let's go."

There was a bit of a chill in the evening air, but both women had pulled on jackets, so they didn't mind. At the ice cream stand, Bessie was pleased to see a different man behind the counter. It was silly, but she didn't want to be recognised as having already had ice cream earlier in the day.

"Two scoops," she told the man. "One vanilla and one chocolate."

"I'll have the same," Doona added.

They walked slowly around the lake as they ate their treat, enjoying the way the park felt as the sun was setting. Most of the family groups were quieter and many were on foot rather than on bikes. Small children dozed in their parents' arms and couples walked together hand-in-hand.

"Let's stop in the grocery shop and get some things in for breakfast and lunch tomorrow," Bessie suggested. "Then we can have a very lazy morning and go out for a nice meal after our watercolour class in the afternoon."

"That sounds like a good idea," Doona replied. "I can lie in and then soak in my jetted tub for a while with one of the books from the book club. I was thinking about trying to get to the pool tomorrow morning, but a bath sounds better."

"We can see how we feel in the morning about having a swim," Bessie suggested.

"I think I'm going to feel lazy," Doona replied with a laugh. "But we'll see."

In the grocery shop, they quickly filled a trolley with everything they wanted for meals in their lodge the next day.

"If you're saving the croissants for breakfast tomorrow," the girl behind the till told Bessie, "the toaster in your accommodation has a pastry warming feature."

"I have the same toaster at home," Doona told her. "That's one of my favourite things about it."

Back in their comfortable sitting room, Doona switched on the television and quickly found an American comedy she was happy to watch.

"I'm just going to head to bed," Bessie told her. "I'll probably read for a little while, but I'm feeling unbelievably tired."

"It hasn't exactly been a relaxing holiday, has it?" Doona asked, sighing.

"Not yet, but we still have several days left," Bessie replied optimistically.

In her room she got ready for bed and then quickly rang John Rockwell. She told him everything that had happened that day.

"I don't like the idea that someone was on your patio and took the knife," he said when she'd finished. "That sounds like someone was trying to frame you or Doona for the murder."

"I hadn't thought of it quite like that," Bessie exclaimed.

"Who knew you two were visiting as Charles's special guests?"

"Mai said Charles was very excited that Doona was coming," Bessie replied thoughtfully. "But most of the staff we've met haven't seemed to know anything about her. The man who took us on the walk this morning and the girl who taught our drawing class didn't give us any special treatment or anything."

"No one other than Mai, then?"

"Lawrence Jenkins must have known all about Doona," Bessie said. "And Harold Butler as well."

"Anyone else?"

"I don't know what Nathan Beck, the French restaurant chef, knew," Bessie said thoughtfully. "He did ask Doona who she was when we had lunch there the other day, though. He'd been told to give us special treatment."

"And he probably told his wife. She's called Monique, right?" John asked.

"Yes, that's right," Bessie said. "I don't know if Joe Klein knew we were coming. I can't really see why the head of security needed to know."

"But he might have," John said. "Of course, it's a huge holiday park and you've by no means met everyone. What we need now is a motive for any of them to have killed the man."

"I'll see what I can find out," Bessie said.

"I wasn't suggesting that," John replied quickly. "Remember, one of them is a murderer. I don't want you investigating, but if you do hear or see something that suggests a possible motive for any of them, I'd like to know."

"I wonder how much Jessica Howe knows about Doona," Bessie said.

"That's a good question. I believe you said she was threatening to kill him at the welcome dinner?"

"She was. I suppose that means she had a motive."

"Indeed. Didn't you say her husband threatened him as well?"

"Yes, I'd assumed because he'd found out about the affair. I'm not sure why Jessica was so angry."

"Maybe Charles dumped her because Doona was coming to visit," John suggested.

"I don't know," Bessie said, letting her frustration into her tone. "I was hoping Inspector Hopkins would have everything worked out by now. Why can't these things ever just be obvious?"

John chuckled. "That would be nice," he agreed. "But it's beginning to seem as if this murder was carefully planned. I'm starting to think I ought to come over and try to help."

"I'm not sure Inspector Hopkins would like that," Bessie said.

"She probably wouldn't," John agreed. "In the same way I wouldn't want her interfering in a murder investigation here. But I could come as Doona's friend, just for moral support."

"I don't think things are that bad yet," Bessie told him. "Doona seems to be holding up so far. If I start to feel as if the inspector is looking at Doona as a serious suspect, I'll let you know."

After the call, with her mind racing, Bessie slid down under the covers and tried to relax. The idea that someone could have been on their patio and taken the knife without her ever hearing them worried Bessie. She couldn't find a comfortable position and every noise had her sitting up in bed and listening intently. Finally she got up and walked out into the corridor. She was nearly run over by Doona, carrying one of the dining area chairs, when she did so.

"What are you doing?" she asked her friend.

Doona flushed. "I keep thinking about how someone must have been on the patio the night of the murder. I was going to put this chair under the door handle so that whoever it was can't actually get inside the cabin. What are you doing up? I hope I didn't wake you?"

"No, I was just thinking almost the exact same thing," Bessie told her. "I rang John to give him an update and afterwards, that was just about all I could think about."

Together the women shoved the chair up against the door.

"It's the wrong height to wedge under the doorknob," Bessie said.

"It's the wrong type of knob, anyway," Doona said. "But at least, if someone does open the door, they'll hit the chair. Hopefully that will wake us up."

"It should wake me. I'm right down the hall," Bessie said. "Maybe I'll sleep with my door open."

"I intend to the do the same," Doona told her. "I also put a row of chairs in front of the sliding door to the patio. They won't stop anyone coming in, but hopefully if someone has to move them, it will make noise."

"I want to go home," Bessie said angrily. "This is supposed to be a lovely holiday, and instead we're having to blockade ourselves in our cabin."

"I'm sure we're overreacting," Doona said soothingly. "Even if someone did steal the knife from the patio, there's no reason for them to break in here."

Unless they want to kill again, Bessie thought. Or plant some sort of evidence here to help with framing Doona.

"You're thinking too much," Doona said. "I can see it on your face."

"What if the killer wants to plant something here that makes you look guilty?" Bessie had to ask.

"Inspector Hopkins and two of her men searched the entire place after she questioned me today," Doona replied. "The inspector knows we have nothing to hide."

"She didn't tell me they'd searched our cabin," Bessie said with a frown.

"I gave them permission to do so," Doona said. "I should have checked with you first, but the inspector wouldn't let me talk to you. I was afraid if I didn't agree right away, that she'd think I was hiding something."

"It's fine," Bessie assured her friend.

"I should have told you earlier," Doona said. "But I've so much on my mind, I completely forgot."

"It's fine," Bessie repeated herself. "We should get some sleep."

"Or at least try."

With the cabin as secure as they could make it, the two women headed back to their bedrooms. For Bessie it was a long night. It was very quiet, but that didn't seem to help. She still slept very little and felt even more tired at six than she had when she'd gone to bed.

After a shower, she dressed and then headed to the kitchen. Doona was already there, making coffee.

"I thought you were going to have a lie-in," Bessie exclaimed.

"So did I," Doona replied. "But I couldn't sleep."

"I was going to walk around the lake this morning," Bessie told her. "Not the one in the middle of the park. I've been around that a dozen times. I was going to walk around the big lake behind us."

"You go and enjoy the peace and quiet," Doona told her. "I'm going to run a bath and soak in my tub for a while with one of the books for Saturday. I haven't read any of them yet, and it's already Wednesday."

After a cup of coffee and a warmed croissant, Bessie headed out. The weather was a bit cooler, and she was glad she'd brought her jacket, as a strong wind seemed to be blowing as she left the building. The map of the park showed a paved footpath all the way around the lake, and Bessie found that it was relatively unoccupied at this hour of the morning.

A handful of people were out walking, including one very tired-looking woman pushing a pram with a crying baby in it, but everyone Bessie saw seemed to walking in the opposite direction to her. She enjoyed the solitude and the chance to think. The only thing she could think about, of course, was Charles's death. The holiday park was so large and had so many guests that it seemed as if anyone could have killed the man. Still, Bessie couldn't help but think that the men and women she'd talked about with John the previous evening seemed like the most likely suspects.

By the time she'd finished going around the lake, she'd decided that either Jessica or Herbert Howe had to be the culprit. She didn't much like either of them and they'd both threatened Charles. I just hope Margaret Hopkins sees things the same way, Bessie thought as she turned the key in the cabin's front door. Although Bessie had taken her time on her walk, even pausing to sit for a while and watch some of the boats on the lake, it was still nowhere near time for lunch when she got back.

"Doona, I'm home," she called as she shut the door behind herself.

"I'm still in the tub," Doona shouted. "It has a heater, so it stays warm forever. I suppose I'll have to get out soon, because I'm awfully wrinkled, but it is so lovely in here and I'm laughing over Bill Bryson's book while I soak."

"Don't rush out on my account," Bessie replied. "I'm going to curl up with a book myself."

She took both the Agatha Christie book and the Bill Bryson one with her out onto their patio. Having read the Christie story many times before, she started with the other, chuckling her way through a number of chapters before switching to reacquaint herself with Christie's wonderful prose. It was only when her tummy rumbled that she thought about lunch.

Doona was bustling around the kitchen when Bessie went back inside.

"I've started getting lunch ready," she announced. "I was going to come and get you in a minute."

Bessie was relieved to see that her friend was looking much better than she had the previous evening. Because she knew her so well, Bessie could tell that Doona was still feeling stressed, but her colour was better, at least.

"I didn't realise how late it was," Bessie said. "We'll have to eat quickly if we're going to get to our watercolour class by one."

"It's only really a snack," Doona said. "We'll go out for a proper meal after class."

"Where do you want to go?" Bessie asked.

"There's an American restaurant," Doona said. "But I imagine that will be burgers and chips, won't it?"

"I expect so," Bessie said. "We never did get to the Italian restaurant yesterday. Why don't we go there?"

"That sounds good," Doona agreed. "Maybe we should try the American place for lunch one day. Then, if we don't like it, we can have a big dinner to make up for it."

Bessie laughed. "That sounds like a good plan," she agreed.

It had just begun to rain when Bessie and Doona headed out to the Rainbow Centre. They both grabbed umbrellas before they left, but as it was still windy, they both also got quite wet on their walk.

"I feel as if I'm dripping," Bessie said as she folded up her umbrella in the small lobby of the building.

"Stuart, it's raining," a woman sitting in the lobby said loudly to the man next to her.

He glanced over at Bessie and Doona and then shrugged. "What can I do about that?" he demanded.

"You can go back to the cottage and get the rain cover for the pram and my umbrella," the woman replied. "We don't want Jocelyn-Mae getting wet, now do we?"

Stuart shrugged again and then got to his feet. "Of course not, darling," he said mechanically.

The woman gave him a smug smile and then returned to her magazine. The lobby was very full, and Bessie and Doona gave up on finding seats and simply walked over to stand near the windows.

"It's busy today," Doona remarked.

"I'm hoping this class finishes at one," Bessie whispered.

A moment later, the door to the classroom swung open and an exhausted-looking Andrea appeared in the doorway.

"We've finished just a few minutes early," she announced to the crowd. "I'll bring the children out now."

A moment later a swarm of toddlers emerged from behind Andrea. Bessie and Doona pressed themselves to the wall, hoping to stay out of the way, as tiny children threw themselves into waiting arms. The excited babble of tiny voices had Bessie wishing she'd taken headache tablets before they'd left the cabin.

Bessie watched as one little girl raced up to the woman who'd sent Stuart out into the rain. She was covered pretty much head to toe with blue paint. For some reason her hair was dripping wet, but at least the drips looked like water rather than paint.

"Jocelyn-Mae, what happened to you?" the woman demanded stridently.

"I'm afraid Jocelyn-Mae decided to dump a pot of paint over her head," Andrea answered for the little girl. "I washed as much of it as I could out of her hair."

"But her clothes are ruined," the woman said.

"That's why we tell you to bring the children in old clothes," Andrea replied.

"You were negligent," the woman snapped.

"We can't do a finger painting class without giving the children paint," Andrea retorted.

"I'm going to complain to your supervisor," the woman said.

"Here," Andrea replied, handing the woman a slip of paper. "This is the manager's name and phone number. Feel free to give him a ring and talk to him. I've already spoken to him about the incident and I will be filing a full report this afternoon."

"I will certainly be ringing him once I've cleaned up my daughter," the woman said.

"In light of what's happened, I'm sure you won't want her to do finger painting again tomorrow. We can cancel that booking and refund your money."

The woman gave her a shocked look. "Of course I want her to take the class again tomorrow," she said. "She needs constant stimulation of her creative energies."

Bessie looked around, Jocelyn-Mae was at that moment rummaging through her mother's handbag, helping herself to what seemed an unlimited supply of chocolate biscuits.

"Yes, well, you'll have to talk to the manager about that as well," Andrea told her. "Under the circumstances, we'd have to add a member of staff to help deal with her and I'm not sure we have anyone available."

"We'll see about that," the woman sniffed. "Come on, baby girl, into the pram. Daddy has gone to get the rain cover so you don't get wet."

Jocelyn-Mae looked at her mother and then stomped her foot. "No pram," she yelled. "No go. Paint more."

"I'm sorry, darling, but we're all done with painting for today," the woman said. "We have to go."

"No go!" Jocelyn-Mae shrieked. "No go, no go, no go."

Bessie and Doona watched with morbid fascination as Jocelyn-Mae continued to scream while her mother attempted to cajole her into the large and obviously expensive pram. The rest of the children were all whisked away by parents who looked either sympathetic or relieved as they left. Finally, Stuart walked back in, carrying the plastic cover and an umbrella.

"Daddy," the child shrieked. She threw herself into her father's arms, causing him to drop everything he was carrying.

"Why is she blue?" he asked his wife.

The woman rolled her eyes and then stormed out of the room past him, pushing the empty pram. After a moment, he shrugged. Andrea picked up the things he dropped and handed them to him wordlessly while he balanced Jocelyn-Mae in one hand and the rest in the other. With the child still shouting and crying in his arms, he turned and followed his wife out into the rain.

"Just when I think my life is a mess, I realise how lucky I am that I don't have a spoiled, over-sugared, blue toddler that I have to live with," Doona remarked.

"She did eat rather a lot of biscuits," Bessie said, shaking her head.

"She ate several during our break, as well," Andrea told the pair. "Whenever I turned my back, she'd take another from the plate. When I finally moved the plate, she started taking them from the other children."

"How old is she?" Bessie had to ask.

"Two," Andrea replied. "They don't call them the 'terrible twos' for nothing."

"I hope you aren't going to be in too much trouble with Harold," Bessie said. "Tell him that we're witnesses to just how badly behaved the child was."

"It's fine," Andrea assured her. "Jocelyn-Mae has already been kicked out of several of the activities here as well as the crèche. She's just never told 'no' at home and doesn't understand how to behave. I actually feel sorry for her, but I hope I don't see her again."

The door to the outside opened and Jack and Nancy Strong rushed in. "I do hope we aren't late," Nancy said. "The rain slowed us down."

"Because you have to run and jump in every puddle," Jack told her.

"Well, yes, rather," Nancy agreed cheerfully.

As she was wearing pink polka-dotted Wellington boots, Bessie could see the attraction of puddle jumping.

"I'm probably last again," Andrew Cheatham said from the doorway.

"Actually, Mai is probably last," Andrea told them all. "She's usually a few minutes late. If she isn't here by ten past one, I'll get you started."

The little group chatted easily about the weather as they waited. With about thirty seconds to go before Andrea's deadline, the door swung open and Mai stomped in.

"Let's get started," she said grimly.

CHAPTER 10

$\mathcal{M}$ai walked over to the door to the classroom and pushed it open. Bessie and the others followed. Inside the room, in the corner where they'd had their pencil sketching class, Andrea was on her hands and knees, cleaning up blue paint. She looked up and nodded at Mai, who ignored her completely.

"Right, everyone should find an easel at the windows," Mai told the group.

Bessie chose one near the centre of the row that was just about the right height for her. She looked out at the dark and rainy day and frowned. She wouldn't need any bright colours for her painting today.

The weather seemed to match Mai's mood perfectly. The girl waited for everyone to choose an easel with ill-concealed impatience. Doona and Andrew again were on either side of Bessie, with Nancy and Jack leaving an empty easel between themselves and Doona.

"Right, I'll just pass out some paints," Mai said. She went over to a large cupboard and began pulling out trays of paints. Then she carried a covered tray to each person in turn.

"If you'll come over here, you can collect your water and your brushes," she told them.

They formed an orderly queue at the sink and Mai handed

each of them a small cup of water and a pack of different types of brushes. Back at her easel, Bessie set the cup down carefully and then opened the paints and the brushes. She was excited to learn about watercolour painting, and she looked at Mai expectantly.

"As you can see, you have an excellent view of the lake for you to paint. Try not to get the tablets of paint too wet, at least in the beginning. You can always add more water for a lighter colour, but once the paint gets really wet it takes a long time to dry. I'm here if you have any questions," Mai said. She walked over to a chair in the corner and pulled out her mobile phone. Within a minute, she was talking to someone in a low voice.

Bessie looked over at Doona. "But I don't know anything about watercolour painting," she whispered.

"Me, either," Doona replied. "I don't even know where to start."

Andrea had finished cleaning the floor and now she walked over to them. "You should approach this like you did my class," she said, glancing nervously at Mai as she spoke. "Start with a few simple shapes and get the feel for how the paints work. You have nearly three hours and as much paper as you need, so take your time and play with techniques and brushes. Then spend the last hour working on painting what you see in front of you."

"Andrea, isn't this your lunch break?" Mai called from her corner of the room. "You need to get going so you're back to set up for the cartoon drawing class."

"I'll be back," Andrea said sharply. "You might want to think about setting up some flowers or a still life or something for your class to paint, as the view outside is pretty miserable today." With that, Andrea left the room.

Mai looked at everyone and then shook her head. "I'm sure you'd much rather paint the lake, even if it is a bit damp." Before anyone could reply, she was back on her mobile, talking and laughing with someone.

"I'm not finding a soggy October afternoon especially inspiring," Andrew told Bessie after a few minutes.

"I'm just painting a circle," Bessie replied. "I'm not ready to tackle the view yet."

They both heard a sheet of paper being torn off an easel and looked at Jack Strong.

"My circle was rather more soggy than I'd planned," he told the others. "I shall try again, I suppose."

After a few more minutes of working in silence, everyone jumped when the studio door opened suddenly. Lawrence Jenkins stuck his head in. He looked around the room, and when he spotted Mai, shook his head. She disconnected her call as Lawrence crossed to her.

Bessie worked on her circle, wishing she could hear the conversation going on in the corner of the room. After a few minutes, she decided that she really needed some fresh water to rinse her brushes in. She walked to the small sink and slowly emptied her cup.

"...doesn't matter. Harold will fire me as soon as he's officially back in charge," Mai was saying in an angry whisper.

"Maybe not," Lawrence answered. "I still have some say about what happens here, even without Charles's support. And I'm working on getting someone else on my side, as well. But in the meantime, you have to do your job and teach your classes. You can't sit here on your phone and ignore the guests."

"I'm tired of the guests," Mai complained. "You said this would be a fun job, but all I do is run around listening to complaints all day."

"I still own that plastics factory in Birmingham. If you'd prefer, you can spend a few months putting deodorant containers together," Lawrence snapped back.

Mai made a face. "I don't see why I can't just have some time off," she replied crossly.

"We aren't having this conversation now," Lawrence told her firmly. "You get to work. I need a word with one of your students."

He spun around and nearly tripped over Bessie, who quickly turned the tap on and filled her cup. For a moment he looked angry, but then he gave her what looked like a fake smile.

"Mrs. Cubbon, isn't it?" he asked.

"It's Miss Cubbon," Bessie replied.

"Oh, of course. Well, I do hope you're enjoying your stay," he told her.

"I am, aside from what happened to Charles Adams, of course," she replied.

"Yes, of course, that was tragic," he said, waving a hand as if dismissing the man's murder. "Anyway, if there's anything I can do to improve your visit, do let me know."

"I didn't realise you work for Lakeview," Bessie said in a questioning tone.

"I'm a shareholder in the company that owns the property, along with many others," he replied.

"Ah, and Charles was as well?" Bessie asked.

"More or less," was the evasive reply. "Anyway, I just need a word with your friend, Mrs. Moore," he told Bessie, walking quickly away from her.

Bessie followed more slowly, not wanting to eavesdrop on the man's conversation with her friend. If Doona wanted her to know what they'd discussed, she'd tell Bessie later.

Whatever Lawrence said to Doona had her quickly following the man out of the room. Bessie watched her friend leave, suddenly worried. Doona was back, alone, within a few minutes, but Bessie could tell that her friend was upset.

"Are you okay?" she asked as Doona picked up one of her brushes.

"No, but we'll talk later," Doona whispered.

Before Bessie could work out the correct reply to that, Mai spoke. "Okay, I'm sorry about that," she announced. "I had to ring a couple of people about issues they're having with their stay and it took much longer than I expected. Let's see how you're all doing."

Apparently, Lawrence's lecture had been effective. For the next two hours, Mai taught them several different watercolour painting techniques. Then she gave them the last half hour to work on painting their view of the lake. While Bessie was eager to talk to Doona, she enjoyed the class and even thought her lake painting wasn't terrible when four o'clock rolled around.

"That's very nice," Mai told her as she made a circuit of the room.

"Thanks. I don't hate it," Bessie replied.

"Are you taking the follow-up class on Friday?" Mai asked.

"We are."

"We can work then on refining a few techniques," Mai told her. "And, if we're lucky, it will be sunny. That always improves everyone's pictures."

As Mai wandered off towards Jack and Nancy, Bessie looked over at Doona's painting.

"You really do have talent," she told her friend, frowning slightly. While Doona's picture was well executed, just looking at it made Bessie feel sad. The colours were dull and muted and it was obviously raining and miserable in the two-dimensional world Doona had captured.

"Thanks," Doona muttered as a reply.

Bessie turned and looked to see how Andrew had done. His painting was much brighter, almost as if he were seeing the lake in sunshine.

"I thought I might as well paint what I wanted to see, rather than what I can see," he told Bessie with a wink.

"It's wonderful," Bessie replied.

"It isn't bad," he conceded. "I might actually keep this one for myself."

The door to the classroom swung open and Andrea walked in. She glanced at Mai and then raised an eyebrow.

"Ah, Andrea is here, so that means our time is up," Mai said brightly. "You're welcome to leave your work on your easels so that they can dry properly. If you are taking the follow-up class on Friday, you can collect today's work at that time. Otherwise, stop in anytime between nine and five any day before you leave. Whoever is here will be able to find your paintings for you."

"Are you taking Friday's class?" Bessie asked Andrew as they queued at the sink to dump their water and wash their brushes.

"I'm signed up for it," he replied. "So I'll probably take it, unless something more exciting comes along."

"I would have thought you'd rather spend time with the grandchildren," Bessie said.

"I'm spending a lot of time with them," he told her. "Starting with breakfast and going on from there. Having a few hours to myself, even if it means making a mess of painting, is a nice break."

"Your painting wasn't bad," Bessie argued.

"It was better than my pencil drawing," he said with a laugh.

"You're doing Friday's class, right?" Bessie asked Nancy.

"Wouldn't miss it," Nancy said with alacrity. "I'm really enjoying these classes."

"I'll be here too," Jack added. "Although I'm less excited than my lovely wife."

With the tidying finished, Bessie and the others headed out of the classroom. The lobby was full of small children who seemed to be chasing one another every which way.

"Okay, boys and girls," Andrea shouted from the centre of the space. "If you can line up in a straight line, we'll march into the craft room and get started."

Bessie walked quickly through the door, eager to get away from the chaos. Outside the rain had stopped, at least temporarily, but the air was still chilly.

"Bessie, I need to ring a few people," Doona said abruptly. "I'm going to go back to the cabin. Can I meet you at five at the Italian restaurant and we'll get dinner?"

"Of course," Bessie agreed quickly, feeling a little hurt that her friend clearly didn't want her around for the calls.

Doona just nodded and then rushed away, leaving Bessie with Andrew as Nancy and Jack walked off towards their accommodation.

"I wonder what Lawrence said to her," Andrew said. He glanced at Bessie and then shook his head. "Sorry, that's incredibly nosy of me. I suppose you never stop being an investigator, even when your retire."

"I'd like to know what he wanted as well," Bessie confided. "Doona seemed quite upset when she came back from talking to him."

"Are you okay?" Andrew asked.

The pair fell into step together, heading towards the centre of the village.

"I'm fine," Bessie replied without thought.

Andrew stopped and put a hand on her arm. "But how are you really?" he asked when she looked at him.

"I'm worried about Doona," she confessed.

"A little bird told me that the murder weapon came from your cabin," Andrew said quietly.

"I thought as much from the questions Margaret Hopkins was asking," Bessie told him. "And it probably had Doona's fingerprints all over it, as well."

"If it did, I think Margaret would have arrested Doona by now," the man replied.

"If it was our knife, it should have had Doona's prints on it," Bessie argued. "She used it the night of the murder to open some boxes."

Andrew shrugged. "Maybe the police could only get partial prints or something," he said. "They make it look easy on telly, but very few people leave nice complete and usable fingerprints on things that they use."

"So did your little bird have anything else interesting to tell you?" Bessie asked.

"They're considering a number of different suspects," he replied. "There are quite a few people who seem to have had motives."

"Like who?" Bessie demanded.

Andrew shook his head. "I really can't talk about an active police investigation," he said, "even if I'm not really with the police anymore."

"Doona and I made a list," Bessie told him. "If I run through it with you, will you tell me if we've missed anyone?"

"Bessie, this is a police investigation. You shouldn't be getting involved," he argued.

"My dearest friend is a suspect and it looks as if the murderer may have found the weapon on our patio," Bessie replied tartly. "We're already involved, whether we want to be or not."

"Who's on your list, then?" he asked.

Bessie frowned and then rattled off all of the names she could think of. "Lawrence Jenkins, Harold Butler, Mai Stratton, Jessica Howe, Herbert Howe, Joe Klein, Nathan Beck and probably Monique Beck as well," she said.

"I'm not sure what motive you can assign to some of them," he told her. "But all of those people are certainly on my list as well."

"But your list must be longer than mine," Bessie replied.

"Not really," Andrew said. "Margaret has to consider every single person at Lakeview, from guests to staff, but the vast majority of people didn't know Charles and were tucked up in bed, fast asleep, when he was killed."

"There must be other members of staff who've made your list," Bessie suggested.

"By this time of year, the park is running on limited staff. If Charles had been killed in August, when the park is at its busiest, Margaret would have had a much bigger job. As it is, aside from a few waitresses that Charles had flirtations with, very few of the staff seemed to have had much interaction with the man at all. Harold was still handling most of the day-to-day operations of the park."

"So what was Charles doing?"

"Cost cutting," Andrew said dryly. "Which is why he'd had trouble with Nathan Beck. Charles wanted to use a single source for all of the food that the park purchases for use in the various restaurants. Nathan has his own suppliers for L'Expérience Anglaise and he wasn't happy about the proposed changes."

"Seems a weak motive for murder," Bessie remarked.

"People have been killed for less," Andrew told her.

They'd now reached the village centre and before Bessie could reply, several members of his family surrounded Andrew. Bessie just waved to him as two small girls demanding his immediate attention swept him into the Squirrel's Drey. He smiled and waved back, leaving Bessie on her own to consider what they'd discussed.

Not wanting to go back to the lodge and disturb Doona, Bessie got herself a cup of tea from one of the takeaway counters and sat down in the food court. She sipped her tea and watched as people came and went through the building. Margaret Hopkins had a huge job on her hands if she had to investigate every single guest, she thought, even if she can eliminate those under eighteen.

From her quiet corner, Bessie watched as Mai wandered in. The girl glanced around the large space as if looking for someone. After a moment, she headed straight towards Bessie. There was a Lakeview brochure on the table, and, without thinking, Bessie picked it up and began to leaf through it. Mai didn't even seem to notice her; instead she walked past her and took a seat at a table a few places away from Bessie's.

As Bessie sipped her tea, she spotted Harold Butler coming out of the door marked "staff." Bessie was surprised when he headed towards Mai. He was clearly focussed on the girl and didn't seem to see Bessie, who kept her head down, ostensibly studying the brochure. Bessie watched with interest as the pair greeted one another, seemingly politely. Harold slid into the seat across from Mai and Bessie could only wish she were close enough to overhear the conversation that followed.

They'd only been together a few minutes when it appeared that things were getting quite heated. Bessie looked away as Mai rose to her feet. There was a mirror on the opposite wall, and Bessie found that she could see the pair quite easily while pretending to look away from them. Mai's voice was getting louder and Bessie could suddenly make out a few words.

"....should I have to cover for her? I've worked hard enough today without having to wait tables tonight."

Harold's reply was too quiet for Bessie to hear, but Mai wasn't trying to keep her voice down anymore.

"So close the restaurant," she said loudly.

When Harold answered, Bessie could hear Mai's bitter laugh before she replied.

"Yeah, you're right, I would have to listen to the complaints, wouldn't I? I suppose I don't have a choice. At least you could look a little less smug about it, though."

Harold stood up, and then to Bessie's surprise, gave the girl a hug that looked affectionate. Bessie waited for Mai to object, but the girl returned the embrace, looking up into Harold's eyes and whispering something to him. He nodded and then glanced around, as if suddenly nervous that someone had seen them. Mai sank back down into her seat, while Harold strode quickly away.

Mai was looking down at the table, which gave Bessie her chance. She picked up her cup and headed straight towards the girl.

"Mai, this is a surprise," she said brightly. "May I join you? I hate sitting on my own, even if I'm only having a cuppa."

Bessie sat down opposite the girl, not waiting for a reply. Mai looked up in surprise, and then smiled mechanically.

"Of course, feel free," she muttered without enthusiasm.

"Oh, dear, something tells me you aren't having a good afternoon," Bessie said. "I do hope everything is okay."

"Oh, I'm fine," Mai said. "I've just been working really hard. We had a much larger staff in the summer, and now everyone who is still here has to work twice as hard to keep things running smoothly."

"I'd have thought managing guest services was a busy enough job on its own," Bessie said.

"It is, really," Mai replied. "But I actually volunteered to teach the watercolour class. I love painting, and teaching the class lets me spend time with guests who aren't complaining, which is nice."

Bessie chuckled. "I suppose that's a help," she said. "But I can't imagine many guests complain. The park is so lovely."

"You'd be surprised," Mai replied darkly. "Some people will complain about everything in the hopes of getting a discount. And a lot of parents have very high expectations for anything and everything that their children do, as well."

"I suppose I can see that," Bessie said thoughtfully. "I do hope you're done for the day and can just go home and relax now."

"I wish," Mai said, frowning. "I've just been told that I have to wait tables in one of the restaurants tonight. It seems Monique Beck isn't feeling well and I have to take her place."

"Oh, dear," Bessie exclaimed. "What's wrong with Monique?"

"Who knows? She's always taking time off. If her husband wasn't such an amazing chef, she'd have been fired a long time ago."

"Well, I hope she feels better soon," Bessie said.

"Oh, I'm sure she just didn't feel up to working today," Mai said airily. "I just hope Harold won't put up with as much nonsense from her as Charles did."

Mai lowered her voice and leaned towards Bessie. 'Charles thought Nathan was incredible, and he was willing to pay Monique just to sit in a corner all day if it kept Nathan happy," she whispered.

"Really?" Bessie murmured.

Mai stood up abruptly. "I'd better get to work," she said with artificial cheer.

Bessie turned to see what had caused Mai's mood change, but the only person she recognised behind her was Doona, who was walking towards them.

"Mrs. Moore, I hope you enjoyed the class this afternoon," Mai said brightly "I'm looking forward to working with you again on Friday."

Before Doona said anything, Mai dashed away.

"That was odd," Bessie said.

"Just more VIP treatment," Doona said with a shrug.

"I suppose," Bessie replied. "Anyway, are you ready for something to eat?"

Doona sat down at the small table. When she looked over at Bessie, Bessie could see tears in her eyes.

"What's wrong?" Bessie asked.

"Let's go for a walk," Doona suggested, as a large party headed towards their corner.

"Of course," Bessie agreed quickly.

The pair walked out of the building and made their way around the lake. Doona was silent and Bessie walked along beside her, wishing she knew how to help her friend.

A large car with "Security" written down the side of it was parked in front of the Rainbow Arts Centre.

"It seems weird to see a car," Bessie remarked. "We haven't really seen any since Sunday."

Doona murmured something that Bessie didn't quite catch. Just then the door to the building swung open and Joe Klein walked out, a scowl on his face. As his eyes met Bessie's, he at least attempted a smile.

"Good afternoon, ladies," he said.

"Good afternoon," Bessie replied. "I do hope everything is okay?"

"Everything is fine," Joe assured her. "We had a small problem here, but it's nothing to worry about."

"Whenever people say that, I always worry," Bessie told him with a smile.

Joe chuckled, but it sounded forced. "After what happened on Monday, I'm not surprised you're worried," he said. "But compared to that, this was a minor inconvenience."

"Do you have any theories about what happened to Charles?" Bessie had to ask.

Joe looked at Doona for a moment and then shook his head. "Not my place to be developing theories," he told her. "Inspector Hopkins has that job and she's welcome to it."

Joe took a couple of steps towards his car, with Bessie following closely. Doona wandered a few paces in the opposite direction, finally sitting down on a bench near the building's front door.

Bessie glanced at Doona and then smiled at Joe. "Obviously, Doona's very upset about Charles's death," she said.

"Obviously," the man echoed.

"Did Charles have any enemies?"

Joe shrugged. "As I said, it isn't my place to get involved," he said, glancing around nervously.

"Is Harold going to get his old job back now, then?" Bessie asked. "He seems like such a nice man."

"That's up to the company that owns the park," Joe said. "I just do my job and try to avoid getting caught up in the management's hassles."

"But you're head of security. That's an important job."

Joe laughed. "Mostly I walk around the park and listen to parents tell their children that if they don't behave I'll take them away," he said, his tone somewhat harsh. "Once in a while someone will misplace something and start shouting about it being stolen, but in the two years I've been here, we've always managed to find whatever was lost. This murder was the first real crime we've had since I've been here, but of course it's not my place to get involved."

"I do hope the inspector isn't taking that attitude," Bessie said. "You've all the insider knowledge that she needs to work out what happened."

Joe opened his mouth and then snapped it shut. After a moment he sighed. "Let's just say the inspector has her own way of doing things," he said quietly.

It seemed clear to Bessie that the man resented being sidelined during the murder investigation. "I don't know about Lawrence Jenkins," Bessie said, keeping her tone conversational. "I'm not even sure what he does here. What is his job title?"

"He's here from the corporate headquarters," Joe told her. "He showed up about three weeks ago and started giving orders."

"I've heard that Charles was interested in cutting costs. Is that what Lawrence is here for, as well?"

Joe shrugged. "When Charles first arrived he cut my security team in half," he replied. "I suppose you could call that cost cutting, couldn't you? I've barely spoken to Lawrence, but I can't see where they could reduce my staff any further, so maybe he doesn't need to talk to me."

"Maybe if the park had better security Charles wouldn't have been murdered," Bessie suggested.

"Sort of ironic, isn't it?" Joe replied with an unpleasant grin.

"I understand Monique isn't feeling well," Bessie said, changing the subject abruptly to see what sort of reaction she'd get.

"She's off sick more than she's in work," Joe told her. "If Nathan wasn't so devoted to her, I think Harold would have fired her a long time ago."

"I'm surprised she survived Charles's cost cutting."

"Oh, she and Charles got along well," Joe replied. "He had enough problems with Nathan with regard to food costs. He wasn't going to fire the man's wife."

"What do you know about Jessica and Herbert Howe?" Bessie asked, changing the subject yet again.

"Jessica was here a lot," Joe said. "She arrived for a week right after Charles came and she's been back regularly since. I think Charles had finished with her, but she was having trouble accepting that."

"Really? What about Herbert? Does he always come with her?"

"No," Joe shook his head. "He came with her for a week last month. All they did all week long was argue all over the park. Harold finally had to speak to them both about their behaviour."

"But he came back again with her this time," Bessie said thoughtfully.

"And they've been arguing up a storm again," Joe replied. "Although for the most part they've kept the fights more private. Mostly they've been shouting at each other in their lodge. We've had a few complaints from the neighbours, but not that many."

"So why do they stay together?" Bessie asked.

"She's stays for the money," Joe said. "Why he puts up with her is beyond me, though."

"What's Mai's connection with Lawrence?" Bessie tried a different direction, hoping the man would continue to be forthcoming.

"I'm not sure, but there's something there," he replied. "She's another one that gets special treatment. From Charles and from Lawrence, though I don't know why."

"Bessie, we need to talk," Doona's voice carried across the space.

Bessie smiled at Joe. "It's been interesting talking with you," she told the man.

"Likewise," he said. He nodded at Doona and then crossed to his car.

Bessie watched as he drove away, then she joined Doona on the bench.

"What's wrong?" she asked her friend, suddenly concerned by how pale and miserable Doona looked.

"I'm pretty sure Margaret Hopkins is going to be back to ask us more questions later," Doona told her. "And there's something you need to know before she starts."

"What?"

Doona shook her head. "I'm sorry I wasn't totally honest with you," she said, her voice shaking.

Bessie took Doona's hands and held them tightly. "Whatever it is, it can't be that bad," she said soothingly. "I'm your friend and I love you. It will be okay."

Doona stared into Bessie's eyes for a moment before looking away. "I'm sorry," she repeated quietly. "The thing is, Charles and I were still married."

CHAPTER 11

*B*essie sat in stunned silence for a moment, her mind racing. Doona pulled her hands away and covered her face. Bessie quickly put her arm around her friend.

"I'm sure you can explain," she said, her voice a bit too loud.

"Of course I can," Doona replied without looking up. "I never set out to lie to you, but things just got so complicated."

Bessie rubbed Doona's shoulders and then gently took her hands again. She pulled them away from her friend's face and stared into Doona's eyes. "I thought you told me, two years ago, that you and Charles had divorced," she said, working to keep from sounding accusatory.

Doona shrugged. "Do you remember when we first met, I told you that working out the divorce was complicated?"

Bessie thought back and then nodded. "There was some problem because you hadn't been married for very long," she remembered.

"Exactly, you can't even apply for a divorce on the Isle of Man until you've been married at least a year," Doona told her. "And then you have to have a good reason for applying as well."

"Surely adultery is a good reason," Bessie said.

"It is, if you can prove it."

"But you had all the things you were sent."

Doona sighed. "When I got back from the trip after I saw Charles with Jessica, I gathered together everything that Charles had ever given me and I had a huge bonfire with it. And when it was really blazing, I threw the envelope on the fire."

"Oh," Bessie said flatly.

"I know," Doona replied. "I was so upset that I simply wasn't thinking straight. I didn't really know anything about divorce law on the island. When my first husband and I split up, it was amicable and neither of us really cared how long it took to work its way though the courts." She looked down at the ground and Bessie could see the tears flowing down her face.

"So without the evidence, you couldn't get the divorce?" Bessie asked.

"I had to wait until we'd been married a year to even apply," Doona told her. "When I talked to my advocate, we agreed that the easiest thing to do would be to wait until we'd been separated for two years and then apply, using the separation as the reason."

"Surely you could have gathered more evidence of his cheating?" Bessie suggested.

Doona flushed. "I didn't really want to pursue that," she admitted quietly. "I didn't want everyone on the island to know that Charles had cheated on me. I was embarrassed."

Bessie hugged her friend. "It certainly wasn't your fault that the man cheated," she said indignantly. "You had nothing to be embarrassed about."

"I suppose," Doona said with a shrug. "Anyway, I think I told you that my advocate and I had worked everything out once we'd decided to wait the two years. I meant to give you the impression that the divorce was settled, even though it wasn't. I'm sorry, but I simply wanted to put the whole ugly episode out of my mind."

Bessie hugged her again. "I understand," she said. "And I can see you not wanting to have to think about it. Having to wait the two years is hard enough, without constantly having to think about it."

"I thought about it quite a bit anyway," Doona admitted. "But I didn't want to have to talk about it. Doncan rang me a month ago to let me know that he'd sent the paperwork to Charles's solicitor. All we needed was Charles's signature and it would have all been over."

Doncan Quayle was Bessie's advocate as well, so Bessie was certain that Doona was getting the best possible advice and assistance. "But Charles didn't sign before he died?" Bessie guessed.

"According to his solicitor, he wasn't going to sign," Doona said. "And without his signature, I'd have to wait another three years to get the divorce."

Bessie swallowed hard. It seemed as if Doona had an even stronger motive for the murder than she'd realised. "And Margaret Hopkins knows all of this?"

"She knew some it almost immediately," Doona replied. "I told her, when she first questioned me, that the divorce wasn't final yet. I gather Charles's solicitor has now been questioned and he's told her that Charles wasn't going to sign the papers."

"So where does all of this leave you?" Bessie asked.

"I'd imagine it leaves me as Margaret's chief suspect," Doona said sadly. "It also leaves me in a weird position here."

"What do you mean?"

"Charles owned some part of the company that owns the park," Doona explained. "Lawrence suggested to me that I might still be Charles's heir."

"Surely someone will contest the will," Bessie said thoughtfully.

"I've no doubt Lawrence will want to fight it, if such a will even exists," Doona replied. "But for the moment, everything seems to be on hold. Apparently Charles's solicitor won't even consider a formal reading of the will until the murderer is caught."

"Can he do that?"

Doona shrugged. "I've no idea. I think I'm his chief suspect as well."

Bessie frowned at the misery in her friend's voice. "Well, that's just nonsense," she said stoutly. "I know you didn't kill Charles, even if you had plenty of provocation."

"And a very strong motive," Doona added.

"So what?"

"And access to the murder weapon," Doona continued. "That's assuming that the knife from our lodge was the murder weapon, but I think that's a fair assumption."

"Doesn't matter," Bessie said firmly.

"And, of course, plenty of opportunity," Doona concluded. "I've admitted to going out for a walk that night. I've even admitted that I saw Charles outside the Squirrel's Drey. I can't prove that I hid from him and walked away."

Bessie shook her head. "Motive, means and opportunity aren't everything," she said. "There's a human element that matters as well. You simply aren't a murderer."

"I know that, but I'm not sure anyone else does," Doona said with a sigh.

"Maybe we need to work out who is," Bessie suggested. "Before Margaret Hopkins starts looking in the wrong direction."

"I've been trying to think it through," Doona said. "But I simply can't think straight."

"It seems to me," Bessie said thoughtfully, "that just about everyone had means and opportunity. Charles was alone in the building, or at least alone with the killer. Anyone could have arranged to meet with him there after hours, couldn't they?"

Doona nodded. "I thought that as well. I know we have a list of suspects, but really anyone in the park could have made an appointment to see him, or even just turned up and surprised him."

"So we're back to suspecting every single person at Lakeview," Bessie said with a sigh.

"Except we haven't talked about motive," Doona reminded her.

"And we've no idea who might have known Charles in the past," Bessie said. "Maybe one of the guests had an affair with him ten years ago, and when she saw him again, she just had to kill him."

"Anything is possible," Doona admitted. "I think we have to hope that isn't the case, though. We need to focus on the people we know had a motive."

"So Jessica and Herbert Howe, Harold Butler, Lawrence Jenkins, maybe Nathan Beck; who am I forgetting?" Bessie asked.

"I'd add Monique Beck and Mai Stratton to the list," Doona said. "And Joe Klein, just because he makes me nervous."

Bessie sat back on the bench and closed her eyes, trying to think. It felt like there was something she was missing, but she couldn't work out what it was. Her stomach growled loudly and interrupted her thinking.

"Maybe we should talk after dinner," Doona suggested with a faint smile.

"I'm fine," Bessie said, ignoring another rumble.

"Let's go get some food," Doona said, getting to her feet. "I'm pretty sure I'm due for more questioning. Maybe we can eat before the questions this time."

Bessie and Doona headed back towards the Squirrel's Drey. Bessie was aware that she was watching closely for Margaret Hopkins as they went.

"I keep thinking every woman is Inspector Hopkins," Doona whispered as they went past a large group of men and women.

"I know what you mean," Bessie agreed.

They reached the short row of restaurants. There was a short queue in front of the Italian restaurant and an even longer one in front of the American one. Only the French restaurant looked quiet.

"We said we'd try the Italian, didn't we?" Bessie murmured.

"I'm not sure I want to wait in the queue," Doona replied. "But I'm not sure I want to eat at *L'Expérience Anglaise* either."

"Maybe we can ask Nathan a few discreet questions," Bessie suggested. "Apparently Monique isn't well. Maybe she killed Charles and the guilt is proving to be too much for her."

"I doubt it," Doona said. "She strikes me as the type who could stab a man without batting an eyelash."

Bessie looked at her friend, surprised at the harsh assessment of the young girl. "I take it you don't like Monique," she said.

"I don't like anyone right now," Doona said with a sigh. "Don't mind me. I'm just looking for someone I can blame Charles's murder on. I really just want this all to be over."

"Let's go get some dinner and see what we can find out," Bessie said, turning and heading towards *L'Expérience Anglaise*. Doona followed.

"Ah, customers," Mai said as they walked in. "What a nice surprise."

"All the other restaurants are quite busy, and we're very hungry," Bessie told her.

"And we're very quiet because everyone has heard how bad the food was the other day when Nathan was having his temper tantrum," Mai said, too loudly.

"I do hope he's feeling better tonight," Bessie said.

"I haven't had any complaints," Mai said. "But then, we haven't had all that many customers. Follow me."

Bessie was surprised at how empty the dining room was when they walked in. Only three other tables were occupied; a total of six other customers in all.

"How about a quiet booth at the back?" Mai suggested, leading the women to the far side of the restaurant.

"This is fine," Bessie said, happy to be at a table almost as far as they could be from where they'd sat on their last two visits to the place.

Mai handed them each a menu and then took their drink order. Bessie and Doona had a quick chat about the menu, both deciding to try something completely different. Once Mai had delivered their glasses of wine and taken their food order, Bessie sat back, determined to try to relax. Mai delivered a basket of fresh bread rolls and butter, and the friends were pleased to find that they were delicious.

Bessie was focussed on her wine when she realised that Doona had turned pale. It only took a second to realise why, as Bessie watched as Mai led Jessica and Herbert Howe to a table not far from theirs.

Jessica frowned as she looked over at them. She said something to her husband and then walked over to Bessie and Doona's table.

"So, you're Charles's wife," she said sneeringly. "He used to tell me such cute little things about you. You were so in love with him."

"Charles could be incredibly charming," Doona replied steadily. "Fortunately it didn't take me long to see through his superficiality. I only wasted a couple of months on him."

Jessica flushed and then shook her head. "But you were getting back together," she said. "He told me that you were coming here to give him a second chance. That's why we split up, at least temporarily."

"You were misinformed," Doona said dryly.

"Charles never lied to me," Jessica replied angrily.

"Then you must have misunderstood him," Doona said with a shrug. "It has nothing to do with me."

"Except when you saw him again, you killed him," Jessica shouted.

"If we were getting back together, why would I kill him?" Doona asked. Bessie could tell that her friend was working very hard to keep her voice calm.

"I imagine Charles must have changed his mind," Jessica said. "Yeah, that's probably it. You came here to get back with him and then he said he wasn't interested after all and you killed him."

"That's an interesting theory," Doona replied. "But it's wrong on every possible account."

"I seem to recall you threatening to kill him if you saw him," Bessie interjected. "Were you that upset that he'd finished with you?"

Jessica glared at Bessie and then tossed her head. "I don't have to answer your questions, you old cow," she hissed. "Charles and I had something very special that you'll never understand."

"And your husband threatened to kill him as well, didn't he?" Bessie added. "I'm not sure what his motive was, though."

"Herbert wouldn't hurt a fly," Jessica said, glancing over at her husband, who was studying the wine list with fierce intensity. "He and I had an understanding about Charles."

Mai appeared then, carrying Bessie and Doona's starters. As she set them on the table, Lawrence arrived, a huge, fake-looking smile plastered on his face.

"My dear Jessica, you look lovely tonight," he said smoothly. "But if you leave poor Herbert alone too long he'll get quite lonely."

"He's fine," Jessica snapped. "I was just offering my condolences to the devastated widow." She gave Doona a contemptuous look and then turned and strode back to her own table.

"You mustn't mind Jessica," Lawrence murmured as he sat down across from Doona. "In a weird way she really cared for Charles."

"And how did you feel about the man?" Bessie asked.

Lawrence looked at her and then chuckled softly. "We were business partners in a number of schemes," he replied. "We weren't necessarily friends."

"So you weren't surprised that he'd never introduced you to Doona," Bessie suggested.

"Actually, I was very surprised," he said. "I never thought he'd get married. He didn't like the idea of commitment."

Doona laughed bitterly. "No kidding," she muttered.

"But he did care about you," Lawrence said. "He really did invite you up here to try to win you back."

"I don't believe it," Doona said flatly. "I don't know what he was up to, but I'll never believe that he suddenly realised he still had feelings for me. We hadn't spoken in two years."

"He spent a lot of that time travelling on the continent," Lawrence told her. "He wanted to get away from a lot of things." He glanced over at Jessica as he spoke.

"I bet she visited him, wherever he went," Doona said.

"It's difficult," Lawrence replied. "Herbert is another investor in many of the projects that Charles was involved with or managed. That's how Charles met Jessica, actually."

"So Herbert didn't mind that she was sleeping with another man?" Doona asked incredulously.

Lawrence shrugged. "As Jessica said, they had some sort of agreement. Herbert likes having a trophy wife, from what I hear."

"I'll never understand some people," Doona said, shaking her head.

"If they had an agreement, what was Herbert so upset with Charles about?" Bessie asked, remembering the man's threats the first time she'd seen him.

"I believe the issue was business rather than personal," Lawrence replied. "Charles was doing a number of things here that were upsetting investors. That's one of the reasons I came up."

"What sorts of things?" Bessie asked.

"Nothing I'm prepared to discuss right now," the man replied with an insincere smile. "Everything has been taken care of now and Harold is doing an excellent job keeping things running while we work out what to do next."

He looked over at Doona who was nibbling at her food without interest. "That's where you come in, of course," he said. Doona's left hand was on the table and Lawrence picked it up and squeezed it.

"There's a very good chance that you're Charles's heir," he told her. "I'd like to talk to you about buying out your shares in the management company. I'm prepared to offer you fair market value plus ten per cent."

"I think we need to wait and see what the will says," Doona replied, pulling her hand away. "And then, if I have inherited anything, you'll have to deal with my advocate."

Lawrence frowned. "I'd much rather deal with you personally," he said. "You were important to Charles and he was my friend."

"I'd be touched by that if you hadn't said earlier that you were business partners but not friends," Doona retorted. "Once the will is read, I'll give you contact details for my advocate, if that's appropriate."

The man looked as if he was going to argue, but Mai reappeared with their entrees. "I'll leave you to your meal, then," he said as he stood up. "Enjoy."

He turned and walked away. Doona stuck out her tongue at his back, making Bessie laugh.

"He is rather disagreeable," she said.

"If I do inherit anything, I don't want him to get it," Doona replied. "Just because he's horrible."

They ate for several minutes in silence. "This is good," Bessie said eventually.

"Not as good as the first night, but much better than lunch the other day," Doona agreed.

"I do hope you're enjoying your meal," Harold's voice interrupted.

Bessie smiled up at the man, who returned the look with a matching smile. "It's very good," she replied.

"Excellent," he said. "I know this hasn't exactly been the holiday you were hoping for, but I do hope you're managing to enjoy your stay in spite of the tragedy. You must let me know if I can do anything to make your visit better."

"Thank you," Bessie said.

"Mrs. Adams," he said, addressing Doona, "I've heard a number of rumours about Charles's will. It isn't my place to ask, but, well, I was wondering which ones are true."

"First of all, I'm Mrs. Moore, or rather Ms. Moore," Doona replied. "I never took Charles's surname and I'm not about to start using it now. Secondly, I have no idea what's in Charles's will. I hadn't spoken to the man in two years and didn't even know where he was. I understand his solicitor is hoping that the police will complete their investigation before he has to read the will to the interested parties."

"Well, if you do inherit some shares in this place, I'd love to buy them from you," Harold said in a very low voice. "I have a better chance of keeping my job if I actually own a piece of the park, don't you think?"

"I don't know anything about how the park is run," Doona said. "Or about Charles's will. If I do inherit anything, I'll give you the contact details for my advocate and you can talk to him."

"How is everything?" Mai asked brightly as she joined them.

"Oh, it's good," Bessie replied.

"Excellent," Mai said. "Harold, Nathan would like a word with you in the kitchen when you're done out here."

She was gone before Harold could reply. He rolled his eyes and then laughed. "Someone always wants something," he grumbled jokingly. "I'm not quite sure why I ever went into management. You'll have to excuse me, ladies."

He stood up, stared hard at Doona for a moment and then strolled away, smiling and chatting with the other guests scattered around the room as he went.

"If you have inherited something from Charles, it sounds as if there's going to be a battle for it," Bessie remarked.

"I don't want anything from Charles," Doona said bitterly. "It isn't

165

like we were married for any length of time. I don't even feel as if I deserve to inherit from him."

"Let's not worry about it for tonight," Bessie suggested. "Let's try to enjoy dinner."

Mai cleared their empty plates and brought a second round of drinks for them. They were just considering having pudding when Nathan wandered out of the kitchen. Bessie watched as he looked around the room. When he spotted them, he headed towards them.

"Ah, good evening, ladies. I'm so pleased that you allowed me another chance to feed you after that dismal lunch the other day."

"It was a strange day in many ways," Bessie said.

"Yes, well, I hope you enjoyed your meal more tonight?"

"It was very good," Bessie assured him.

"And you, Mrs. Moore?" Nathan asked.

"Oh, it was good, thanks," Doona answered.

"I understand you may soon own shares in our little park," he said to Doona. "I do hope you'll be as supportive of my work as Charles was."

"How's Monique?" Bessie asked, trying to spare Doona from having to come up with a suitable response.

"Monique? She's fine," he replied. "She gets homesick sometimes and then she doesn't feel up to working. Charles was always very understanding about it."

"Seems a bit hard on Mai, though," Bessie suggested. "Since she's the one who has to cover for her."

Nathan shrugged. "Mai always seems to enjoy helping out here," he said. "She's a really sweet girl."

"But she's the manager of guest services and teaches classes as well," Bessie replied. "Having to work in the evenings after working all day seems like too much."

"Charles got rid of a lot of the staff," Nathan replied. "We used to have enough waitresses to cover when one was off. Charles more or less halved the number of wait staff in every restaurant."

"I'd heard he was doing a lot of cost cutting," Bessie replied.

"Anyway, I'd better get back to the kitchen," Nathan said. Bessie saw that Mai was beckoning for him in the kitchen doorway. "I'll send out something special for you both."

He was gone before the women could argue. Bessie watched as he and Mai had a whispered conversation in the doorway before Nathan walked through it. Mai looked upset for a moment but she had a smile back on her face as she walked around the room, talking to various guests. A few minutes later, she brought plates with huge slices of chocolate gateau on them to Bessie and Doona.

"Enjoy," she said after she'd set them down.

Bessie stared at the delicious looking cake for a brief moment before diving it. It was almost tastier than it looked, and even Doona seemed to have found some enthusiasm for it as she ate.

"That was wonderful," Bessie said as she pushed her empty plate towards the centre of the table.

"It truly was," Doona agreed. "I wasn't even hungry."

Bessie glanced at her friend's empty plate and smiled. "Good thing," she remarked.

"Would it be terrible to get small ice cream cones for the walk home?" Bessie asked as they exited the restaurant.

"Yes," Doona replied. "But let's do it anyway."

There was, as always, a queue, but it was moving fairly quickly and the pair didn't mind. This time they both ordered only a single scoop of ice cream from the stand.

"Pardon me, Ms. Moore, isn't it?" the deep voice carried through the small crowd around the ice cream counter.

Bessie looked over at Herbert Howe and frowned. She felt as if Doona had had quite enough chatting with suspects for one day.

"Mr. Howe, isn't it?" Doona said politely.

"It is, yes," he replied, bowing slightly. "I won't keep you, but I wanted to let you know that I'm very interested in purchasing any business interests you might inherit from Charles Adams. I didn't realise he was married, or that you were his wife, until yesterday."

"If I inherit anything, and I consider it highly unlikely that I will, you'll have to deal with my advocate on the Isle of Man," Doona replied.

"Excellent, I'd rather deal with professionals," he told her. "They generally appreciate financial gains over sentimental value."

"As your wife seems to have had some sort of relationship with the man, perhaps Charles made her his heir," Bessie suggested, feeling brave about confronting him with a small crowd surrounded them.

Herbert just laughed. "Jessica was nothing to Charles," he said firmly. "She and I have a very volatile relationship, but she'd never leave me, certainly not for a man like Charles."

"Meaning what?" Bessie asked.

"Jessica likes money more than anything," he replied. "Charles was a very successful businessman and he was good at investing wisely, as well. He'd managed to build up a decent-sized share in the management company that owns this park and the chain of hotels he worked for, but he wasn't wealthy, at least not by Jessica's standards. She enjoyed his company, but he was never more than a diversion."

Bessie bit her tongue as a dozen different replies sprang to her lips.

"I was all wrong for Charles, then," Doona said. "I actually expected him to be faithful."

"Monogamy isn't part of my marriage," he said with a shrug. "On either side. I don't expect you to understand," he added, presumably reading the look on Bessie's face correctly. "And I'm not going to try to explain, either. All I wanted to do was make sure you knew I was interested in buying up Charles's shares in the company. No doubt Harold and Lawrence have also made offers. I'll happily outbid them both, once we know exactly what's at stake."

He nodded at both of them and then walked off, without waiting for a reply.

"Maybe, if Charles did leave me something, I should just keep it and watch them all beg for a while," Doona said with a sigh.

"Eat your ice cream," Bessie told her. "It will make you feel better."

The pair walked in silence back to their cabin, enjoying their frozen treat. Bessie was lost in thought, wondering if everyone's eagerness to get their hands on Charles's shares in the company might give any of them a motive for murder.

Just across the small bridge, Doona sank down on a bench. Bessie joined her and they sat and watched the tiny waves rippling on the miniature lake for a moment.

"I need to find out more about this company," Doona said eventually. "It seems as if Charles owned a fairly large piece of it, from what everyone is saying."

"We know that Lawrence and Herbert were also shareholders. I wonder how many others there are?"

"Maybe thousands," Doona said. "It could be a huge publicly traded company for all I know."

"But it doesn't sound like it," Bessie replied.

"No, it doesn't," Doona agreed.

They sat for a few minutes longer before Bessie spoke again. "Am I the only one who thinks it's strange that Herbert didn't mind his wife cheating on him?" she asked. "I know I'm old-fashioned about such things, but he isn't all that much younger than me."

"But if you were jealous of the relationship and then the man suddenly ended up murdered, wouldn't you start going around telling everyone how you didn't mind at all?" Doona asked.

"Of course I would," Bessie agreed. "I didn't think of that."

"You know, I'm afraid Margaret Hopkins is waiting back at Foxglove Close to arrest me," Doona said.

"If she does, John will be on the next flight across," Bessie told her.

"While that makes me feel a bit better, I'd still rather not be arrested," Doona replied.

Bessie shook her head. "Inspector Hopkins is probably at home tucked up in bed, watching something inane on the telly."

"Maybe," Doona said doubtfully.

"Pardon me?" a voice whispered. "May I join you?"

Bessie recognised the soft French accent before she spotted Monique in the fading light.

"Of course," she said, sliding over to make more space for the girl.

"The police, they are waiting at your lodge for you," Monique said intently to Doona. "But I had to talk to you. I have to know if it's true that you're Charles's wife."

CHAPTER 12

*D*oona glanced at Bessie and then looked at Monique. "Charles and I were married," she said slowly. "But we'd been separated for two years when he died, and I'd applied for a divorce."

"You aren't what I expected," Monique said sadly. "He told me about you."

"Really?" Doona asked.

"Yes, he was sorry for how he treated you," she said. "He still cared about you."

"At least that's what he told you," Doona said sourly.

"He didn't lie to me," Monique replied.

"I thought that once," Doona told her. "But I was wrong."

Monique brushed away tears. "I don't blame you for not believing me," she said after a moment. "I know he hurt you very badly."

"It was a long time ago," Doona said dismissively. "I've moved on."

"He hadn't," Monique said.

They all stared at the lake for a moment before Bessie broke the silence.

"I hope you're feeling better," she told the girl.

"I'm okay," she said with a shrug. "Sometimes it's easier to be alone.

Taking care of guests takes so much effort. Being polite and rushing about with heavy trays isn't fun."

"Perhaps you should look for a different job," Bessie suggested coolly.

"I have thought about it," Monique said. "But Nathan needs me. He counts on me to help with everything. We're a team, even when we don't get along."

Bessie opened her mouth to ask another question, but Monique rose to her feet.

"I must go," she said, her gaze darting back and forth. "Someone will miss me."

She slipped away into the darkness before Bessie or Doona could reply.

"We should go and see what the inspector wants," Doona said, clearly reluctant to do so.

"Or we could go for a walk," Bessie suggested. "Maybe get some more ice cream and then find a quiet spot to sit and watch the world go by."

"Don't tempt me," Doona told her. "But I won't be forced into hiding. I didn't do anything wrong and if the inspector has more questions for me, I need to answer them."

The pair got to their feet and walked slowly towards Foxglove Close. When they turned the corner into the cul-de-sac Bessie spotted the inspector standing in front of their cabin. She crossed to them, a tight smile on her face.

"Mrs. Moore, I'm afraid I have more questions for you," she said as a greeting.

"Shall we talk out here so that Bessie can get some sleep?" Doona proposed.

"I think I'd rather talk to you in my office," Margaret replied. "If you don't mind."

"You're arresting me," Doona said flatly.

"Not at all," the inspector countered. "I'm asking you for your cooperation."

"It's quite late," Bessie said. "Maybe she could come to your office in the morning."

"I'd rather not wait," Margaret said smoothly. "This is a murder investigation, after all."

Bessie opened her mouth to object, but Doona held up a hand. "It's fine," she said tiredly. "You go and get some sleep and I'll try to be extra quiet when I get back. We can catch up in the morning."

"Are you sure?" Bessie asked, taking Doona's hands in hers and staring into her eyes.

"I'm sure," she said, her eyes meeting Bessie's without blinking. Bessie could see many emotions in her friend's eyes. She gave Doona a tight hug and then, reluctantly, stepped back and watched silently as the inspector and Doona walked away. As soon as they were out of sight, Bessie headed for the cabin.

"The inspector had just taken Doona to her office for questioning," she told John Rockwell as soon as he answered his phone.

"I'll ring her and see what I can find out," he replied. "Don't worry."

Bessie laughed at his words, but John had already disconnected. With nothing to do but worry, Bessie paced around the small building, walking from room to room, staring at her mobile and willing it to ring. It felt like hours, but was really only about ten minutes later when John rang her back.

"Margaret is under a lot of pressure to solve this thing," he told Bessie. "Doona had a very strong motive, the murder weapon came from her accommodation, it has fingerprints on it that are a partial match for hers, and she's already admitted to seeing Charles the night of the killing. The only surprising thing in all this is that Margaret hasn't actually arrested her. She's only taken her in for additional questioning."

"But Doona didn't do it," Bessie said angrily.

"Margaret doesn't know Doona at all," John said calmly. "And even if she knew her well, she has to work from the evidence she's collecting. If I were in her place, I'd probably arrest Doona myself."

"You aren't making me feel any better," Bessie said grumpily.

"I talked to one of Margaret's assistants, and they may well keep Doona overnight," he told her.

"Poor Doona," Bessie exclaimed.

"She'll be well looked after," John told her. "They have a couple of rooms for overnight guests that are secure but not cells. She'll be able to sleep there and Margaret will make sure she gets fed as well."

"So what happens tomorrow?" Bessie asked.

"Tomorrow we hope they find evidence that someone else did it," John replied. "I'm going to fly across if I can get a flight. I'll let you know when I'm going to arrive and we can go from there."

"I'll feel better with you here," Bessie said.

"I'll feel better being there," John replied.

Bessie told John about the various conversations she'd heard or overheard during the day. "It seems like there are a lot of motives out there," she concluded.

"And it sounds as if there's quite a bit of money at stake," John added. "Which is worrying, as it's just another thing that strengthens Doona's motive, if she really is Charles's heir."

"I wish I knew what Monique wanted tonight," Bessie said. "It was a strange conversation that went nowhere."

"It sounds like she was quite close to Charles," John remarked. "I wonder how close."

"What are you suggesting?" Bessie asked.

"Nothing and everything," John replied. "Until I get there and actually meet the concerned parties, I'm just thrashing around in the dark."

"Let me know when you'll be arriving," Bessie told him. "We'll have to sort out a place to meet."

"You'll be the first to know," John assured her.

After they disconnected, Bessie continued to pace around the cabin. Eventually she decided that she needed to get some sleep, but as she got ready for bed, all she could think about was Doona. Bessie knew she was overtired and her imagination was overactive, but in her imagination poor Doona was sitting in a hard wooden chair with a bright light shining in her eyes while the inspector shouted question after question at her.

Bessie grabbed her stack of book club books and curled up in bed. She read a chapter in each book, finding nothing that could hold her interest. Finally she gave up and turned out the light. After an hour of tossing and turning, she got back up and went out on the patio. She curled up in one of the comfortable lounge chairs and stared up at the sky. When she woke up hours later, she was stiff and cold and the sun was starting to come up.

With nothing productive to do, Bessie decided to have an early morning walk around the lake. She took a quick shower and then got dressed and headed out. She locked the door behind her and turned towards the road. Andrew was just emerging from number seven.

"Good morning," he said cheerfully.

"Good morning," Bessie replied with as much enthusiasm as she could muster.

"What's wrong?" he asked immediately.

Bessie stifled a sigh. "Inspector Hopkins arrested Doona last night," she said. She took a deep breath and then tried again, aware of how angry she'd sounded. "The inspector took Doona to her office for additional questioning," she corrected herself.

"I presume there's quite a bit of evidence against your friend," Andrew said. "I don't think she did it, myself, but Margaret has to investigate every possibility."

"Doona would never kill anyone, not even her ex-husband," Bessie said confidently.

"Except they weren't divorced, were they?" Andrew asked.

"Well, no, technically not," Bessie said slowly.

"Let's go for a walk," Andrew suggested as someone emerged from a lodge a few doors away. He offered his arm, and after a moment's hesitation, Bessie took it. They made their way down the path around the lake. Eventually, Andrew broke the silence.

"I've been calling in a few favours to find out what's going on with the investigation," he told Bessie. "Let's talk about what I know and see if we can work anything out."

"We can try," Bessie said doubtfully.

"Allegedly, Charles dumped Jessica Howe recently. She seems to have quite a volatile temper," Andrew said.

"Are you suggesting she killed him?" Bessie asked.

Andrew shrugged. "I can believe it of her more readily than of Doona," he replied. "Her husband had his own reasons for hating Charles. From what I've heard, they were both personal and professional."

"I can't imagine why he was willing to work with Charles even though he knew Charles was having an affair with Jessica," Bessie said, shaking her head.

"People do odd things for money," Andrew said. "And apparently Charles was very good at making money for the company."

"So we know they both had motives. Did they have means and opportunity?" Bessie asked.

"As far as getting to Charles, just about anyone could have done that. The Squirrel's Drey was meant to be closed, but Charles could have let someone in, the killer could have had a key, or a door somewhere in the building could have been left open. Security wasn't as much of a priority as it should have been."

"Did they alibi each other?" Bessie asked.

"Actually, just the opposite," Andrew told her, shaking his head. "They both claimed to have been alone in their lodge the entire night."

"Well, clearly one of them is lying, then," Bessie exclaimed.

"Probably both of them," Andrew said dryly.

"So why isn't the inspector dragging them in for questioning?" Bessie asked.

"Because there's no evidence that they knew who Doona was until after the murder," Andrew replied.

"What does that have to do with anything?" Bessie demanded.

"If Doona didn't kill Charles, someone took a risk climbing onto your patio to take that knife to try to frame her. Whoever that was must have known that she had a motive for killing Charles."

Bessie stopped suddenly, her mind racing. "I never really thought about that," she admitted. "I should have realised."

"Of course, the murderer wouldn't necessarily admit to knowing about Doona, even if he or she did," Andrew added.

"Someone sent Doona an envelope full of evidence that Charles was cheating on her two years ago," Bessie said. "That person certainly knew about Doona and about Charles's affair with Jessica."

"Doona doesn't know who sent the envelope?"

"She said she thought it was Herbert Howe," Bessie replied.

"Why did she think that?"

"I don't know," Bessie said with a frown. "You'd have to ask her."

"If it was Herbert Howe, that certainly makes him more likely as a suspect," Andrew said.

"Has anyone admitted to knowing about Doona?" Bessie asked.

"It's a good thing I'm retired," Andrew replied with a chuckle. "And I'm only repeating what I've heard secondhand through miscellaneous connections. If I were still working for the police, I could get fired for discussing an active investigation."

"So has anyone admitted to knowing about Doona?" Bessie repeated herself.

"Mai suspected, because she wrote out the place cards for the welcome reception," Andrew told her. "And Monique said she knew because she and Charles were good friends and he confided in her."

"How good of friends were they?" Bessie asked.

Andrew shrugged. "She said Charles was like a big brother to her. She and Nathan had been having trouble and Charles provided a shoulder for her to cry on."

"Hmm," Bessie murmured.

"Other than that, apparently Charles told everyone that you two were coming and were very important people, but nothing further."

"I find it hard to believe that Charles never told Lawrence, his business partner, about his wife," Bessie said.

"And yet, as I understand it, Doona didn't know anything about Lawrence, either," Andrew countered.

"What about Harold?" Bessie asked.

"He said he and Charles had a decent working relationship, but never discussed their private lives. As Charles took Harold's job and was highly vocal in his criticism of how the park was run when Harold was in charge, I can't imagine they spoke much at all."

"So why did Harold stay?"

"He started working here right out of university," Andrew replied. "Over the years, he worked his way from being an assistant in guest services all the way up to site manager. He's never worked anywhere else."

"Why didn't Charles fire him, then?"

"I can only tell you what I've inferred from things that have and haven't been said," Andrew said. "I suspect Harold knows too much to be let go."

"About running the park?"

"About any number of things," was Andrew's cryptic reply.

"Have we left anyone out?" Bessie asked, thinking back through their conversation.

"Nathan Beck wasn't happy with the changes Charles was making in suppliers, from what I understand," Andrew replied.

"He seems to have quite a quick temper," Bessie said. "Maybe he didn't approve of Monique's friendship with Charles, either."

"But there's nothing to suggest that he knew anything about Doona," Andrew said.

"Maybe the killer just happened across the knife while walking across the grass or something," Bessie suggested.

"It would be a pretty big coincidence, he or she just happening to find a knife on the patio of the property where the victim's wife was staying," Andrew said. "Anything is possible, of course, but it seems highly unlikely."

"I suppose," Bessie replied. "Are there any other suspects?"

"I think we've covered the main ones," Andrew replied. "One of the reasons they aren't looking too closely at the huge number of other guests is the connection to Doona. I do hope that doesn't turn out to be a coincidence. Margaret can't keep everyone here until she finds the killer."

"Tomorrow is an arrival and departure day, isn't it?" Bessie asked.

"We're booked through the weekend, but not everyone will be. Is Margaret making anyone stay?"

"As I understand it, no, but then most of the main suspects are employees. Jessica and Herbert are booked through the end of the month. I gather as an investor he gets special rates."

"It doesn't seem as if we've made any progress," Bessie complained as they finished their circuit of the lake and arrived back where they'd started from.

"There is one other suspect we haven't mentioned," Andrew said after a moment.

"Who?" Bessie demanded.

"Well, you, of course," Andrew replied.

Bessie took a step backwards, feeling stunned. For a moment she felt angry with the man. She forced herself to count to ten before she replied.

"I've managed to live into my late middle age without ever feeling the need to kill anyone," she said steadily. "And you can be sure that if I ever did decide I needed to do so, I would do it in such a way that I would never be a suspect."

Andrew looked at her for a moment and then he laughed. "You're right, of course," he said after a while. "You're much too smart to use a knife from your own kitchen, especially in the middle of all those restaurants. There were dozens of knives for the killer to choose from. The only reason to use the one from your cabin was to frame someone."

"Surely all the knives in the various restaurants were locked up for the night," Bessie replied. "Not that I'm trying to incriminate myself or anything," she added hastily.

"I had a long talk with Joe Klein about just that," Andrew said. "All of the restaurants on the site are owned by Lakeview, including everything in the food hall. That means they only have a single locking door between the public areas and the staff areas where you can access all of the kitchens. Any member of staff with a master key could have opened the door, and Joe said it was often left unlocked during the day to let staff get in and out easily. There's no way to tell if it was locked or not on the night of the murder, but as nearly all of the suspects have master keys or access to them, it doesn't really matter."

"Did Joe know who Doona is?" Bessie asked, realising they hadn't discussed the security head.

"He told me he didn't," Andrew replied. "I get the feeling he wasn't involved in the day-to-day running of the place in any way."

"Except for providing all of the security."

"Well, yes, but I don't think Charles took that very seriously."

"Maybe he should have," Bessie said dryly.

"Indeed."

They'd been standing still for several minutes. Now Bessie moved over to the nearest bench and sat down.

"It doesn't seem as if we've worked out anything," she said grumpily.

"No, it doesn't," Andrew agreed as he sat down next to her. "I have to tell you that I'm quite enjoying the mental exercise. Retirement doesn't really agree with me. But I don't suppose that makes you feel much better about your friend."

"No, it really doesn't," Bessie told him sharply.

He flushed. "I'm trying to do everything I can on her behalf," he said. "But I have to be careful not to get in the way of the official investigation."

"So you really don't think Doona did it?" Bessie checked.

"No, for much the same reasons I don't think you did it," Andrew replied. "Even if she snuck out of your cabin intending to kill Charles, I can't see her taking that particular knife with her. And if she did, I think she'd be smart enough to have removed the knife from the crime scene. She could have thrown it in one of the lakes and I doubt anyone would have ever found it."

"But the killer left it there to incriminate Doona," Bessie said. "Surely Margaret Hopkins must be thinking the same way you are. She must know Doona's being framed."

"But she still has to investigate every lead," Andrew said in a soothing tone. "Doona had motive, means and opportunity, after all."

Bessie nodded reluctantly. "How long will she keep Doona, do you think?"

"I suspect Doona is doing her best to cooperate with Margaret," Andrew replied. "Which means she won't be insisting on being allowed to leave. Under the circumstances, Margaret might be keeping her for her own safety as well."

"What do you mean?" Bessie demanded.

"More than one killer has tried to cover his or her tracks by killing another suspect and trying to make it look like suicide," Andrew said. "This killer has already tried to frame Doona. That suggests a certain animosity towards her, at least to my mind."

Bessie shook her head. "Talking to you isn't making me feel any better," she said.

"I'm sorry," Andrew replied, sounding sincere. Before he could continue, Bessie heard voices calling his name. They both stood up and Bessie only just spotted the quick grimace that flashed over Andrew's face before he smiled at the group that now descended upon them.

"Time for breakfast," a young man said heartily.

"Hungry," a small child chirped from the middle of the group.

"You all start for the Squirrel's Drey and I'll meet you there in a minute," Andrew suggested.

A middle-aged woman frowned, giving Bessie a cold look. She opened her mouth to speak, but it looked as if Andrew caught her eye, causing her to change her mind. Instead, she spun on her heel and began to walk away. The others followed, chatting loudly amongst themselves.

"I'm sorry I didn't introduce you to anyone," Andrew said as he watched them leaving. "It just seemed too much like hard work."

Bessie laughed. "I rather agree with you," she said. "I'd never remember them all, anyway. There are far too many of them."

"I'll have to try to arrange a meal with you and one or two of them at a time," he replied. "They're all good people, just a bit overwhelming when taken as a group."

"You'd better go," Bessie told him. "I'd hate for them to come back looking for you."

He smiled at her and then gave her a quick hug. "Let's have dinner, just the two of us," he suggested. "We can talk more about the case. Who knows, maybe Margaret will solve it between now and then."

"My friend John Rockwell, from the Isle of Man Constabulary, is meant to be coming over some time today," Bessie replied. "If he's here, we should include him in dinner."

"Of course," Andrew agreed quickly. "And Doona as well, if she's back," he added.

"Six o'clock at our cabin?" Bessie asked. "We can have something delivered for however many people there are."

"Excellent," he said. "In the meantime, just remember: the good guys always win the end."

Bessie found herself smiling again as she watched the man walk away. He was charming and kind and she was glad they'd met, even under such difficult circumstances.

She glanced at her watch and frowned. It was still rather early in the morning and she had no idea what to do with the rest of her day. She felt as if she was simply waiting around to see what was going to happen next, which wasn't a good feeling.

As she'd skipped breakfast in favour of the walk, she headed back into the cabin to get something to eat. She put some bread in the toaster and drank a glass of orange juice while she waited it for it to pop. She was just washing up her dishes when her mobile phone rang.

"Hello?"

"Bessie, it's Doona," a tired voice said.

"Are you okay?" Bessie asked, letting every bit of the concern she was feeling into her tone.

"I'm fine, just tired," was Doona's reply. "The inspector thought I might like to ring you in case you were worried about me."

"Of course I'm worried about you," Bessie replied. "When will you be back here?"

"Probably not today," Doona told her. "I'm trying to help the inspector work out who sent those photos and things to me two years ago. We're working through a lot of things and I can't see us finishing soon."

"Are you under arrest?"

"No, not officially, anyway. I suspect if I kicked up a fuss about leaving the inspector would let me go back to Lakeview, but I'm trying to cooperate. I want Charles's killer found at least as much as anyone else does."

"But we're supposed to be on holiday," Bessie said. She frowned when she realised she was more or less whining. "Sorry," she said. "I don't mean to moan."

"It's fine," Doona told her. "This certainly isn't the holiday I was hoping for, but we didn't have anything on the schedule for today, did we?"

Bessie glanced at the sheet on the table where Doona had written down all of their scheduled activities. "No, nothing today," she said.

"That's what I thought. If I'm still here tomorrow morning, I'll start fussing," Doona told Bessie. "I don't want to miss that second watercolour class or our trip around Torver Castle."

"John should be here later today," Bessie said. "I suspect he'll be in touch with Inspector Hopkins when he arrives."

"I'll feel better when he's here," Doona said quietly. "Although I do think Inspector Hopkins is doing a good job."

"Meanwhile, Andrew and I have been talking about the suspects," Bessie said. "He suggested...."

Bessie stopped when Doona suddenly began to cough violently. It seemed to take a while before the coughing fit finally died down. "Are you okay?" Bessie asked. "Do you need a doctor?"

"I'm fine," Doona replied. "Did I mention that the inspector was kind enough to let me use the phone in her office to ring you?"

"No, I suppose that was nice of her, but...." This time Bessie stopped herself as she realised what Doona was trying to tell her. There was a very good chance someone else was listening to the call. "Anyway, John should be here later," Bessie repeated herself. "Is there anything you need?"

"No, I'm okay. I can survive another twenty-four hours or so if I need to," Doona assured her. "You should relax and enjoy your day. Maybe try out the pool. We haven't done that yet."

"Maybe," Bessie said vaguely.

"I'll probably see you in the morning," Doona told her. "Please try to have fun and relax. Don't worry about me."

"Easier said than done," Bessie murmured after Doona had disconnected. Bessie put her phone down and paced around the tiny cottage. Doona hadn't sounded too distressed, but she'd known someone was probably listening to the conversation. Going to the pool held no appeal at all for Bessie, so she sat down with her book club books and tried to get lost in their pages. After only a short time, she was grateful when her mobile interrupted.

"Bessie, it's John. I'm still working on flights and a hire car."

"So you don't know when you'll be getting here?"

"No, but it isn't going to be today," he replied.

Bessie sighed. "I was really looking forward to seeing you," she said.

"I know. And I'm eager to get there, but a few things came up here this morning and by the time I sorted through them all it seems I'd missed quite a few of the flights for the day."

"There aren't as many flights this time of year as there are in the summer months," Bessie said.

"And I'd rather not fly into London and have to drive all the way up there," John told her. "I was hoping to fly into Liverpool or Manchester, but I missed both of the morning flights, and the afternoon ones are both full. I could go to Ronaldsway and wait and see if there's a cancellation, but it seemed wiser to just book a morning flight and go from there."

"I suppose," Bessie said, trying not to sound as disappointed as she felt.

"Have you heard anything from Doona?"

Bessie filled him in on her brief chat with Doona and also told him about her conversation with Andrew.

"I'm looking forward to meeting Mr. Cheatham," he told Bessie when she'd finished. "He's quite well known in police circles."

"Really?"

"He worked for Scotland Yard for many years and he and his team solved some very difficult cases."

"I've never heard of him," Bessie said.

"He's always kept a very low profile, but he's very good at investigative work, or he used to be. He's been retired for many years now, of course."

"Did you get a flight booked for tomorrow, then?" Bessie asked.

"I'm flying into Manchester a few minutes after ten," he replied. "I'm still working on arranging for a hire car, but assuming I get that sorted, I should be at Lakeview by midday."

"Let me know if anything changes," Bessie requested.

"I will do," he replied.

It wasn't until after they'd disconnected that Bessie wondered why John hadn't simply taken the ferry. That was something she'd have to ask him when she saw him, she decided.

It was still only late morning, but Bessie couldn't get excited about reading any more in her books. Instead, she headed out to the Squirrel's Drey to do some shopping. Maybe she'd cook something for herself and Andrew for dinner that evening, rather than ordering from one of the restaurants.

Nothing in the small grocery shop tempted her in the slightest, and the smell from the Chinese restaurant had her mouth watering, so Bessie changed her mind again. She picked up a sandwich and a bag of crisps for her lunch and then found a quiet bench where she enjoyed her meal.

Somehow she managed to waste the afternoon, walking around the park, watching boats on the lake and laughing at the antics of the small children in a huge play area made up of soft foam obstacles. She was back at number eight at half five, ready for her guest.

CHAPTER 13

$\mathcal{A}$ ndrew was right on time, and after a short discussion, they agreed to go and eat at the Chinese restaurant rather than have food delivered.

"This way we don't have to clean up after ourselves," Andrew said brightly.

"And I think I need to get out of the cottage," Bessie told him.

The restaurant was moderately busy, but the hostess was able to find a table for two in a quiet corner for them.

"Let's get a bottle of wine," Andrew suggested. "We'll drink it slowly and just let it relax us."

"I could do with some relaxing," Bessie admitted. "Between the murder and Doona's arrest, I'm not really sleeping well."

"Doona hasn't been arrested," Andrew told her. "She's working with Margaret on figuring a few things out. Margaret feels that keeping Doona away from Lakeview for the moment is for the best."

"Does she think Doona's in danger?" Bessie asked.

"I don't think so, at least not immediate danger. But you have to admit that she's definitely safer where she is."

Bessie frowned, even as she nodded. "I still wish she were here.

And I wish we were just enjoying our holiday, not dealing with all of this."

"No one can blame you for that," Andrew replied.

The waiter delivered the wine and Andrew performed the necessary tasting ritual before the waiter filled both of their glasses.

"To new friends," Andrew suggested, holding up his glass.

Bessie touched hers to his gently. "And old friends," she added.

They ordered far more food than they expected to eat. "I can put leftovers in our cabin's refrigerator for my lunch tomorrow," Bessie said, justifying the extravagance.

"Or we can just eat it all tonight," Andrew said with a grin.

"So, I take it your friend from home didn't manage to get here today, at least not yet," he said after a moment.

"He couldn't get a flight today," Bessie explained. "He should be here tomorrow around midday."

"I understand from Margaret that she might have something to announce around that time," Andrew told her.

"Something to announce? What does that mean?"

"I'm hoping for your sake and Doona's that it means an arrest," Andrew replied. "But I couldn't get her to tell me anything at all."

"I just hope she isn't planning to announce Doona's arrest," Bessie said worriedly.

"She isn't," Andrew told her in a confident voice. "She would have warned me if that were the case."

"I hope you're right," Bessie muttered.

"I know I'm right," Andrew said.

"So who is she going to arrest?" Bessie had to ask.

"I don't know," Andrew admitted. "I don't even know if she's going to arrest someone. She might be announcing something else altogether."

"Like what?"

Andrew shrugged. "We could go around and around all night, trying to work it out," he said, "but it would be a waste of time and energy. I can think of a great deal more interesting topics to discuss."

Bessie wasn't sure she agreed, but she didn't object. She couldn't see any way their conversation would help Doona, so she let Andrew choose a subject.

For the next two hours, they ate more food than Bessie had imagined they could, sipped their way through the bottle of wine and told one another all about their lives.

"I must come and see the Isle of Man for myself," Andrew said eventually. "You make it sound incredible."

"It's home and I can't imagine living anywhere else," Bessie said simply.

"I've never felt that way about anywhere," Andrew mused. "I travelled a great deal in my army days, and then once I was married and the children were arriving, we moved every few years into bigger and bigger houses in different parts of London to accommodate them. London is a great city, but it never felt like home to me."

"I haven't been to London for many years," Bessie said. "I'm not fond of big cities."

The waiter arrived to take their sweets order, but both were too full to even consider a pudding.

"I wish I could," Bessie said as she glanced down the menu. "Everything sounds delicious, but I'm quite full."

"We can pack something up for you take back to your accommodation," the waiter suggested.

"Oh, don't tempt me," Bessie said with a laugh.

He brought them their bill, along with two fortune cookies. Andrew quickly handed the man his credit card.

"Dinner is on me," he told Bessie firmly. "And you get first choice of fortune cookie as well."

"Would it do me any good to argue?" Bessie asked.

"I'll chose a cookie first, if you prefer," Andrew replied, deliberately misunderstanding her.

Bessie thought about challenging him, but decided against it. Instead, she picked up a cookie from the plate. She broke it open and found her fortune.

"You have many good and true friends," she read. "Well, I hope that's true."

187

Andrew opened his cookie and smiled. "New friends add new spice to life," he read.

"I don't suppose either of us can complain about our fortunes, anyway," Bessie said. "Or about the food here. That was excellent."

"It really was," Andrew agreed.

They both got to their feet as the waiter returned with Andrew's card. "Thank you, sir," he said as Andrew handed him the signed credit slip.

"Let's walk back the long way around the lake," Andrew suggested, as they exited the Squirrel's Drey.

"I think I need to walk off all that food and wine," Bessie agreed.

They walked slowly in a companionable silence for several minutes. Bessie suddenly felt as if she didn't want the evening to end. She felt relaxed by the good food, excellent company and the alcohol she'd consumed. The last thing she felt like doing was going back to her empty cabin to worry about Doona more.

"Let's play crazy golf," Andrew suggested as they reached the far side of the lake.

"Crazy golf?" Bessie echoed, certain she was hearing things.

"Sure, why not?"

Bessie looked at her watch. It was nearly nine o'clock and it felt too late to be out playing games.

"When was the last time you played?" Andrew asked her.

Bessie thought for a minute and then shook her head. "I don't know if I've ever actually played crazy golf," she told him.

Andrew sighed. "You've missed out on so much," he said. "Come on."

Still shaking her head slightly, Bessie followed Andrew to the small stand at the entrance to the crazy golf courses.

"You'll only be able to play one course for tonight," the young man behind the counter told them. "Last entry is at nine."

"One course will do," Andrew assured him.

The man handed them each a club and a ball and then handed Andrew a small score card and tiny pencil.

"Surely we don't need to keep score," Bessie said.

"We don't have to," Andrew agreed. "But I'm keeping the tiny pencil for my granddaughter. She'll love it."

Bessie laughed and followed Andrew into the enclosed crazy golf area. Aside from a family of four who were just finishing the last hole on one course, they were the only people there.

"Do you want to do the 'rabbit' course or the 'squirrel' course?" Andrew asked in a serious voice.

"What's the difference?" Bessie asked, looking around in confusion.

"The 'rabbit' course is a par 36, which means they expect you to sink every ball in two shots. The 'squirrel' course is a par 38, which means two of the holes must be slightly trickier."

"Oh, in that case, I think we'd better try 'rabbit,' if it's easier," Bessie said.

"'Rabbit' it is," Andrew told her. He led her over to the first hole, designated by a small flag with a number "1" on it. "I'll go first, shall I? You can just follow what I do."

Bessie nodded and watched as Andrew set his ball on the ground and then carefully hit it down the short green. There were a few small bumps along the side of the green, but nothing hindered the ball's progress right down the centre. It stopped just short of the hole and Andrew easily tapped it in.

"Your turn," he said with a smile.

Bessie put her ball down and then shrugged. "I'm not even sure how to hold the club," she confessed.

Andrew quickly showed her and Bessie found herself lining up her shot, feeling incredibly foolish. She hit the ball gently and watched, amazed, as it rolled down the green towards the hole. It took her two additional shots to actually sink it, but she felt exhilarated when it fell in.

"I did it," she exclaimed in surprise.

"And in only three shots," Andrew said. "That's excellent for your first try."

An hour later, Bessie felt as if she'd laughed more in the previous sixty minutes than she had in several years. The holes got "crazier" as they went along, with various obstacles to get around, over or through. Andrew patiently coached her through different techniques for dealing with each one and Bessie ended the round feeling as if she hadn't totally humiliated herself.

"You did very well," Andrew told her as they returned their clubs.

"It was actually rather fun," Bessie said, surprise in her voice.

Andrew laughed. "It's meant to be fun," he told her.

"Have a nice evening," the man behind the counter told them both. As soon as Bessie and Andrew took a few steps away, he was quickly turning off lights and shutting down for the night.

"The poor man was just waiting for us to leave," Bessie whispered. "I should have played more quickly."

"We didn't do too badly. I walked past last night at half ten and there were still a dozen people playing," Andrew told her. "I'm just glad you had fun."

"It was wonderful to do something out of the ordinary. It took my mind off everything."

"And now, hopefully, you're tired enough to sleep well tonight."

Bessie nodded. "I feel as if I will," she said, pleased with the idea.

Andrew walked her to her cottage door. "Thank you for a very pleasant evening," he told her. "I hope your friend gets here safely tomorrow, and that you no longer need him to be here."

"Oh, I do hope so, too," Bessie said with alacrity.

Inside the cabin, she got ready for bed and then grabbed her pile of book club books. She wasn't more than half way through any of them and the club was meeting in only two days. At least she'd read *Emma* before, although now that she was rereading it, she was surprised to discover that she'd forgotten much of the story.

Now she curled up in bed with the book and read until her eyes began to close. After she switched off the light, she fell into a deep and restful sleep, not waking once until the next morning, a little bit past her usual time.

After showering, Bessie made herself a bowl of cereal with milk for breakfast. It was raining a steady and soaking rain outside, so she wasn't in any hurry to take her walk. After she ate, she finished reading *Emma*, sighing with satisfaction as Austen tied up all the loose ends and gave everyone his or her happily ever after.

The weather hadn't improved, but Bessie struggled into her water-proofs and went out for her walk anyway. She kept it short, just a quick circle of the smaller of the two lakes, and returned back to her cabin without seeing another person who'd ventured outside in the miserable weather. After hanging her things up to dry, she decided she might as well work on another book. Before she got settled in, though, her mobile rang.

"I just wanted to let you know that I'm on my way," John told her when she answered. "I should be with you around midday if every-thing goes well."

"Ring my mobile when you arrive at the park and I'll let you know where I am," Bessie suggested. "I have a watercolour class at one o'clock, so I'll probably be getting some lunch around midday."

Bessie had barely disconnected when someone knocked on the front door. She crossed to the door, wondering who had braved the rain. When she pulled the door open, she could only stare at Doona for a moment.

"I'm getting rather wet," Doona said as Bessie gaped at her.

"Oh, goodness, but do come in," Bessie said, stepping backwards to let her friend through the door.

"My keys are somewhere in the bottom of my bag," Doona told her. "It was raining so hard I didn't want to open it. Then I was afraid you might be out somewhere," Doona explained. She stood for a moment in the doorway, waving to the man driving the police car that was stopped outside their door. He waved back and then drove slowly away.

"I thought cars weren't allowed in the village," Bessie said.

"Clearly they make an exception for the police," Doona replied.

Bessie shook her head to try to clear it and then gave her best friend a big hug. "I missed you," she whispered.

"I missed you as well," Doona replied. "Although everyone I met at the police station was very nice and they treated me very well."

"It still wasn't much of a holiday, though," Bessie complained.

"No, but anyway, I'm back now," Doona said brightly. "In time for the watercolour class and the castle tour tonight."

"Why did the inspector let you go?" Bessie asked. "Did she finally realise you didn't do it?"

"I think she just got rather busy with other things," Doona replied.

"What other things?"

"She's arrested Lawrence Jenkins."

"For Charles's murder?" Bessie asked excitedly.

"Unfortunately, no. He's been arrested for things related to his business ventures. I gather she uncovered some evidence of fraud or money laundering or something. She wouldn't give me any details, but she suggested that my solicitor might want to be on standby if I really did inherit anything from Charles."

"That doesn't sound good," Bessie said, frowning.

"No. I suppose even if I am Charles's heir, I won't be inheriting millions," Doona said.

"But if Lawrence has been arrested, what about Herbert Howe?"

"As far as I know, only Lawrence has been arrested. That doesn't mean Herbert isn't next, of course."

"I wonder if Andrew knows more than you do," Bessie said speculatively.

"Why don't you ring him and invite him over?" Doona suggested.

Bessie tried his mobile number, but no one answered.

"Never mind, I'm sure we'll all find out more as the day goes on," Doona said. "Margaret is going to hold a press conference at five to announce the arrest."

"So does she also think he's the killer?" Bessie asked.

Doona shrugged. "I think she'd like him to be. It would be neat and tidy and get two big cases off her desk at one time, but she won't be charging him with murder until she's absolutely certain he did it."

"Which means you aren't off the hook yet," Bessie said with a sigh.

"No, but at least everyone will have something else to talk about for a while," Doona replied.

"I'm just so glad you're back," Bessie exclaimed, giving her friend another hug. "John's on his way over. He should be here around midday."

"I hope he isn't in too much trouble for just taking off like this," Doona said. "But it will be nice to have him here."

"I'm not sure where he'll stay, but we can sort that out when he gets here. What do you want to do now?"

"Really, I'd love a long nap, but I'll settle for a long and very hot shower," Doona replied. "And then, when I feel properly clean again, I'd like to get some lunch. I'm starving and I feel as if I haven't eaten anything in days."

"We'll go over to the Squirrel's Drey and you can get something from every single food court vendor," Bessie suggested.

"Perfect," Doona laughed.

Bessie sat down with her books again, in a much happier frame of mind. She read the last few chapters of *The Murder of Roger Ackroyd*, enjoying the story even though she knew the twist that was coming. By the time Doona was ready for lunch, Bessie had finished with Agatha Christie and was laughing her way through Bill Bryson.

"I hate to interrupt your reading, but I need lunch," Doona said when she walked into the small sitting room where Bessie was curled up. "Even if we do have to fight our way through the miserable rain to get it."

Bessie looked out the window and frowned. The rain was still coming down heavily. Bessie's waterproofs were still damp, but she put them on again. She hadn't bothered with an umbrella earlier, but now she picked hers up from the small foyer. "I hope it isn't too windy for this," she remarked.

"Let's hope," Doona replied, waving her own umbrella.

The wind was only light and the pair were quickly walking single-file down the path towards the Squirrel's Drey under their protective covers. Although there were a few more people out and about than there had been during Bessie's earlier walk, the village still felt much quieter than normal.

"It's checking in and out day," Bessie exclaimed as she noticed the cars that were beginning to line the side of the roads.

"It is," Doona agreed. "Everyone who is leaving must be out before midday and then the new arrivals can't arrive before two. I suspect it will be very quiet in the Squirrel's Drey."

Doona was right. The large and usually bustling food court was almost empty.

"Too bad we don't have time to go to the pool now," Doona commented as they studied the various food choices. "We'd have the place practically to ourselves."

"But we have our class at one," Bessie said.

"If we ever visit again, we'll plan it better," Doona told her. "And plan to spend the whole afternoon during check-in at the pool."

"That's what my children are doing," a voice from behind them announced.

Bessie turned around and smiled. "Andrew, how nice to see you again."

"And you," he said with a small bow. "And it is especially nice to see you again," he said to Doona. "You don't look too distressed after your ordeal."

"Everyone was as pleasant as they could be under the circumstances," Doona replied. "But the food wasn't terrific."

Andrew laughed. "Let's stop talking and focus on finding you some food, then," he suggested.

Doona quickly decided on Indian, ordering herself enough food for two people. Bessie placed her own smaller order at the same counter. When they turned around with their trays, Andrew waved from a corner table where he was sitting with a slice of pizza and a fizzy drink.

"We tried to ring you earlier," Bessie told him when they'd joined him. "We were wondering if you'd heard anything about Lawrence's arrest."

"Only that it was going to happen," he replied. "And that it has to do with the business, not murder."

"So we aren't any closer to finding out who killed Charles," Bessie said with a sigh.

"I'm sure Margaret is looking even more closely at Lawrence for it," Andrew said. "And maybe at Herbert Howe as well."

"Speak of the devil," Bessie muttered as Herbert and Jessica walked into the building.

"I thought you'd been locked up for killing Charles," Jessica called across the room, staring hard at Doona.

Bessie glanced around, relieved to find that there were only a handful of people in the room who might have heard Jessica's words. None of them seemed to be paying Jessica the slightest bit of attention.

Jessica strolled over to their table. "Don't tell me you didn't do it?" she demanded of Doona.

"Of course I didn't do it," Doona replied angrily.

"But then who did?" Jessica wailed dramatically.

"Now, now," Herbert said as he joined them. "You mustn't upset yourself. I'm sure Inspector Hopkins will work it all out soon enough."

"Have you seen Lawrence today?" Jessica asked abruptly.

"No," Doona replied. "Should I have?"

"Maybe not," Jessica said with a shrug. "Only he was supposed to be meeting us here and he isn't around."

Bessie exchanged glances with Doona. Clearly news of Lawrence's arrest hadn't reached the Howes yet.

"Let's get something to eat," Herbert suggested to his wife. "When Lawrence gets here, he can join us."

Jessica shrugged and turned away from Bessie and her friends. Without another word or a backwards glance, she walked off. Herbert glanced at Bessie and then quickly followed his wife towards the food counters.

"What a thoroughly unpleasant pair," Bessie said when they were out of earshot.

"Ah, Doona, there you are," a voice called across the large space.

Bessie sighed at yet another interruption. She wanted to talk to Andrew and spend some time with her friend. She still managed a smile when Harold joined them a moment later.

"I rang the police this morning and Margaret told me she was letting you go," he said to Doona. "I was so pleased to hear that. I wanted to talk to you about my job here, and, well, some other things."

Doona shook her head. "I don't think I'm the person you want to talk to," she said.

"But I heard you were inheriting Charles's share of the company," Harold protested. "We really must talk."

"I don't know that I'm inheriting anything," Doona replied. "Let's have this chat after the will is read, okay?"

Harold frowned. "I suppose," he said, clearly reluctantly.

Doona ignored him and began to eat her lunch. After an awkward moment, he turned and walked away.

"You're very popular today," Andrew remarked.

"Lucky me," Doona retorted.

"And another one," Bessie murmured as Nathan Beck walked into the food court. He looked around the room and then headed straight for them.

"Where's Lawrence?" he demanded, staring at Doona.

"I haven't seen him in days," Doona replied, returning the stare.

"We were supposed to meet to discuss suppliers this morning," Nathan told her. "He never showed up."

"I'm not sure why you think I'd know where he was," Doona said.

"You're partners now, right? That's what I heard, anyway."

"We aren't anything of the kind," Doona replied sharply. "I barely know the man."

"Well, he told me you were his new partner, what with Charles gone and all. I want to change back to my old supplier and Lawrence said he'd listen to my reasons. If he isn't around, I suppose I can tell you."

Doona held up a hand. "I don't know anything about suppliers," she said. "And I'm not Lawrence's partner. You'll have to wait for him."

"But I wanted to start making the changes," Nathan said, in something close to a whine.

"Maybe you could talk to Herbert Howe," Bessie suggested, smiling at Nathan's scowl. "I understand he owns part of the company as well."

"I'd rather not," Nathan replied shortly. He glanced around the room and then shook his head. "Never mind," he muttered before turning and walking away.

"Eat quickly," Andrew suggested. "Before anyone else arrives."

They all laughed, but then did just as he'd recommended. Bessie was just swallowing her last bite when her mobile rang.

"John's here," she announced after the short call. "He's picked up a map and is walking over now."

"That's good news," Doona said.

It seemed only a moment later that the man strode in. Bessie felt a rush of relief when she saw his familiar face.

"John," she called, rising to her feet. He had hugs for both her and Doona before they introduced him to Andrew.

"It's a pleasure to meet you, sir," he said formally. "I've read a lot of your books."

"You write books?" Bessie asked.

"Not really," Andrew said, flushing. "Just training manuals and the like."

"Excellent ones," John added.

Andrew shrugged. "Anyway, welcome to Lakeview Holiday Park," he said to John.

John glanced at the remains of their lunch. "I hope you don't mind if I grab a bite to eat," he said. "I skipped breakfast."

Bessie pressed her lips together. It wouldn't do to lecture him now, not when he'd been travelling all day to get here for Doona. She made a mental note to speak to him another time about taking proper care of himself. He was still far too thin, mostly, she suspected, from the stress of his impending divorce.

When John returned with his tray of food, Doona brought him up to date on the latest developments of the case. He ate quickly and then pulled a notebook out of his pocket.

"I've been taking notes all along," he said. "Hoping I wouldn't need them. As means and opportunity are rather open, I've been focussing on motive."

"That's how I've been approaching it as well," Andrew said.

John smiled, obviously pleased at the agreement. "So, we have Jessica, who may or may not have just been dumped by Charles. Her husband, Herbert, may have personal or professional reasons for killing the man. Lawrence was his business partner, who was doing something illegal, from what I've heard just this morning. Harold lost his job to Charles. Nathan was upset about the cost cutting that Charles was doing. I'm less clear on motives for Mai and Monique."

"Monique had some sort of relationship with Charles," Doona said. "She claims they were just friends. She's also very protective of her husband, even though she also says they were having difficulties."

John nodded and made a note. "And Mai?"

"There's something going on between her and Lawrence," Bessie said. "They had a very intense conversation in the arts and crafts studio and she said something about Lawrence getting her the job here. Apparently Mai used to get Charles to give her special privileges as well. Maybe that was connected to her relationship with Lawrence, whatever that is."

"You don't think it's a romantic relationship?" John asked.

"No, it certainly didn't feel that way to me," Bessie answered. "Mai must be half his age, anyway."

"Which proves nothing," Andrew pointed out.

Bessie frowned, but didn't disagree.

"Did I miss anyone?" John asked.

"Joe Klein, the head of security, is on my list as well," Andrew told him. "He wasn't happy with the many changes Charles was making here either. As far as I'm concerned, he's last on my list. I think, if he were really unhappy here, he'd have just quit. Murdering your boss is a pretty dramatic step to take, even if you really hate your job."

"And there is always the possibility of an unknown person or persons," John said. "Someone who is operating under the radar."

"Margaret's team has done a lot of background digging into the many guests staying here at the moment. So far she hasn't found anyone that appears to have known Charles. The staff is being looked at as well, but apparently Charles spent most of his time in his office, pushing paper around. Harold dealt with the day-to-day running of the site."

"So where does that leave us?" John asked. "Does anyone have a favourite suspect?"

"Lawrence," Bessie said firmly. "They were business partners and Lawrence was stealing from the company."

"I hope it was him," Doona said. "Just so it can all be over."

"The business angle is an interesting one," Andrew said. "I wish I knew more about how Charles, Lawrence and Herbert all fit together."

"From the description of the crime scene, I'm not convinced," John said. "Stabbing someone repeatedly suggests a great deal of anger and a more personal motive."

"Maybe Herbert was finally fed up with Charles sleeping with his wife," Bessie said.

John closed his notebook and shrugged. "I really want to meet all of the suspects," he said. "I can't formally question them, but at least I can get a look at them."

"Jessica and Herbert are over there," Bessie told him.

"Come on, I'll introduce you," Doona said.

She got to her feet and she and John crossed the room to where the couple was sitting. Bessie followed a few steps behind, unable to resist listening in on the conversation.

"I just wanted to introduce you to my friend, John, who has come to join us for the last few days of our holiday," Doona said.

"Is he your solicitor?" Herbert asked.

"No, he's just a friend," Doona replied.

"It's very nice to meet you," Jessica said, standing up. "Any friend of hers is a friend of mine." She threw her arms around John and hugged him tightly, whispering something in his ear. John didn't reply, but his face turned bright red.

"That's enough of that," Herbert snapped at her. "Sit down and behave."

"I'm going back to the chalet," Jessica said. "If Lawrence turns up, you can ring me." She flounced off, pausing at the door to turn back and give them all a little wave. "Remember what I said," she shouted, presumably to John.

"Never marry a younger woman," Herbert said, getting up from the table. "You'll end up paying for it." He stormed off after his wife, leaving Bessie and her friends to rejoin Andrew.

"What did she say to you?" Bessie had to ask.

John blushed again and shook his head. "I'd rather not repeat it," he told her. "Let's just say it was an inappropriate suggestion."

"Maybe we can have dinner at *L'Expérience Anglaise* tonight so you can meet Nathan and Monique," Bessie suggested.

"That sounds good," John replied.

"Harold is always around somewhere," Doona said, glancing around the nearly empty room. "There he is, at the pizza counter."

She waved and Harold walked over to them. "Is there a problem?" he asked.

"No, not at all," Doona assured him. "I just wanted you to meet a friend of mine. John Rockwell has joined us for the last few days of our holiday."

"How nice," Harold said in a distracted manner. "Your lodge is capable of sleeping six, so you should have plenty of room. You didn't want a bigger one, did you? I'm not sure we can accommodate a change at this point."

"No, no, it'll be fine," Doona replied.

"If he wants to join in any of your scheduled activities, just tell them I've okayed it," Harold said. "Enjoy your stay," he said to John, before walking quickly away.

"There's a man with something on his mind," John said.

"I imagine the situation with Lawrence will cause all sorts of unexpected backlash," Andrew said.

"But at least I've met another suspect, even if that was rather unsatisfactory," John replied.

"You'd have to ring Margaret if you want to talk to Lawrence at this point," Andrew said. "And I don't think he'll want to talk to anyone other than his solicitor."

"That just leave Mai," John said.

"And you can meet her now," Doona replied. "It's time for our watercolour class. You may as well come along and meet her before we get started. Harold said you can even join in if you want to."

John laughed. "Maybe I'll just sit and watch," he said.

CHAPTER 14

The sun was now shining and Bessie found that she was quite looking forward to doing some more painting. After trying to capture the lake in the rain, she was eager to have a chance to attempt the scene in bright sunshine. They arrived at the building to find the door locked. A moment later, Jack and Nancy Strong joined them.

"Where's Mai?" Nancy asked. "We thought we were late."

"You are, a little bit," Bessie answered, glancing at her watch. "I think Mai is running behind as well."

She introduced John to the couple and the small group chatted amongst themselves for several minutes while they waited for Mai.

"I'm surprised Andrea isn't here, doing classes for the little ones," Bessie remarked.

"I don't think many families stay through," Andrew said. "My children have visited in the past, and they said there isn't usually much on offer on the Fridays. Everyone is too busy either coming or going."

"But this class was definitely today," Bessie said. "I'm sure of it."

"It was supposed to be, anyway," Nancy agreed.

A few minutes more passed before Bessie saw a familiar face hurrying towards them.

"I'm so sorry," Andrea gasped as she fumbled with her keys. "Friday is my day off and I was half an hour away when Harold rang me to come in."

"Where's Mai?" Bessie asked.

Andrea shrugged. "Harold didn't say. He just asked me to get here as quickly as I could to take over this class. It's the only thing happening at the Rainbow Arts Centre today, which is why I usually get the day off."

She ushered them all into the building, locking it behind them. "We don't need any unexpected visitors," she muttered, more to herself than the others, as she did so.

"Everyone can find an easel and I'll start passing around supplies. Basically, this class is a follow-up to the previous one. I won't be showing you any new techniques, just helping you get better at the ones you've already learned."

"I wasn't here last time," John said, giving the girl a friendly smile.

"Sorry," she said, blinking at him. "I was so distracted by everything I didn't even see you." She looked him up and down and then winked. "I won't make that mistake again."

"If I'm going to be a problem, I'll sit quietly and just watch," John told her.

"Oh, goodness no," Andrea said. "I'll assume you've sorted payment for the class and registered properly." She winked at him again. "You can choose an easel, and after I've given everyone their supplies, I'll come and help you get started."

"Helps to be young and good-looking, I think," Andrew whispered to Bessie as they headed towards the easels.

Bessie glanced at John. She often forgot just how attractive the man was, even though his brown hair was just beginning to look as if it needed cutting. She worried about how thin he was at the moment, but she supposed that he probably looked fit and athletic to those who were just meeting him for the first time. He worked out regularly, having converted a spare room at the Laxey station into a gym for himself and the rest of the staff.

Doona had already found a space in front of the windows. so

now Bessie moved to the easel next to her. John took the one on Doona's other side and Andrew moved over next to Bessie. Nancy and Jack settled in about as far from Bessie and her friends as they could get.

"Nothing personal," Nancy called across the small space. "But we were on that side last time. I want to try to paint the boathouse this time, and this is a better angle."

Andrea had quickly filled cups and set up paint trays. Now she moved around the room passing them out to everyone.

"Would you like music?" she asked after she'd finished distributing supplies. When no one replied, she laughed. "I'll put a local radio station on low volume. If it bothers anyone, we can switch it off."

Bessie worried what local radio might play, but the station that Andrea found was playing a fairly innocuous selection of easy listening songs. She settled in to paint, letting the music fade into the background. She could hear Andrea's voice as the girl worked with John, going over the basics, but Bessie ignored that as well and focussed on the blank page in front of her.

The afternoon seemed to flash past as Bessie worked on painting the beautiful lake that was sparkling in the sunshine in front of her. She was shocked when Andrea spoke loudly.

"I'm afraid that's all we have time for today," she announced. "It's just gone half four, which is a little later than advertised, but I wanted to make up for the late start."

Bessie looked around at several surprised faces. It seemed everyone else had also been concentrating quite hard on his or her artwork.

"That went too fast," Doona complained as she handed Andrea her brushes.

"I feel as if I didn't work hard enough," Andrea told her. "You were all so focussed I didn't want to interrupt, but I didn't really do more than check in with you each once or twice. I hope you don't feel shortchanged."

"Not at all," Bessie assured her. "I wouldn't have welcomed any interruptions, actually."

"Everyone should take a minute to look at all of the paintings," Andrea said. "They are all very good."

Bessie had to agree with Andrea's words, at least on every picture but her own. While they were all still obviously painted by amateurs, everyone had clearly put in a great deal of effort, and Bessie was sure all of the others had improved from the first class.

"You have real talent," she told Doona as she stood in front of her friend's painting. "You should take more classes at home."

"I just might," Doona told her. "This is the first time in days I've managed to forget about everything going on around me."

"Leave your paintings to dry," Andrea instructed them. "You can collect them tomorrow or Sunday before you leave."

"Can I just throw mine away?" Andrew asked.

"Don't be silly," Bessie chided. "It's lovely and it will be a wonderful memento of your holiday."

"I think it looks as if a six-year-old did it," Andrew replied.

"A very talented six-year-old, maybe," Bessie said with a laugh.

"Maybe we should add painting classes to our schedule at the station," Doona said to John. "You know, aerobics, weight training, and watercolours. I'm sure the constables would love it."

John shook his head. "I didn't love it," he replied.

Bessie walked over and looked at his picture. "It isn't bad," she said firmly. "Remember, this was your first class. We're all a class ahead of you."

Jack and Nancy headed out, but Bessie and the others helped Andrea clean up. Andrea was just locking up the supply cupboard when the five o'clock news headlines came over the radio.

"A local businessman's arrest might mean trouble for Lakeview Holiday Park. Two footballers were fined for inappropriate behaviour after last night's match, and the weather calls for more rain tomorrow."

Andrea hurried over and turned up the volume.

"Lawrence Jenkins, a partner in HAJ Enterprises, which owns Lakeview Holiday Park, has been arrested by local police. While we have been unable to get any official comment, we have reason to believe that his arrest is not in connection with the tragic murder of one of his business partners, Charles Adams, on Saturday. Police had been questioning a female park guest in relation to the murder, but we understand that she has been released without charge. No word yet on why Mr. Jenkins has been arrested or on any arrest for the murder."

Andrea switched the radio off, a stunned look on her face. "But what's Lawrence done?" she asked, glancing at Bessie.

"I'm sure we'll hear about it in due time," Bessie answered, evading the question slightly.

"I'd better go and talk to Harold," Andrea said. "If he hasn't heard, he needs to, and if he has, well, maybe that explains why Mai's not around."

"What do you mean by that?" Bessie asked.

Andrea shook her head. "Nothing, I'm just babbling," the girl replied. She ushered them all out now, quickly locking the door behind her.

"Don't forget to pick up your pictures," she said before she rushed off down the path towards the Squirrel's Drey.

Bessie looked at her friends. "Does that mean it's time for dinner?" she asked.

"It better be," Doona replied. "Our castle tour starts at seven and *L'Expérience Anglaise* isn't always the fastest place to eat."

The little group made their way to the French restaurant. It appeared that they were its first customers of the evening.

"We'll be busy later, after everyone has unpacked," the girl behind the hostess desk told Bessie.

She showed them to a table for four and left them with menus.

"What's good?" John asked as he opened the menu.

"That rather depends on what sort of mood the chef is in," Bessie replied wryly. "The first night everything was excellent, but we had lunch here the next day and it was very disappointing. It was better on our third visit, but still not as good as that first night."

Before John could reply they heard a loud crashing noise from the kitchen. A moment later a pretty brunette came out and glanced around the restaurant. Apparently not seeing who or what she was looking for, she walked back over to the kitchen door and pushed it open tentatively. The hostess joined her in the kitchen doorway and the pair had a short, whispered conversation. As she returned to her desk by the door, the hostess gave Bessie and her friends a bright and obviously fake smile.

Another crashing noise was followed by the kitchen door opening again. This time Monique strode out, her cheeks flushed and her head held high. She looked around quickly and then plastered a bright smile on her face.

"Good evening, how are you?" she said as she walked across the empty restaurant.

"How are you?" Bessie asked pointedly.

"Me? I'm just great, thanks," the girl replied, not meeting Bessie's eyes. She read the day's specials off a card and then suggested drinks.

"Maybe a bottle of wine?" Andrew suggested.

"I don't drink on, um, er, that is, I'd rather stick to soft drinks," John said.

"Well, I could do with a bottle of wine," Doona said stoutly. "It's probably best if I share it with the rest of you, though."

Bessie grinned. "Let's get one, then. We are meant to be on holiday, after all."

John ordered a fizzy drink while Andrew read through the wine list. As neither woman much cared what sort of wine they drank, he ordered a dry white wine. Monique nodded and disappeared back into the kitchen.

"I'm thinking things aren't great in the kitchen," Bessie whispered to the others. "I wouldn't suggest ordering anything too complicated."

"Maybe we should eat somewhere else." Andrew said.

"John wanted to meet Monique and Nathan," Doona reminded him.

"Maybe we could just do a quick introduction and then go and get Chinese," Andrew replied.

Monique stomped back into the dining room before anyone else spoke. She handed John his drink.

"The sommelier will be here in a moment with your wine," she announced before returning to the kitchen.

"Did they have a sommelier the last time we were here?" Bessie asked Doona.

"I don't think so," Donna said with a shrug.

When Harold Butler appeared a moment later, Bessie couldn't help but glance at Doona and grin. He was carrying their wine and he made a big fuss of the opening and tasting. Andrew gave his approval and Harold served everyone.

"You don't normally act as sommelier here, do you?" Bessie had to ask.

"Nathan wants to make *L'Expérience Anglaise* feel more like a proper restaurant and less like a holiday park," Harold told her. "And we really want to keep Nathan happy right now."

"Why?" Doona demanded.

"He's an excellent chef," Harold said. "He's had offers from several other holiday parks and a few restaurants in London as well. I was always warning Charles not to upset him, but Charles was all about the bottom line. He kept cutting corners and Nathan was increasingly unhappy here."

"I thought Charles liked Nathan," Bessie remarked, trying to remember everything she'd heard.

"Charles liked anyone who could make the guests happy," Harold retorted. "But mostly he liked people who could make the guests happy cheaply. That wasn't ever going to be Nathan."

"So why did Nathan stay?" John asked.

Harold shrugged. "I suppose Monique likes it up here. Even though he was getting other offers, apparently no one quite matched up to what he has here. It was just a matter of time, of course, before someone did, but Charles didn't see it that way."

"Harold?" a voice roared from the kitchen.

"I'd better get back," Harold said, looking around nervously. "I'm helping out in the kitchen as well as serving the wine."

He was gone before Bessie could ask why.

It felt like a long time before Monique came back to take their order. Bessie was just about to suggest that they pay for the wine and leave when Monique swung back out from the kitchen. Everyone ordered from the specials menu, hoping that would be best, considering that Nathan seemed to be having another bad day.

As Monique turned away, the hostess showed a party of eight into the dining room. Monique made a face at her before returning to the kitchen.

The new group had clearly just arrived and seemed intent on having fun. They were all adults in their early to mid-twenties and Bessie immediately realised that they had already been drinking before dinner. When Monique reappeared to take their drinks order, they requested four bottles of wine between them. Bessie thought she looked relieved that Harold was going to have to deal with them.

Although they had been seated on the opposite side of the room from Bessie and her friends, the new group was so noisy that conversation proved almost impossible for Bessie's table. Instead, Bessie sipped her wine and let her mind wander. It was hard to believe that it was less than week since the first time she'd sat in this restaurant, having just met Doona's not-quite-ex-husband.

She looked around the room, wondering if something that had happened that evening had been the catalyst to Charles's murder. A momentary lull in the conversation on the other side of the room let Bessie and others hear yet another crash from the kitchen.

"What is he doing in there?" Bessie asked.

"Banging pots for effect," Doona suggested.

Monique brought out their meals not long after Harold delivered the other table's wines. The room felt strangely quiet as Bessie and her friends began to eat and the other group began to work their way through their bottles.

"This isn't bad," Bessie said after a few bites.

"Neither is mine," Doona said. "Still not as good as the first night, but not bad."

"I'm enjoying mine, but I didn't get much lunch," John said.

"I'm enjoying the company and the wine more than the food," Andrew said. "But I've had worse food."

"That's hardly a compliment to my husband," Monique said angrily from behind Bessie.

"It wasn't meant to be," Andrew said calmly.

"He's working ever so hard," Monique told him, tears forming in her eyes. "It isn't easy, with all the things going on around us. First Charles was murdered and now Lawrence has been arrested. I don't know how Nathan can work at all under the circumstances."

"He's doing fine," Bessie assured the girl. "Everything is good."

"Hey, waitress," a man from the other table shouted. "Where's our food, then?"

Monique rolled her eyes and then hurried over to the other table. Bessie watched her go.

"She's very quick to defend her husband," she remarked to the others.

"I still want to meet Nathan," John said.

The foursome watched as Monique spoke to the other group for several minutes before heading back to the kitchen. A few minutes later, Nathan himself stormed out.

"I understand you have a problem," he said loudly to one of the men in the large group.

The man looked at the powerfully built chef and shook his head. "No, we're good," he said quickly. "Just hungry."

"Your food will be out when it's ready," Nathan replied. "I can't rush proper preparation." He turned and glanced over at Bessie's table. After a brief hesitation, he walked over to them.

"I hope you're enjoying your meal," he said stiffly.

"It's fine," Bessie said. "Quite good, actually."

"Great," Nathan muttered, turning to leave.

"You should meet our friend, John," Bessie said loudly.

Nathan turned and smiled vaguely. "I didn't know you had a friend joining you," he said.

John held out a hand. "John Rockwell," he said. "I'm good friends with both Bessie and Doona."

"Welcome to Lakeview Holiday Park and *L'Expérience Anglaise*," Nathan said. "I hope you enjoy your holiday."

They all watched silently as the man walked away.

"He's seems off tonight," Bessie murmured. "Like he's drunk or something."

"Drugs?" John said, looking at Andrew.

"Could be," Andrew replied.

By the time Monique came back with the sweets menu, the group had decided to get ice cream at the little stand outside, which was right next to where the bus to Torver Castle was collecting them.

"Dinner is on Nathan," she told them when Andrew asked for the bill. "He feels as if he isn't doing his best right now and he doesn't want Lakeview's guests to pay for that."

"That's going to get expensive," Bessie commented as she looked at the large group whose food had just been delivered by the hostess.

"Oh, they'll pay," Monique said with a shrug. "They're too drunk to know if the food was good or not."

Bessie decided she couldn't argue with that, so she and her friends headed out. Andrew and John fell into step together, chatting in low voices while Doona and Bessie followed at a slower pace, talking about nothing much as they enjoyed the night air.

They were only a short distance from the ice cream stand, and from there they were only a few steps away from the sign for the castle tours. With fifteen minutes to fill before the bus was due, Bessie and Doona started to discuss the books for the next day's book club. Doona hadn't had much time to read and Bessie was happy to give her a quick summary of each book.

The bus arrived a few minutes early, and when the doors opened, Bessie was surprised to see Andrea climb out of it.

"Hello again," she greeted Bessie. "And before you ask, this is meant to be one of Mai's jobs as well, but she's still not around. I used to do this, before Mai arrived and started taking all of my favourite jobs away from me, so don't worry about me not knowing what I'm doing."

"But what's happened to Mai?" Bessie asked.

Andrea shrugged. "No idea, but I suspect it has something to do with Lawrence. Maybe she thinks with both Charles and Lawrence gone she'll get fired anyway. Harold isn't her biggest fan, after all."

Before Bessie could ask any more questions, Jack and Nancy Strong came rushing up.

"Oh, thank goodness we didn't miss the bus," Nancy said. "I'm so excited about this tour."

"Because we've only been around Torver Castle twice before," Jack muttered from behind her.

"Last time I felt something," Nancy said in a confiding tone. "I'm sure it was one of the ghosts."

"I'm sure it was something you ate," Jack said.

"Oh, hush," Nancy admonished him. "Just because you don't believe in ghosts doesn't mean they aren't real."

"If it did, I'd try not believing in your sister," Jack whispered just loudly enough for Bessie to hear. She quickly turned her head so that Nancy wouldn't see her laughing at the man's words.

"If you'd all like to board the bus, I'll check you off my list as you do so," Andrea said.

Bessie and her friends climbed on board, with Andrea making a note that John Rockwell had joined the party. They took seats near the front of the bus and watched as a dozen or so other people joined them. Nancy and Jack were the last to board and they took the seat right behind the driver.

"We're just waiting for two more people," Andrea announced from the doorway. "If they aren't here in a few minutes, we'll go without them."

"We should go now," a loud voice called from the back. "We're already late and I'd hate to miss any of the show."

"It's a tour, sir, not a show," Andrea said, coming up the steps into the bus. "You'll have plenty of time to tour the castle. It isn't a long drive."

"Yeah, but the spooky ghost noises and flashing lights and all that are pre-arranged, right? I don't want to miss that stuff," he said.

"I can assure you that nothing is pre-arranged," Andrea replied. "Whether the ghosts are active or not is entirely up to them."

"Ooooh, scary," the man said mockingly.

"Ted, stop it," the woman next to him said. "You don't want to upset the ghosts."

The man laughed and then glanced at his watch. "If we don't get moving, they'll have all gone to bed when we get there."

Andrea smiled tightly and then climbed down out of the bus. From her seat, Bessie watched the girl look around anxiously. After a moment, she shook her head and turned back towards the bus.

"We're here," a voice called out loudly. "We're here. Don't go without us."

Bessie frowned when she recognised Jessica Howe as the woman stumbled towards the bus. Herbert wasn't far behind her. Jessica stopped just outside the bus and took a deep breath. She straightened her very tight and short dress and then ran a hand through her hair.

"We were having a nap," Jessica said to everyone from the bus doorway. She shimmied down the aisle, winking at John Rockwell on her way. Herbert followed, clearly out of breath. Bessie looked at his red face and wondered how strong his heart was. He fell heavily into the seat behind Bessie and Doona, shaking the entire bus as he did so.

"Right, that's everyone then," Andrea said from the doorway. "Here we go." She perched on the stairs as the driver pulled away from the village centre. Everyone fell silent as they made their way out of the holiday park and into the countryside.

"Do you think we'll see any ghosts?" Doona asked Bessie in a quiet voice.

"I doubt it. I do believe we can't explain everything in our world," Bessie answered. "But whether that includes people's spirits coming back to haunt the living or not, I don't know. I know when Matthew died I felt as if I could feel his presence for a long time afterwards. It made me feel better, so I don't see any harm in it."

Doona patted Bessie's arm. "I'd much rather believe in benevolent ghosts than the scary sort."

"Me, too," Bessie agreed. "But from what I've read, if there are ghosts at Torver Castle, they aren't the friendly kind."

"I don't want you to think I'm crazy, but I keep worrying that we'll bump into Charles's ghost," Doona whispered.

"He won't be at Torver Castle," Bessie said firmly. "If he's haunting anywhere it will be his office at Lakeview, because that's where he was killed."

"I suppose you're right," Doona said. "But I'm still not sure about this tour."

"We can wait on the bus while the others take the tour, if you want," Bessie offered.

Doona shook her head. "I don't want you to miss out on the fun just because I'm sort of skittish at the moment."

Bessie took her friend's hand. "I can tour a haunted castle anytime I want back at home," she said. "Actually, both Castle Rushen and Peel Castle are haunted, so I even have a choice. Your mental health is more important than seeing another old stone building."

Doona laughed and then sighed. "I'm being silly," she said. "I'll take the tour. I can always head back to the bus if I start to feel spooked."

A strange noise from the seat behind them interrupted their conversation. Bessie glanced back and shook her head. Herbert Howe had fallen asleep and was now snoring loudly. A moment later Jessica's heels clicked back down the aisle. She glanced at her husband and then dropped into the seat next to Bessie and Doona, where John and Andrew were sitting. She nearly landed on John's lap, and he quickly slid over to make room for her.

"Oops," she said, giggling. "Sorry, handsome stranger. I didn't mean to land on you."

"I'm John Rockwell, Doona's friend," John replied. "We met earlier."

"I can't believe I don't remember meeting you," Jessica cooed. "I didn't have that much to drink."

Bessie glanced over at Doona and found her friend staring intently at the exchange across the aisle.

"Is your husband okay?" Bessie asked the woman pointedly.

"Oh, I'm sure he's fine," Jessica replied, waving a hand. "He'll probably just sleep on the bus while we do the tour." She turned her attention back to John. "Maybe you could hold my hand as we go around, in case I get scared," she suggested, licking her lips.

"I don't think so," John replied stiffly.

Jessica giggled. "You can't blame a girl for trying," she said, pouting slightly.

"Surely your husband will want to go around the castle," Bessie said.

Jessica shrugged. "Maybe," she said. She glanced over at Doona and smiled nastily. "I'm surprised the police let you go," she said. "It seems like you had the best motive for murdering poor Charles."

"I didn't have any motive," Doona countered in a cool voice. "He was no longer part of my life."

"But it looks as if he left you a fortune," Jessica said.

"I highly doubt that," Doona replied.

"He really did care about you, you know," Jessica told Doona. "He was actually going to break up with me right after your wedding. I had to work hard to make sure that didn't happen."

Bessie squeezed Doona's hand, hoping the woman's nasty words weren't upsetting her friend too much.

"You sent me the photos, didn't you?" Doona demanded.

"What photos?" Jessica asked, giving Doona what Bessie assumed was meant to be an innocent look.

Doona opened her mouth to reply and then snapped it shut again. She turned her head and looked out the bus window.

"He cared for you, but he would never have stayed faithful," Jessica said loudly. "He wasn't faithful to me, even when we were together. He always had to have at least two or three women at his beck and call." She shook her head. "I don't know why I put up with him for so long."

Doona didn't reply, but Bessie could feel that she was taking long and slow breaths, trying to control herself.

"I think that's quite enough," Bessie said to Jessica. "Why don't you head back to your seat and leave us alone?"

"Ah, but I'd miss my handsome new friend if I went back there again," Jessica said, patting John's knee and then running her hand slowly up his thigh. The hand didn't get far before John pushed it firmly away.

"I think you need to move," he said tightly.

Jessica laughed lightly. "You know, it's a big castle with lots of tiny, dark rooms. I'm sure we could find a place to slip away and get better acquainted. Do think about that," she said before she got back to her feet and wandered back down the aisle.

"Hello, gorgeous man," Bessie heard her saying to someone further back in the bus.

"He's very married," an angry voice replied. "And I'll thank you to stay well away from him."

Bessie heard Jessica laugh again and then Andrea's voice came over the tannoy.

"We're just about to arrive at the castle. We will be the only guests here tonight. When we arrive, a tour guide from the castle will be coming on board to share the history of the site, and then you are welcome to either take a guided tour or simply explore the castle on your own. We will meet back at the bus at exactly half nine. Please don't be late, as the site will be shutting down at that time."

"I thought we were meant to finish at nine," Bessie murmured to Doona.

"Maybe they extended it because we got such a late start," Doona replied.

A moment later they passed through the castle's gates and pulled up in front of the building itself. A woman in her mid-thirties, dressed in Elizabethan garb, climbed on board the bus as soon as it stopped.

"Welcome to Torver Castle," she began. "The first settlement on this site has been dated to the Iron Age, with the earliest fortified buildings being started in the Roman era. We're quite close to the Scottish border, of course, and we suspect...."

Bessie tuned her out. She'd read the history of the site in a guide-book when she knew she'd be coming, so now she turned her thoughts to the things Jessica had said. If Jessica was right and Charles was always involved with more than one woman, whom had he been seeing when he died?

There were many attractive young women on the staff at the park, and Bessie could only assume that they'd all been questioned. As far as she knew, no one had admitted to being involved with the boss. She still wondered about the exact nature of Charles's relationship with Monique Beck, but now she started thinking about Mai and Andrea as well. She was startled when everyone around her began to stand up. The costumed tour guide was leaving the bus and everyone was getting ready to follow her.

"The history is fascinating," Doona said. "But I'm still not sure I want to go in there."

"We'll be fine," Bessie said confidently. "We'll take a proper tour and stick together. Ghosts hate that sort of thing."

Doona laughed, but it sounded forced. There were several guides available for tours and Bessie selected an older woman who looked kindly. She pointed out a few things in the courtyard area and then led the foursome into the castle itself.

As they walked through the castle, their guide kept up a steady stream of information. It felt to Bessie as if nearly every room was said to be haunted by some spirit or other. It took them an hour and a half to tour the entire building, and when they got back to the court-yard, there was no one else around.

"That was interesting," Bessie said.

"And not at all creepy," Doona added happily. "I didn't see or hear or feel any ghosts."

There were several benches spread out around the space, so they sat down and waited for the rest of the group.

"Tomorrow is meant to be our last full day," Doona said. "We're supposed to go home on Sunday, but I'm not sure that Margaret will let us."

"I'm going to talk to her in the morning," John said. "I'm hoping to persuade her to let you go home, as long as you promise to come back if circumstances warrant it."

Jack and Nancy were next out of the castle and they were quick to join Bessie and the others.

"I saw him," Nancy said excitedly.

"Who?" Andrew asked.

"Sir William," Nancy replied. "The ghost in the chapel. Only the most famous ghost in the whole castle."

"How exciting," Bessie said politely.

"It was only a glimpse," Nancy admitted. "Sort of out of the corner of my eye, but I'm sure it was him."

Jack shook his head, but didn't speak. Within minutes, other groups began to arrive. Andrea appeared from somewhere and she knocked on the bus door. When the driver opened it, she suggested that everyone might want to climb back inside.

"I'll just start checking you all in," she said brightly. "And if we're all here, we can head back."

Bessie and her friends joined the queue. While Bessie waited, she tried to work out if anyone was missing or not. She wasn't surprised to find that Herbert and Jessica weren't anywhere to be seen.

"I'm not sure where my husband has wandered off to," the woman at the front of the queue was telling Andrea. "We split up because he was bored and wanted to skip half the rooms. I assumed he just came back here."

"I'm sure he'll turn up," Andrea said, making a mark on her list. "You can go ahead and find a seat."

Bessie was back in her seat near the front when Herbert Howe wandered into the courtyard. From where Bessie was sitting, he seemed to have come from the road, rather than from inside the castle.

"Nice little pub across the street," he announced as he lurched down the aisle. "No ghosts there."

Andrea climbed in after him. "We're just waiting for two more people," she said, looking and sounding quite tired. "I'm sure they'll be along shortly."

"As my wife is one of them, I'd be willing to bet the other is a man," Herbert shouted from his seat behind Bessie. "He'll be younger and better looking than me, that's for sure." He laughed bitterly and then shut his eyes. Within seconds he began to snore.

"What a strange marriage those two have," Bessie whispered to Doona.

"Whoever is with Jessica might find himself divorced," Doona replied, looking down the aisle at the woman whose husband hadn't arrived back at the bus yet.

"If he's with another woman, I'll kill him," the woman said angrily.

Before anyone could reply, a man came running out of the castle and up into the bus. His shirt was buttoned incorrectly and his face was smudged with the same pink lipstick Jessica Howe favoured. Under the makeup, his face was pale.

"I think she might be dead," he said to Andrea. "She just stopped breathing. It wasn't my fault."

CHAPTER 15

*A*s everyone on the bus began to talk at once, John and Andrew got to their feet and walked down the aisle.

"Ring 999," John said to Andrea. "Request an ambulance and ask for Margaret Hopkins to be sent immediately."

Andrea nodded.

"Tell them that there are two police officers checking on the woman and securing the scene, but we're both out of our jurisdiction," he added before turning to the man.

"Show me," he said sternly.

The man shook his head. "I'm not going back in there," he said. "There were all sorts of weird noises and flashing lights in every room as I came out. You'll find her. She's in the third room along on the left side once you go up the main stairs."

"That's very specific," John said.

"She asked me to meet her there," he replied sheepishly, glancing at his wife, who was giving him an angry look.

"Sir, I'm going to ask you to have a seat on one of the benches in the courtyard," John said. "Doona, can you sit with him, please? I don't want him talking to anyone."

"Hey, he has a lot of questions to answer," his wife shouted from her seat.

"He does indeed," John said. "But mine take priority in this instance."

The woman opened her mouth to argue, but John was already ushering the man out. Andrew and then Doona followed. Bessie had to stand up to let Doona out, and she was tempted to leave the bus as well, but she didn't want to get in anyone's way. Herbert was still snoring and Bessie wondered if she should wake him to tell him about his wife, but decided against it. John would probably rather do the telling when the time came.

It wasn't long before the police arrived, and an ambulance wasn't far behind. Bessie was relieved when the stretcher that finally emerged from the castle was carrying a woman clearly getting treatment. John stepped back on the bus and gave Bessie a hint of a smile as he walked past her.

He stopped at the next seat and spoke to Herbert. "Mr. Howe? Herbert? Can you please wake up?"

"What? Hey, what's going on?" the man said loudly. "Are we back at Lakeview, then? Did my wife ever turn up?"

"She did turn up," John said. "But she seems to have fallen ill. There's an ambulance transporting her to hospital. The police have arranged for an escort to take you as well."

"Ill? Hospital? My Jessica?" Herbert jumped up and followed John back down the aisle. Bessie was surprised by the seemingly genuine concern she'd heard in his voice. Whatever problems the couple had, he seemed badly shaken by the news.

A few minutes later John, Andrew and Doona all climbed back into the bus. John had a quiet word with Andrea and then she spoke to the driver.

"We'll just get underway, then," Andrea said cheerfully over the tannoy.

"What about my husband?" the very angry woman at the back shouted.

"He's talking to the police now," John told her. "They'll bring him back to Lakeview when they've finished speaking to him."

"They'd better take him to his mother's lodge, not mine," the woman replied. "I'm sure I don't want him back."

John didn't answer; he just slid into his seat. Doona was back next to Bessie. No one spoke as the bus made its way back to the holiday park.

"I hope you all enjoyed your visit to Torver Castle," Andrea said with little enthusiasm as they drove through the entrance to the park. She was first off the bus, and stood ready to help the others as they made their way down the stairs.

Bessie gave her a small smile as she exited. "Not exactly the best evening," she murmured.

"I've actually had worse," Andrea told her. "We had a group of guys in their early twenties on the tour once. They discovered the pub across the road as well and got unbelievably drunk in the ninety minutes we were there. Several of them got sick on the bus on the way back and two of them got into a fight as well and started throwing punches."

Bessie shook her head. "I don't understand people," she said sadly.

Andrea shrugged. "And people wonder why I don't drink," she said.

Bessie sat down on the nearest bench and watched as the rest of the guests made their way off the bus. John spoke for several minutes with the woman whose husband had been with Jessica. She was clearly still very angry, and Bessie didn't blame her a bit. Doona came and joined Bessie on the bench as they waited for John to finish. After a moment Andrew crossed to them as well.

"She's very upset," he commented quietly, nodding towards the pair who were still talking.

"I don't blame her," Bessie replied.

"No, me either," Doona said.

By the time John finished his chat, the woman was looking less angry. As he turned to walk away, she said something that caused John to turn bright red. He shook his head and then walked quickly over to Bessie and the others.

"What did she say at the end there?" Andrew asked the question Bessie was too polite to put to her friend.

"She suggested it would be good for her husband to find me keeping her company when he got back," John said.

Something about the way he said it told Bessie that the woman had actually suggested something rather different than merely "keeping her company." Bessie shook her head and then got to her feet. It had been a long day and she was suddenly eager to get back to the cabin and into her bed.

She and Doona fell into step together, neither bothering to make conversation. John and Andrew followed, and Bessie could hear the low murmur of their voices as they made their way down the path towards their little cul-de-sac.

"They were supposed to drop my bag off at your cabin," John told them as they reached the cabin door.

Doona opened the door and went inside. "They did," she yelled from the sitting room. "We just have to sort out where you're going to stay."

"Andrew has suggested that I stay with him," John replied. "He has two bedrooms and he's only using the one."

Doona reappeared, carrying a small overnight bag. "Are you sure?" she asked.

"I'm sure," Andrew answered. "It will be easier for everyone."

Bessie felt as if she should argue, but John would be far more comfortable in the spare bedroom in Andrew's cabin than on the couch in theirs.

"I'll be over around half seven or eight," John told them both. "And I'll ring Margaret before I come over to see what news there is on Jessica."

"I'll probably come as well," Andrew said. "If I'm up early, I'll go into the Squirrel's Drey and get some fresh pastries."

"I'll plan on doing the same," Bessie said. "You can never have too many pastries at breakfast."

With their plans made, John and Andrew headed next door and Bessie and Doona went inside.

"The castle was interesting," Bessie said as she sank down in a chair in the sitting room. "But I wonder what happened to Jessica."

"John seemed to think she'd overdosed on something," Doona replied. "She was certainly drunk, anyway."

Bessie thought of a dozen things to say, but she was too tired. "I need some sleep," she said.

"Me, too," Doona said, yawning. "And I'll need coffee in the morning, I'm sure."

They headed to their rooms. Bessie got ready quickly and then crawled into bed. She glanced at the books on the bedside table, but she was too tired to care that she hadn't finished them all. She was asleep as soon as she'd switched out the light, and she slept soundly until her internal alarm woke her at six.

There were no sounds coming from Doona's room after Bessie had showered and dressed, so she made herself a piece of toast and washed it down with some orange juice. Coffee or tea could wait until they were all together sharing pastries later. Bessie let herself out quietly. It was too early to go to the Squirrel's Drey for the breakfast treats, so she headed out around the large lake for a nice long walk.

There was a definite autumnal chill in the air, but she'd worn her jacket, so she didn't mind. As it was meant to be their last day at the park, Bessie found herself looking around and noticing more than she had in the last few days. She watched a red squirrel running up a tree and saw several rabbits chasing one another around in circles. When she reached the far side of the lake, she sat down on a bench and looked back towards the cabin that had been home for the previous week.

The lake was calm, and Bessie watched as a member of the park staff began to open up the boat rental stand. There was a small family standing nearby, presumably waiting to hire a boat. After a few minutes, Bessie got up and headed back along the path. There was a second path that went off into the woods just a few steps away. Bessie had noticed it before but not paid it much attention. Now she gave way to curiosity and turned to follow it.

It wasn't long before she found herself on the outskirts of a large section of holiday cabins. The buildings looked somewhat smaller than the one that Bessie and Doona were sharing. There were cars parked in front of several of them, in spite of the fact that it was Saturday and no one should have been coming or going. Bessie followed the path past several cabins, stopping when a door suddenly opened and someone she knew emerged from the last house in the row. Bessie smiled and increased her pace to say hello.

"Monique? How are you?" she said as she reached the girl's side.

Looking startled, Monique glanced around before she spoke. "What are you doing here? This area is for staff only," she said.

"I didn't see any signs," Bessie said. "So these are staff cottages?"

"Yes," Monique replied, seemingly reluctantly. "Most of the staff live in the area and drive back and forth every day, but some of us live on-site."

"That's convenient for you, since you and Nathan keep such late hours," Bessie said.

"Yes, I suppose so," Monique nodded. She glanced around again and then inched closer to the car that was parked in front of the cabin, its boot open and packed full of boxes and suitcases.

"Oh, but I'm keeping you from getting somewhere," Bessie said. She looked at the car. "And from the suitcases in the boot, I'm guessing you're going away."

Monique looked at the car and then at the cabin before she spoke. "My, um, my father isn't well," she said. "I'm going home for a few days to see him."

"I'm so sorry to hear that," Bessie said. "I hope he gets better quickly."

Monique flushed. "Yes, well, thank you," she said. "I must get going."

Bessie watched as the girl shut the boot and then jumped into the car and drove away. *I wonder if Inspector Hopkins knows she's leaving?* Bessie thought to herself as she continued down the path into the woods.

The path continued for a short while and then stopped abruptly at a large fence. Bessie could hear traffic whizzing past on the other side of the fence, but couldn't see the road through the trees. She shrugged and turned around to retrace her steps. While she did so, she pulled out her mobile. She'd just ring John and let him know about Monique, she'd decided.

He didn't answer. Bessie was just trying to find Andrew's number on her phone when she found herself back in front of the row of cabins. Nathan Beck was standing in front of the end unit, looking miserably at the empty space where Monique's car had been.

"Good morning," Bessie called out to him.

Nathan jumped. He looked over at Bessie and shook his head. "Not good," he said.

"Monique said she had to go home because her father was ill," Bessie told him. "I hope everything is okay."

"Is that what she told you?" Nathan asked. "I suppose it could have been worse."

Bessie walked up the short path towards the cabin's front door. She stopped in front of Nathan and looked into his eyes. "Is everything okay?" she asked softly.

"Monique thinks I killed Charles," Nathan replied. "She's left me."

"I'm sorry," Bessie said, her mind whirling. "Why would she think such a thing?"

Nathan laughed harshly. "She knows me too well," he said. "I did it for her, but she doesn't believe me. Can you ring the police, please? They can come and get me. She's gone. It doesn't matter anymore."

Bessie opened her mouth, but no words came out. For a long moment she just looked at the man and then she pulled out her phone. As she hadn't reached John a moment ago, she tried Doona's mobile.

"Bessie, where are you?" Doona demanded. "The police just rang. Apparently Monique rang them and said she thinks Nathan killed Charles and that you're wandering around in the woods by their cabin. What's going on?"

"I'm here with Nathan," Bessie said as calmly as she could. "We'll just wait here for Margaret."

"Margaret is on her way," Doona said. "Where will she find you?"

Bessie told her about the path behind the lake and then disconnected. Nathan hadn't moved or spoken during the call. Now he looked at Bessie and shrugged.

"It was all working so well," he said sadly.

"Let's sit down," Bessie suggested, gesturing towards a nearby bench. "The police will be here soon."

Nathan followed her to the bench and sat down beside her. "She was having an affair with Charles and then he dumped her," he told Bessie. "She wanted to leave."

"I'm sorry," Bessie said. She was torn between asking him questions and wishing the police would hurry.

"Maybe I'll get to cook in prison," he said, staring off into the distance. "I'm not a bad cook. Monique was the genius in the kitchen, of course. Without her, I'm just an ordinary cook."

Bessie tried to fit the pieces together as the man spoke. "I didn't know that," she said after a moment.

"Of course you didn't," Nathan replied. "We were very careful to make sure that no one knew. Her father wouldn't let her run their kitchen. He didn't think it was a job for a woman. Lots of people seem to agree, so we always told employers that she was my assistant. The job here was just about perfect, because Harold didn't care what we did as long as the guests were happy. Charles ruined everything."

"I'm sorry," Bessie said, feeling as if everything that came out of her mouth was the wrong thing.

"He cut my staff so much that Monique had to start waiting tables instead of helping in the kitchen. We found ways to work around that, but then he started buying cheaper ingredients as well. Monique was furious."

Bessie watched Nathan's eyes fill with anger. "How frustrating for you," she murmured.

"All I ever wanted was to have my own little restaurant," the man said sadly. "Monique was happy to help me until Charles broke her heart."

"I'm sorry," Bessie said, wishing the police would hurry.

"We had an agreement, Monique and I," Nathan continued, almost talking to himself. "We didn't love each other, but we worked well together. She hated what Charles was doing to the restaurant, but she fell madly in love with the man."

"Poor Monique," Bessie muttered. The words were hardly out of her mouth when she spotted Margaret Hopkins. The woman was walking very slowly towards them, trying to keep out of Nathan's line of sight. It wasn't all that difficult, as the man was staring straight ahead and didn't actually seem to be seeing anything.

"She really fell for Charles," Nathan told her now. "And she was heartbroken when he told her his wife was coming and he was planning to get back together with her."

"That wasn't going to happen," Bessie replied.

Nathan shrugged. "She wanted to leave. She said she couldn't work with Charles anymore. I agreed to go anywhere she wanted, but she didn't want me to come with her. She was going to leave me here, knowing I'd never keep my job without her help. I'm simply not a very good chef."

"I'm sorry," Bessie said quietly, watching Margaret closely.

"Try to keep him talking," the other woman mouthed to Bessie. At least that was what Bessie thought she said.

"So she was going to leave?" Bessie repeated his words.

"I didn't mean to kill him," Nathan said, glancing around and spotting Margaret. "I didn't mean to kill him. I just wanted to talk to him. I was hoping he could persuade Monique to stay, that's all."

"But that didn't happen, did it?" Margaret asked, her voice low.

"No, he wouldn't listen. He said Monique had just been a bit of fun, that's all. I was so angry," Nathan dropped his head into his hands.

Bessie looked up at Margaret and then rose to her feet. "I'm sorry," she said again to Nathan, not entirely certain what she was sorry about.

Margaret waved a hand and several uniformed policemen quickly surrounded the bench as Bessie slowly walked away.

CHAPTER 16

"I didn't get any pastries," Bessie said as she walked into her cabin. "I'm sorry, I completely forgot."

John, Andrew and Doona all jumped up and rushed towards her.

"Never mind pastries," Doona said. "Are you okay? I was so worried about you."

"I'm fine," Bessie insisted as she was pulled into a huge hug. Once Doona released her, John gave her a quick hug as well, and even Andrew wrapped an arm around her shoulders and gave her a small squeeze.

They all made their way into the kitchen, where a huge box of pastries and a pot of coffee waited. Bessie sat down with a croissant and coffee and sighed deeply.

"I'm glad someone remembered the pastries," she said after she'd had a bite of her flaky croissant.

"I said I'd bring them," Andrew told her. "And I had to find something to do while we waited to hear from Margaret that you were okay."

"I was fine," Bessie said with a wave of her hand. "I wasn't in any danger. Nathan just fell apart."

"He started falling apart right after the murder," Andrew said. "His cooking suffered immediately."

"That might have been because Monique wasn't helping him anymore," Bessie said, telling them what Nathan had said about the real talent behind his delicious meals. She took them through her conversations with both Monique and Nathan.

"I wonder why Monique didn't come forward sooner," Doona said when she'd finished.

"I'm not sure we'll ever know," Andrew replied. "But I'm sure Margaret will ask."

"Nathan insisted that he never intended to kill Charles," Bessie said thoughtfully. "He was just upset because Charles wouldn't help him keep Monique here."

"I'd be more inclined to believe that if he hadn't stolen the knife from your cabin," Andrew said.

Bessie gasped. "I hadn't thought about that," she admitted. "That certainly makes it seem more likely to have been premeditated, doesn't it?"

"I would say so," John said. "But I'm sure he'll come up with some sort of explanation."

"You do seem to have a knack for getting confessions from people lately," Doona said to Bessie with a sigh.

"I don't mean to," Bessie replied defensively. "I just seem to be in the wrong place at the wrong time."

"From my perspective, this time it was the right place," Doona told her. "I was sure Margaret thought I did it."

"Well, I'm just glad it's all sorted before we're due to head back," Bessie said.

Everyone ate silently for a few minutes before Doona spoke. "I'm not sure I feel up to going to the book club this afternoon," she said to Bessie. "I hope you don't mind if I skip it."

"I'm not feeling like talking about books much myself," Bessie admitted. "I only finished two of them and I can think of a lot of better ways to spend our last day here."

"Like what?" Doona asked.

Bessie looked over at Andrew and grinned. "We should all go and play crazy golf instead," she suggested. "And get two scoops of ice cream."

"And maybe play Poohsticks on the way back," Andrew added.

They all sat back and ate and drank. Bessie felt as if she were waiting for something, but she wasn't sure what. Margaret called a short time later and had a long conversation with John.

"He's confessed to everything," he told the others when he'd disconnected. "He's even admitted to stealing the knife from your patio. He still says he didn't go to Charles's office intending to kill him, but he can't explain why he took the knife with him otherwise."

"What about Monique?" Bessie asked.

"She told Margaret that she suspected him all along, but she says she didn't want to believe that he was capable of murder. According to her, she was never in love with him, but she thought he was a good person."

"I think we should put it all out of our minds and go and get some lunch and have some fun," Andrew said.

"Andrew's right," John agreed.

"Give us fifteen minutes to freshen up," Doona suggested. "We'll meet you on the bench out front."

The men left and Doona turned to Bessie. "Did Nathan really say that Charles dumped Monique because of me?" she demanded with tears in her eyes.

"Yes," Bessie said.

"I don't even know what to think," Doona said, shaking her head. "Maybe he really did want to give our marriage another chance."

"I suppose we'll never know," Bessie said, hugging her friend. "You should believe whatever makes you the happiest," she suggested.

"That's a thought," Doona replied. "I wish I knew what that was," she added with a small laugh.

"You'll work it out," Bessie told her.

Andrew seemed determined to make sure that everyone thoroughly enjoyed the afternoon. They had lunch at the American-style restaurant and then played several rounds of crazy golf. At the ice cream stand, he bought them all double scoops. They found a bench in a quiet spot and sat down to enjoy their treat.

"This has been a fun afternoon," Doona said between bites. "And it's taken my mind off things, as well."

"That's good to hear," Andrew told her.

John had pulled out his phone and was checking his messages. "I need to ring Margaret," he said with a sigh. He walked a few steps away and punched the numbers of his phone. When he came back a few minutes later, he was smiling.

"Jessica Howe is going to be just fine," he told them all. "Apparently, she'd just had far too much to drink. Herbert hasn't left her side and I gather the two are talking about a second honeymoon and starting over. For some weird reason, I hope it works out for them."

"Did Margaret have anything else to say?" Bessie asked.

"Yes, you and Doona are free to return home tomorrow as planned," John replied. "But Charles's solicitor wants to talk to Doona before you go. He's suggested a meeting tonight."

"I don't suppose I have a choice," Doona said.

"Not really," John replied. "He'll be here at seven unless I ring Margaret back to change it."

"That's fine," Doona shrugged. "At least I can have a good dinner before I hear what he has to say."

As it happened, he didn't have much to say. The foursome had a light dinner together and then Bessie and Doona returned to the cabin to wait for the man. When he arrived, he got straight to the point.

"Mrs. Adams, your husband has left his entire estate to you. A few days ago I would have said you were now quite wealthy, but there seem to be several concerns about the partnership your husband was a part of. All I can tell you at this point is that, if there is any money in the estate after the legal issues are resolved, you will inherit it. I will be doing my best to represent Charles as things move forward."

"So I shouldn't start planning to buy a mansion in the Algarve just yet," Doona replied dryly.

"No, I'd say not," the man replied solemnly. "The only other thing I have for you is a letter," he said, handing Doona an envelope. "Charles wanted you to have this if anything happened to him."

Doona turned the envelope over in her hands. "Thank you," she said eventually.

After the man left, Bessie gave Doona a hug. "I can leave you alone if you want to open the letter," she said tentatively.

"I think, for now, I'm just going to put it in my suitcase," Doona answered. "According to the schedule, there's a disco on tonight. Why don't we put on our dancing shoes and have some fun?"

Realising that her friend was hoping to keep her mind off Charles, Bessie was quick to agree. She rang John and Andrew and they joined them on the walk to the Squirrel's Drey. They could hear the loud music as they approached and Bessie exchanged glances with Andrew.

"My children and adult grandchildren are in there somewhere," he told Bessie. "I keep telling myself it's going to be fun."

"We just might have to work at making it fun," Bessie said with a small sigh. The tables and chairs in the food court had all been removed and the entire space was being used as a dance floor. Flashing lights and loud music assaulted Bessie's senses. She looked over at Doona and decided that this was exactly what her friend needed tonight. They stayed out until they were all exhausted enough to sleep in spite of everything.

The next morning, Bessie was up at six again. As she walked around the lake for the last time she kept her thoughts on home. Doona didn't get up until nearly time to leave, so she had to scramble to finish her packing in time. John and Andrew arrived to help them carry their bags back to their car.

"We don't have enough stuff to warrant driving the car here," Doona said. "Although it was nice having it brought to us when we arrived."

"I think the VIP treatment is over," Bessie said.

"I'm just worried that we'll get a bill for everything," Doona replied.

"We'll work it out," Bessie told her.

"I'll be flying back in a few hours," John told them at Doona's car. "We should get back to the island around the same time."

"And I hope you'll keep in touch," Andrew said. "I meant what I said about visiting the island. I think the little beach houses near you would be perfect for me and my family next spring or summer."

Bessie promised to send him a brochure about the holiday cottages and to keep in touch. Then she and Doona headed back towards Heysham and the ferry terminal.

"That wasn't exactly the holiday I was hoping for," Doona said sadly as they drove away from the park.

"Maybe we should take another holiday somewhere far away," Bessie suggested. "I'll talk to Doncan and see if I can afford to take us both to America or something."

"Maybe once the legal issues are settled, I'll be able to afford to take us both somewhere exotic," Doona said. "Or at least to Liverpool for a long weekend."

Bessie laughed. "Even that would be fun, if we do it together," she told her friend.

"Thank you for being my best friend," Doona said. "I don't know how I'd have made it though this last week without you."

"That's what friends are for," Bessie told her. "You were there for me during all the awfulness in July and after. I'm just hoping we can both have a quieter life for a while now."

"Quiet sounds wonderful," Doona replied with enthusiasm.

GLOSSARY OF TERMS

ENGLISH/MANX TO AMERICAN TERMS

- **advocate** — Manx title for a lawyer (solicitor)
- **bin** — garbage can
- **biscuits** — cookies
- **book** — reserve (like restaurant tables)
- **boot** — trunk (of a car)
- **car park** — parking lot
- **chips** — french fries
- **creche** — a day care center for babies and small children
- **crisps** — potato chips
- **cuddly toy** — stuffed animal
- **cuppa** — cup of tea (informal)
- **disco** — a party with dancing
- **duvet** — a comforter with a removable cover, usually filled with feathers and down
- **en-suite** — an attached bathroom
- **fairy cakes** — cupcakes
- **fizzy drink** — soda (pop)

- **flat** — apartment
- **fortnight** — two weeks
- **gaol** — jail
- **half-term** — a school break, usually a week long, in the middle of the term
- **hire car** — rental car
- **holiday** — vacation
- **jumper** — sweater
- **lie in** — sleep late
- **loo** — restroom
- **midday** — noon
- **motorway** — highway
- **pram** — stroller
- **pudding** — dessert
- **queue** — line
- **return** — round-trip
- **rubbish** — garbage
- **shopping trolley** — shopping cart
- **stabilisers** — training wheels (on a bicycle)
- **starters** — appetizers
- **takeaway** — take out
- **tannoy** — public address system
- **telly** — television
- **till** — check-out (in a grocery store, for example)
- **trainers** — sneakers

OTHER NOTES

As far as I can determine, there really aren't any US equivalents to a UK holiday park. Imagine a huge site where every family can stay in their own private cabin or cottage with two or more bedrooms and multiple bathrooms. Most of the parks offer a central location for a large indoor swimming complex as well as shops and restaurants. Elsewhere on the site will be sports fields, tennis courts, mini golf, possibly a full-sized golf course, indoor sports courts for things like basketball and squash, pool tables, table tennis, etc. Some even offer things like horseback riding or off-roading. Such parks now also offer spa facilities, but those weren't yet popular in the late 1990s when Bessie visited Lakeview. The sites offer an enormous range of activities for guests of all ages, from day-care facilities for the very young to introductory classes in just about every sport you can imagine for children from two or three and up. They also offer arts and crafts, special activities just for teens and their own small supermarkets.

Ronaldsway is the area of the island where the airport is located. Although officially called the "Isle of Man Airport," nearly everyone on the island calls it "Ronaldsway" when talking about it.

Poohsticks comes from the Winnie the Pooh stories by A.A. Milne.

CID is the Criminal Investigation Department of the Isle of Man Constabulary (Police Force).

When talking about time, the English say, for example, "half seven" to mean "seven-thirty."

The emergency number in the UK is 999, rather than 911, as used in the US.

The Lieutenant Governor on the Isle of Man is the Queen's official representative there. Today the role is largely ceremonial.

Hop-tu-naa is a Celtic festival that most closely approximates to US Halloween and takes place on October 31st each year. Traditionally children hollow out and carve turnips and then light them up with candles. They also go door-to-door and sing the Hop-tu-naa song in exchange for treats. (The song varies depending on which part of the island you live in.)

Holidays that include "self-catering" have facilities within the accommodation to allow the guests to cook their own meals rather than having to eat at restaurants each day.

A "full English breakfast" generally consists of bacon, sausage, eggs, grilled or fried tomatoes, fried potatoes, fried mushrooms and baked beans served with toast.

It has been pointed out to me that I talk about different biscuits but don't explain them. Digestive biscuits (usually just called digestives) are round, hard, slightly sweet and probably the most common biscuit in the UK. The closest US equivalent that I can come up with is a graham cracker, but digestives are less sweet and have a harder texture. You can find them covered with a layer of chocolate or even caramel and chocolate, which (to my mind) only improves them slightly.

Waterproofs are rain jackets (and sometimes matching trousers) that attempt to keep their wearer dry in spite of the heavy rain that is common in the UK.

ACKNOWLEDGMENTS

Many thanks to my wonderful editor, Denise, who works so hard on my behalf.

Thanks to my beta readers, Charlene, Ruth, Janice and Margaret.

Thank you to Helene and Anne for suggesting some of the names for characters in this story.

Thanks to Kevin for the wonderful cover photo, yet again.

And special thanks to all the readers who have taken the time to get in touch via Facebook and email. I love hearing your thoughts on Bessie and her friends!

Bessie's adventures continue in...

Aunt Bessie Invites

An Isle of Man Cozy Mystery

By Diana Xarissa

Aunt Bessie invites her dearest friends for a traditional American Thanksgiving feast.

Having spent her childhood in the US, Bessie Cubbon still celebrates an American-style Thanksgiving every November. Now Laxey's favourite "Aunt Bessie" is planning for her biggest feast ever, but when a body turns up on a nearby farm, she finds herself in the middle of yet another murder investigation.

Aunt Bessie invites herself to more than one house as she questions various people about the dead man. But the more she learns, the more complicated the case seems to get.

Aunt Bessie invites the dead man's sister for tea.

But the sister has her own theory as to who might have killed her brother. Can Bessie help the police sort out who really had a motive for murder all those years ago?

This is book nine in the Isle of Man Cozy Mystery Series.

ALSO BY DIANA XARISSA

The Isle of Man Cozy Mystery Series

Aunt Bessie Assumes

Aunt Bessie Believes

Aunt Bessie Considers

Aunt Bessie Decides

Aunt Bessie Enjoys

Aunt Bessie Finds

Aunt Bessie Goes

Aunt Bessie's Holiday

Aunt Bessie Invites

Aunt Bessie Joins

Aunt Bessie Knows

Aunt Bessie Likes

Aunt Bessie Meets

Aunt Bessie Needs

The Isle of Man Ghostly Cozy Mysteries

Arrivals and Arrests

Boats and Bad Guys

Cars and Cold Cases

Dogs and Danger

The Markham Sisters Cozy Mystery Novellas

The Appleton Case

The Bennett Case

ABOUT THE AUTHOR

Diana Xarissa lived on the Isle of Man for more than ten years before returning to the United States with her family. Now living near Buffalo, New York, she enjoys having the opportunity to write about the island that she loves so much. It truly is a special place.

Diana also writes mystery/thrillers set in the not-too-distant future under the pen name "Diana X. Dunn" and fantasy/adventure books for middle grade readers under the pen name "D.X. Dunn."

She would be delighted to know what you think of her work and can be contacted through snail mail at:

Diana Xarissa Dunn

PO Box 72

Clarence, NY 14031.

You can sign up for her monthly newsletter on the website and be among the first to know about new releases, as well as find out about contests and giveaways and see the answers to the questions she gets asked the most.

Find Diana at:

www.dianaxarissa.com

diana@dianaxarissa.com

CPSIA information can be obtained
at www.ICGtesting.com
Printed in the USA
BVOW04s1322040917
493897BV00014BA/355/P